The Orig
Book Two)

Christopher Coleman

OTHER BOOKS BY CHRISTOPHER COLEMAN

Gretel (Gretel Book One)[1]
Marlene's Revenge (Gretel Book Two)[2]
Hansel (Gretel Book Three)[3]
Anika Rising (Gretel Book Four)[4]
They Came with the Snow (They Came with the Snow Book One)[5]
The Melting (They Came with the Snow Book Two)[6]

---

1. https://www.amazon.com/Gretel-Book-One-Christopher-Coleman-ebook/dp/B01605OOL4/

2. https://www.amazon.com/Marlenes-Revenge-Gretel-Book-psychological-ebook/dp/B01LX8R3LD/

3. https://www.amazon.com/Hansel-Gretel-Book-Three-Mystery-ebook/dp/B072L8C5SN/

4. https://www.amazon.com/gp/product/B0784MXFHD/

5. https://www.amazon.com/They-Came-Snow-Post-Apocalyptic-Survival-ebook/dp/B06XPL2Q4L/

6. https://www.amazon.com/gp/product/B07FCW6C2H/r

Chapter 1

"It's this way, Samuel, follow me."

Nootau held his hand above his shoulder and waved two fingers forward, all the while gliding effortlessly along the dirt path toward the sound. Despite the fading light, he dodged the tall loblolly pines and avoided the prickly pear shrubs with the grace of a mustang.

Samuel stopped and took a deep breath, his eyes watching Nootau disappear around the brush, and then he placed his hands on his knees and bent over, searching for air. But he rested only a moment before following Nootau through the thick grass.

"Let's go, Samuel," Nootau called, "we won't make dinner, but we must try to be home before dark."

"Where are we going?" Samuel asked, but the words were to himself, only a whisper; he needed to preserve his strength to keep up with the young Algonquin boy striding ahead of him.

Samuel reached the bank of the sound where Nootau had already unmoored the canoe from an old border fence and was now dragging it across the sand to the water. Samuel stood in awe for just a moment as he watched the brown-skinned boy, about his own age but seemingly twice as strong. He moved so differently than any boy he'd ever known, Samuel thought, moved in a way Samuel knew he could never, no matter the training.

Nootau and Samuel had become friends only days after Samuel and his family arrived from England, landing on the shores of this new world that the Italian explorer Columbus had discovered less than a century earlier. This friendship had developed despite the ebb and flow of tensions between the settlers—including the Cook family to which Samuel belonged—and the natives, and it had strengthened in the last year, a year in which Samuel's father had left with John White to return to England.

It wasn't that the boys didn't feel the obvious strains of the two cultures—men had died fighting over the land, after all—but they had made a silent pact to stay above the cultural rifts, seeming to understand that it was the only way either would survive.

"What are you staring at Samuel? Help me. Please."

Samuel smiled, the added pleasantry at the end of Nootau's sentence so unnecessary yet so appreciated by Samuel. It was his way—polite—even in the throes of a reasonable command. "Sorry, Nootau, what do you need me to do?"

"Place the shrubs back against the fence where the canoe was. It won't fool anyone who is looking for the boat, but at least it won't be obvious if someone comes down to the beach for some other reason, as a sentry or to fish, perhaps. And father will kill me if he knows I took it without permission."

"Where does he think you've gone for the day?"

Nootau shrugged. "It is my day of rest. He doesn't ask anymore. For boys my age, exploration and learning are encouraged without the doting of a parent. It is how we become men."

"Then why would he be mad about the boat?"

"Because it isn't mine, Samuel. He does not encourage stealing."

Samuel knew they were only borrowing the boat, and that the plan was to have it back in its dock, undamaged, before the owner knew it was gone; but he considered there may not exist the distinction between stealing and borrowing without permission in the language or culture of Nootau, so Samuel only nodded solemnly in understanding.

"We won't have long after dusk to make it back. So as soon as we see it, we have to go."

"See what? What is this thing you keep talking about?"

Nootau launched the boat into the sound, and within seconds, the Algonquin boy had hopped inside and was rowing furiously, his thin, sinewy arms tightening and releasing with every stroke. Samuel rushed clumsily into the surf and climbed aboard, positioning himself on the stern seat across from his native friend.

"Nootau?"

Nootau snapped from his reverie and looked up at Samuel who was lamenting his wet trousers and shoes. Samuel stared at the boy expectantly, no longer willing to let Nootau dodge the question. "What is it?"

"I can't explain it, Samuel. I haven't seen it myself."

"What? You haven't seen it? I thought you had something to show me. How do you even know—?"

"I do. I know...Just trust me."

Samuel did trust Nootau, fully, but he also knew that he would have been less likely to agree to this illicit adventure had he known that Nootau had no firsthand knowledge of this mysterious "thing" that supposedly existed somewhere on the beaches of the wide sea.

This exploit scared Samuel, that much was without question, and he would have latched onto any excuse to keep himself from having to face his fear. It was only recently that he had started to become comfortable with the island and his colony there, but beyond the sound, east to the ocean where they were headed now, was another thing entirely. It was unruly there, wild and unpredictable. He had made only a handful of trips to the ocean since they'd arrived in this New World, and on those few occasions, with his father always, he had looked out at the endless water with terror, all the while fostering images of ships emerging on the horizon, an armada of invaders intent on descending upon the thin strip of ocean beach before crossing the sound to the island.

It was, in fact, that same trek that his family and fellow countrymen had made when they came to Nootau's land, and there was no reason Samuel could think of to prevent such a thing from happening again. He could only imagine the fear that the sight of his people's boats must have brought to Nootau and his tribe.

"I'll row us back," Samuel uttered absently, the words immediately embarrassing him. The offer was genuine but filled with guilt, guilt at both his lack of contribution to the current quest, and for his mere presence in Nootau's land.

But despite his earnestness, the proposal was hollow; Samuel knew when the time came, it was Nootau who would be thrusting the oars to bring them home. Nootau knew the way in the dark, and he was stronger in every way than Samuel.

"Okay," Nootau said grinning. "The Viking Samuel, eh?"

Samuel smiled back and clicked his head up in affirmation, and then squinted his eyes to bring into focus the approaching western bank of the barrier island. It was only a little over a half mile from the settlement island to the barrier island, and with the power of Nootau's strokes, it seemed they'd left only a minute ago before the bank was in sight.

"When we arrive, Samuel, don't hesitate. Help me bring the canoe to shore and then keep up your pace until we get to the dunes. I know of a perfect place for viewing it when it arrives. We should have plenty of time, but I don't want to miss our chance."

Samuel felt the adrenaline rush through his body at the sound of the words 'it' and 'arrives.' To this point, Nootau had been excruciatingly vague about the thing they were going to see, but now that they were close to the beach, perhaps only moments away from seeing the object of their quest, the tension was high in Samuel's stomach and throat. "What if it doesn't come?"

Nootau frowned at the thought, and, for the first time since they'd left the village, Samuel saw a real moment of insecurity in the boy's eyes. "Then we'll go again next week."

"That's going to get difficult to explain, you and me leaving every time you get a free day. Even if your father does give you freedom. Someone could follow us."

Nootau locked Samuel's eyes and said, "You don't have to come, Samuel. But I am. I'm returning every week until I see it."

Nootau never broke stride with the strokes of the oars, and Samuel dropped his gaze almost instantly at the boy's declaration.

Within minutes, the two boys were standing on the soft bank of the barrier island, and, as instructed, Samuel quickly assisted Nootau in pulling the canoe ashore, wedging it into the muddy ground. It wasn't a proper mooring by any standards, but the options were few in this part of the country, and they'd brought nothing along to help weigh the boat down.

"Shouldn't we tie it down?" Samuel asked, knowing they had no rope. But it didn't matter, Nootau had already started east toward the dunes, and Samuel ran after him, giving one quick glance back to the canoe. It would be fine there, he thought, they'd pulled it in enough.

But what if they hadn't? What if the tide came in further than they'd estimated and stole the canoe into the sound? They would be stranded. Samuel was no swimmer, so it was that boat, and that boat alone, that would bring him back to the colony.

Samuel chased Nootau up to the dunes, feeling the soft, luxurious burn of sunlight on his neck behind him. There was still plenty of daylight ahead of them, but the sun had begun to dip and take on the orange glow of the looming dusk. They were fine though; night was still hours away, and Samuel made a silent prayer that the intelligence Nootau had received was reliable, and that this thing they had quested to view would show itself sometime around dusk.

But once they saw it, once this magical 'thing' revealed itself, they wouldn't have long to admire it before they would have to rush back to the boat and traverse the encroaching darkness of the sound. Hopefully, they would arrive back at the colony not more than an hour or so after night fell. They would miss supper, of course, and neither boy would eat again until breakfast, but they'd already agreed it was a price they were willing to pay. Besides, the village and colony could use the extra food. Hunger was a new enemy to them both. It was the reason his father had joined Captain White on his mission back to England. Supplies were low, and the colony wouldn't survive for another year without reinforcements.

Samuel appeared beside Nootau on one of the several tall dunes that looked down on the Great Western Ocean, a moniker which seemed rather ridiculous from this side of the world. He tried to keep his breathing steady, to keep the burning weakness of his lungs a secret from his friend. But Nootau paid him little mind, as his eyes were fixed on the sprawling water in the distance, his eyes sparkling, his own breathing heavy and anxious. Expecting.

"Were going to see it tonight," Nootau said, the grin from earlier returning to his face. "I can feel it."

"It's too early, right? You said dusk. That's probably another..." Samuel looked back to the sun in the blue sky behind him. "Forty-five minutes."

"Fifty-six," Nootau replied. "We'll wait down there." He pointed to a short, wide dune about twenty yards in front of them and covered in sea grass. "It will conceal us."

Samuel nodded, hoping this concealment was needed so as not to scare away the mysterious thing they were hoping to espy, and not for their own protection. For his own will's sake, he decided it best not to clarify.

"And from there it should be able to hear me."

Samuel stared at the side of Nootau's face, unblinking, finally forcing the Algonquin boy to turn and look at him. "That's enough, Nootau. No more secrets. I want to know what we're looking for."

Nootau dipped his head and stared at the sand beneath him, pondering whether this was the proper time for the revelation. "You'll see soon, Samuel," he said.

"No. I want to know now. I'm here. I followed you. And I want to be prepared."

Nootau stood motionless for a moment and then nodded slowly. "It is a fair request, Samuel. Come with me to the dune, and I'll tell you what I've heard."

Chapter 2

Danny Lynch sipped his coffee and stared out at the rising sun of the Atlantic. The path of light that flowed from the horizon seemed to lead straight toward him, beckoning him to the ocean shore. The first-story porch upon which he stood was agonizingly low, and the chipped paint of the rotting wood instilled a low level of depression in him.

But Danny could get past the poor upkeep of the porch; it was the height of the deck that really tortured him. The dunes in front of him rose like sandcastles toward the sky, obscuring his view of the shore line.

But an ocean view—even if obstructed—was a must have for any property he rented, and this house, despite its many flaws, checked that box. The other box, of course, was price, and as far as rental properties went, it was the only thing on the water he could afford right now.

Danny flicked his wrist over and checked his watch once again; it was a movement he made now as habitually as blinking, and each time he made it, a dull reminder of the events from two years earlier blazed through his arm, the night a bullet had passed through his shoulder during an escape from a madwoman.

It was only 6:30 am—he had another full hour before the sun would rise—which meant he had a half an hour to get to the beach by 7:00 am to prepare. Thirty minutes before dawn, just like every morning.

Of course, as with each of the past six mornings since he'd arrived here, his expectations were anything but high.

It had been two years since he'd seen it last, and each day tightened around him a little more, like a python around the chest of a pygmy boar.

But there was hope.

A news report of a death on Wickard beach had piqued his interest. He'd seen it on the last page of the Metro section in the Washington Post—one of the dozen or so newspapers he now bought on at least a weekly basis. The mysterious death was the third one on this beach in the last three months. And this was no drunk sorority girl showing off for the boys, or some elderly thrill-seeker, unable, perhaps, to accept the collapsing weight of time on his frail body, risking the ocean surf in some Quixotical quest for youth. This latest victim was a healthy male, thirty-eight, a resident of the town for a little over five years, married and gainfully employed. This was the last type of person who drowns in the sea in the early morning. It was still unclear why he had been on the beach to begin with, but that was an answer Danny intended to obtain.

The other two deaths were semi-explainable, less exotic, more fitting members of a demographic group that one would expect to drown in the ocean. The first of these two was a frequent swimmer with a history of heart problems, so a heart attack while swimming was the assumed cause of death.

The second death was a child. Eight years old. A strong swimmer, according to his father, and not a boy prone to adventure, unlikely to sneak from his home and hazard the ocean the way the report described.

Danny had researched each of the deaths on his own, to the extent he could using the internet and by placing a few phone calls, and he had found a few holes in each of the stories. There were no witnesses to any of the disappearances, and the law enforcement—which, in this town, basically consisted of three guys who were at least ten years older than Danny, as well as a woman who was young enough to be his daughter—had made a lot of assumptions about what must have happened. Neither of the first two bodies ever showed up—only their garments were found tattered and strewn on the sand—and the other body—the young man who'd made the latest edition of the paper—had evidently washed ashore in pieces on the beach. *Sharks must have got 'em*, the police had said, but Danny silently offered another theory.

He could have been wrong, of course—in fact, he assumed he was—but three deaths in as many months was as solid a reason as any to bring him to this beach, to this house which stared like a sentry upon the Atlantic Ocean, searching.

Here was as good a place as any to find the god that had consumed him for the past two years.

And to kill it.

"You looking for something?"

Danny cringed at the sound of the woman's voice behind him. He remained silent, still, hoping that his obvious lack of interest in her question would cause her just to leave.

"You want me to make breakfast?"

Danny closed his eyes and turned around, opening his eyes at the end of his pivot. "No, thank you. I have to be somewhere in fifteen minutes or so, so..." Danny pursed his lips, signaling that she should be able to fill in the rest of the scenario.

"You want me to leave?"

"I mean..."

The woman shook her head slowly, frowning. "Geez, Danny, you're kind of an asshole. I mean, I wasn't expecting us to get married, but Christ."

"You don't *have* to leave," Danny answered, the emphasis on 'have,' implying that he really would prefer it.

"Screw you," the woman said, swinging her body back toward the bedroom, shaking her head ruefully, as if hating herself for allowing this scene to play out once again.

Danny watched her go, searching for a name and, coming up with nothing, accepting the possibility that he never knew it to begin with. He'd only had two beers last night at Mason's—the closest bar, only three blocks away—and he hadn't really gone there for the purposes of coming home with anyone. But the nameless girl who was now stuffing things in a bag in his bedroom had begun flirting with him almost immediately, and less than two hours later she was walking with him on the beach toward his house. She must have said her name at some point, but really, what difference did it make now?

Although, if he had come to the right place—that is, if Wickard Beach was the latest feeding ground of the god—it wouldn't hurt to keep a few contacts in the Rolodex.

Danny took a deep breath and followed the girl into the bedroom. As he passed the bar that bordered his kitchen, he saw the woman's purse sitting tucked in the corner. He paused a moment, and then quickly scavenged for her wallet, pulling it out and checking her driver's license.

Samantha. Probably went by Sam.

He stuffed the wallet back inside and entered the room. "Look, Sam, I'm sorry."

The woman looked up at Danny, a look of gentle surprise on her face, and then she went back to gathering her things.

"Stay. Please. Just until I get back. Which won't be long. I'll be back here by eight and then, instead of you making me breakfast, we'll go out. My treat."

Sam flashed her head up again, this time her brow was wrinkled, confused. "Really?" she asked, as if the offer of someone to take her out for a meal was a practice she didn't quite understand. Danny couldn't imagine why—the woman was no supermodel, but she was attractive by just about any definition.

"Absolutely. You can even get the steak and eggs."

"I'm vegan."

Danny smiled. "Of course you are."

Danny leaned in to kiss Sam on the cheek, but the girl put her hands up in front of her and frowned, suggesting that breakfast was fine, but Danny shouldn't get carried away.

"I'll be back."

Danny grabbed his beach bag from the counter and pushed through the screen door, descending the steps that ran along the side porch of the rental house until he was standing on the battered boardwalk that led to the beach. In less than thirty seconds, his feet were off the splintered wood and he was standing barefoot in the cool sand.

He closed his eyes and luxuriated in the crisp morning air. It was the type of air only found near the ocean, before sunrise, and only on overcast days. Danny opened his eyes reluctantly and stared across the water, watching the cloud-bleached sun push up over the Atlantic. He was suddenly consumed with a spark of déjà vu. That wasn't surprising, of course, this familiar feeling; almost every day for the last two years was the same as the one before it.

Danny thought back on the early days at Rove Beach, just after he and Tammy had moved in. Before the sighting on that morning in late summer. Before he lost his wife. Before he lost his sanity to the creature that emerged on the beach that day.

And before Lynn Shields, the woman who had tried to sacrifice him to the monster and who would alter the course of his life forever.

He recalled those days prior to the sighting with such fondness now, in a way he never appreciated them before. Those were easy days, leisurely, as perfect a life as he could ever have imagined leading. It was almost a fairy tale, really, spending his days in a locale as beautiful as the wife he lived with. He had youth and money and plans for a family. He was still without real purpose in his life, but that would come later. It was time to enjoy his success. It was time to hit the beach.

But it was the beach that would change him. If only his dream had been to live in the mountains. Or in the heart of Manhattan, maybe. How different his life would be now.

But Danny had loved the beach since he was a kid, the smell and sound of it, in particular, and when he had finally started living there, he had come to relish his morning jogs along the coastal highway as much as anything in his life. He felt strong in the morning, and when he would finally reach the sand at the bottom of the overlook, he would take his pre-dawn swim in the Atlantic, grounding him to the earth, connecting him to the lifeforce of the universe.

And when his swim concluded, he would reverse his run back home, almost sprinting the three and a half miles, the salt and sweat encouraging him to reach his house as quickly as his body would allow so that he could feel the wonderful relief of the cool shower.

But that was his life then, mundane though it may have been, and the fragility of it seemed so comical to Danny now. It took only seconds to collapse it like a mountain of marbles. It took one lone, black figure to emerge like a demon above the surf, to stand tall and still on the shores of Rove Beach. One glimpse of that demon-deity and Danny could never have his fantasy life again. Some images lived in a mind forever; every piece of Danny's life from that moment forward would be polluted with the event.

Tammy was gone now, killed violently, a victim of the devil-god from the sea. And Danny himself had become so addicted to the thing's existence that he had constructed a plan to offer up his friends as a sacrifice. He had drugged Tracy and Sarah that first night—had poisoned two people with whom he'd become friends and who had shared the experience of the monster's massacre with Danny. He had become enchanted by the sea beast, addicted to it, and the offering of the women was the only way Danny could keep the spell from dying.

Thankfully, the god hadn't appeared on the beach that night, despite Danny blasting the cries of the minke whales, and Danny knew in his heart that the cycle had finally ended.

That evening, Danny had managed to transport the women back from the grotto—the same prison where Lynn Shields had kept Danny—without either of them the wiser, and he had continued his weekly dinners with both of them, each time with the intention of watching their slaughter by the giant beast.

But he never saw it again. The god had moved on from Rove beach.

Perhaps it was to do with Lynn Shields, he had speculated. The god had lost its master. The woman who had called and fed the beast for so many years, was now gone. How it would have sensed her absence, Danny didn't know, but Tracy had told him the story her aunt used to tell about the 'Master of the Shore,' the person who, over time, could learn to control the actions of the being, at least to the extent that he or she could consistently draw it from the seas. There was no way to confirm that this was the monster's motives for disappearing, but Danny thought it as good a theory as any.

But it was gone, and as each day passed without this false god in Danny's life, the poison of its addiction faded a little further from his soul.

He thought of Tracy and Sarah again, both of whom were still alive and well in Rove Beach. As far as Danny knew, neither had ever suspected Danny of the malice he had once intended. He had laid off the sedatives after that first night, since both women had passed out and woke the next morning with a pair of splitting headaches, and he obviously couldn't have kept that story up for long, using wine and too much to drink as the reason for their lack of memory. Had the Ocean God appeared again, Danny wasn't sure exactly what he would have done, though he supposed he would have found other ways to disable the women and drag them to the beach. Shovels were useful for such things. And hammers.

Danny hadn't heard from Sarah in several months, though he occasionally saw her byline in the Rove Beach Rover (one of the newspapers he continued to receive weekly), writing under her new pen name.

Tracy, on the other hand, he spoke with quite frequently. She continued to reside rent-free in the home Danny had bought from her, the home Lynn Shield's had left to the girl in her will. He had originally purchased it for the purposes of keeping a close watch on the creature, but now that he was a changed man and the beast was no longer in Rove Beach, he was ready to sell. Danny simply couldn't afford it. The royalty checks from his 'Superstar' song still arrived monthly, they just weren't the sizes they used to be.

But as much as he wanted to sell, he felt he owed it to Tracy to keep up the payments and let her stay. His guilt haunted him now. He felt like a serial killer who had been reborn, who had finally recognized the wickedness of his ways before he was ever caught and tried for his crimes, and now had to make amends in other ways.

That was his quest now: to find the Ocean God before it killed again.

He knew he should turn himself in, of course, if not for the attempted murder of Tracy and Sarah—he hadn't overtly attempted anything, really—then for the cover-up of his own wife's murder. He was with her at the time of her death, had seen every gruesome second of it, and thus was obligated to report it to the police.

But Danny couldn't imagine what that would even look like. The police hadn't believed the cell phone picture of the monster, had continued to dismiss it as a hoax, so how exactly could he explain that Tammy's death came at the hands of the monster?

There were only two conclusions he could see coming from his confession: either he would be considered out of his mind and committed to an institution, or he would be tried for the disappearance and murder of his wife and end up in prison. But he wasn't crazy, and he didn't kill his wife, at least not in the way for which he'd be accused, and thus both of those outcomes were unacceptable. He would live with the guilt. For now. Until he could enact his own form of repentance.

Danny took a deep breath and then proceeded down to the water's edge, removing the portable Bluetooth speaker from his bag as he went. He tossed a towel from his shoulder onto the sand and placed the waterproof speaker on top. He then pulled his phone from his pocket and pressed the 'Downloads' icon, pulling up a single file of a .wav recording titled 'Minke.'

He touched the recording with his finger, and a familiar chill tingled down his spine as the sound of the low, alien cries erupted from the speakers. The minke whales. Mating perhaps, or beckoning to potential mates, he had never really known for sure.

Danny glanced around suspiciously and quickly adjusted the volume. It wasn't nosy bystanders he worried about; these types of sleepy, sunny locales were notorious for old beachcombers who didn't think twice about asking a stranger his business. He'd been asked a thousand times what he was doing, and so he always kept a couple of answers chambered, usually to do with some piece of music he was writing. He was a songwriter by trade, after all, so the response came naturally to him.

But Danny didn't feel much like chatting today; he was now obligated to breakfast with Sam, so he wanted the few minutes he had now to be alone with his thoughts.

Twenty minutes passed and Danny turned off the recording and folded up the towel. He would be back again at sundown, and would let the recording go for several hours. It was a new strategy to come at dusk, and it was based on nothing other than he needed to change his methods for luring the beast.

"Whatcha doing?"

The sing-songy voice of a child came from Danny's right, and Danny nearly screamed at the sound. He whipped his head around to see a boy of no more than nine standing with his head cocked to the side, trying to figure out the scene in front of him. He held a large conch shell in his hand and beside him was a beautiful black Labrador retriever.

"I'm working on some, uh, music."

The boy didn't reply, clearly not seeing any connection between what Danny was doing and any music that he had ever heard.

"It's uh, I'm recording sounds for a song."

"What sounds? The ocean? I hear ocean noises in here." He held up the shell for Danny to see. "And I make music with it too." He blew through the shell once, making a low, bellowing sound.

Danny smiled politely. "It's kind of like that, yes."

"But not really?"

When spectators questioned him this way, Danny's normal play was to act like he was getting some marine feedback and had to get back to work. But he sensed this boy wouldn't get the hints.

"They're whale sounds. Minke whales. I'm trying to lure something...from the water." Danny had no idea why he was offering up this much of the truth to this kid; there were so many other explanations he could have gone with. Maybe he needed just to say it once, aloud to another human being, for cathartic reasons.

"The black and purple man?"

Danny quite literally stopped breathing at the sound of the boy's words. It was as if the oxygen in his lungs had suddenly turned to clay. Gradually, he bent over at the waist, tears in his eyes, putting his hands on his knees.

"Are you okay?" the boy asked.

Danny put a hand up and then began to cough. The dog barked nervously in response.

"Should I get my dad?"

Danny shook his head furiously and then stood straight, finally remembering how to exhale. He took in three full breaths and then folded his hands and placed the tips of his fingers beneath his chin. He looked the boy in the eye. "What man?"

The boy turned and faced the water, his face now solemn as he stared out at the waves. "They don't believe me."

Danny turned and faced the water too, examining the ocean where the boy was peering, as if expecting the beast to emerge at that moment. "What's your name?"

"Shane."

"Shane," Danny repeated. "That's a solid name."

The boy shrugged.

"*I* believe you, Shane. I've seen it too."

The boy turned to Danny now, his eyes on fire, a mixture of both hope and fear. "You know the black and purple man?"

The black and purple man.

It wasn't the way any adult of the current day would have described the creature, not in this world awash of racial sensitivity and political correctness. But a child of Shane's age hadn't developed such verbal governors yet, and the description cut right to the bone.

"When do you see it?" Danny asked, afraid of losing the boy's interest, or perhaps his trust, fearing that anything other than one or two simple questions would scare the boy off.

He shrugged again and shook his head. "Not in a long time."

A long time. That could mean anything. A long time in the mind of a nine-year old could mean three or four hours ago. "Did you see it before or—"

"Why do you call it 'it'?"

"What?"

"You said 'it,' 'Did you see *it.*'"

"Him," Danny corrected quickly, "Did you see him—the black and purple man—before or after...um...Christmas let's say?"

The boy looked to the sky a moment and then said, "I saw him on my mom's birthday."

Danny nodded, feeling lucky that with that information he'd be able to get an exact date. "And when was that?"

"Shane!" a male voice called from the distance, south down the beach from where these two unlikely conversation-alists now stood. "Shane, you need to get back over here. Now!" The voice was angry, heavy with an accent from either New York or Jersey. No doubt the father. Danny knew anger was a reasonable reaction to the boy wandering, especially considering the number of 'drownings' that had occurred here in the past few months.

Shane turned toward the voice and the big lab cocked his head once to the side and then took off like a bullet toward the man's call.

"Okay, bye," Shane said, lopping off the conversation abruptly, as if they had come to some point where the conclusion was satisfactory.

"Shane!" Danny said, stopping the boy in his tracks. He needed to get the date.

But it was too late; the father was now upon them. There was no way Danny could ask such a personal question about the boy's mother now, not without either having the police show up at his house later that morning or getting a punch in the nose.

"It was nice to meet you," Danny said before looking up at Shane's father, who was a tall, burly fellow with dark eyes and a hairline like a waning crescent. Danny smiled humbly, but the man only squinted and clicked his head up in return.

Danny brought his attention back to his phone, pretending to be engrossed in his whale-sounds project.

It was only about twenty seconds later, after Danny had begun to process the boy's information, thinking about what steps he would take next, when Danny heard the boy call from down the beach.

"It was on Saturday, mister," Shane called.

Danny snapped his head to the boy, his eyes wide and crazed.

"We had cake and everything."

Chapter 3

"Kitchi was the first to speak of it. At least to me. He told of a large creature that lives among the waves of the Yapam." Nootau never took his eyes from the water as he revealed the source of the information that had propelled the two boys on their adventure.

"Kitchi?" Samuel asked. "But...how would Kitchi know?"

Kitchi was Nootau's cousin, or perhaps his uncle—the relationship had always been unclear to Samuel—and he had been born crippled, unable to walk since birth.

"He was told of it by his grandfather, my great uncle, and then Kitchi told it to me, on a night when he was under the influence of mead. He said he was sworn to secrecy by his grandfather, but Kitchi has little control in the hours after midnight."

Samuel stayed quiet, but he knew that Nootau could sense his doubt. It was a third-hand sighting, a re-telling of another's story, and told to Nootau by a cripple and a notorious drunkard.

"You don't believe me Samuel, that is fine. I know your people think of us as storytellers, as inventors of the truth rather than revealers of it. That has always been one of your people's many misjudgements. And yours is yet another mis-interpretation. We do have our religion, just as you have yours of Jesus and your book of The Bible. But we don't lie, Samuel. If Kitchi's grandfather told him of this creature, and warned him never to tell of it to another, then it—"

Bwoosh!

Nootau and Samuel shot to their feet in unison, as if they'd been pulled by a chain that had been attached to the tops of their heads. It was a counterintuitive move, since they were now exposed, outside the cover of the sea grass. Nootau took a step forward toward the ocean; Samuel took one back, lowering himself down to the height of the reeds.

"What was that?" Samuel asked.

Nootau continued walking toward the water, his head on a swivel, oblivious of Samuel or the potential danger.

"Nootau, stop," Samuel said, his voice lacking the fear and distress that was bubbling inside.

Nootau took three or four more paces and then did stop. He stood motionless for a beat and then slowly craned his neck forward as he pointed out to the water.

Samuel stood tall again and followed with his eyes the direction of Nootau's point, at first seeing only the shadowy surface of the breakers.

"Do you see it, Samuel?" Nootau called back, tilting his head in Samuel's direction without averting his eyes from the water. His voice was a loud whisper, as if his full speaking voice would have made a difference.

"I don't..." Samuel took a half-step on the sand, barely edging outside of the false safety of the sea grass. He squinted but still couldn't see anything unusual.

"Come closer, Samuel! It is...rising." Samuel's voice was loud and deep now, a true summons, and he walked boldly to the very edge of the water, hypnotically drawn to whatever thing he was seeing. "There!"

Had it been anyone other than Nootau, Samuel may have begun to doubt his sanity. But Nootau was grounded, measured, not prone to exaggeration or dramatics as many of Samuel's own people were.

And he wasn't being dramatic.

As thoughts of Nootau's earnestness swirled in Samuel's mind, a black dome took shape atop the water, appearing amongst the waves as if placed there magically before Samuel's eyes. It was a featureless figure, smooth and glistening, like a large lump of opal floating on the water's surface.

"You see it, yes, Samuel?"

Samuel nodded. "I do."

"Then come."

"I thought we were going to hide, Nootau. Why are we out here in the open?"

Nootau was still entranced by the shape, unable to answer, and Samuel had little choice but to allow the moment to play out. After all, he still didn't know exactly what they were expecting to see here. Nootau's third-person account of some sea creature may have, in fact, been the mysterious black saucer bobbing currently atop the surface, perhaps released from some loose bed somewhere beneath the ocean. If this was all it was, what danger was there really?

But Samuel's instincts told him differently. Nootau was not bragging when he said his people didn't lie. Living the reality of the world was as natural to the Algonquin as fishing the waters or the planting of crops. This black dome was just the start; there was more to come.

Samuel closed his eyes for a moment and then opened them wide before summoning the courage to dash up to the water's edge where his friend stood in rapture. "Nootau," Samuel pleaded, gently stretching his arm across the boy's shoulders, attempting to steer him back to the dunes.

Nootau shrugged Samuel's hand away and took a half step to the side, but Samuel persisted, and kept close to his native comrade, grabbing Nootau's right arm with both hands, gripping tightly while dragging him back toward the dunes.

Nootau again tried to pull away, but Samuel held tightly, locking eyes with Nootau, softening his stare in a look that pled for the boy to listen and follow.

And then Nootau's look changed, as if he suddenly found the truth somewhere in Samuel's face. That his friend was right. That they were in mortal danger.

Nootau allowed himself to be pulled away now, all the while keeping his head turned toward the ocean as he jogged with Samuel back to the dunes. They stopped in their hiding place, and the two boys positioned themselves in a stoop behind the clump of seagrass.

Nootau immediately made a wide part in the middle of the clump, opening up the grass so he could have a clear view of the beach. Samuel edged his face in beside Nootau's to get a look as well.

And it was only a matter of moments before he saw it.

The myth of Nootau's people, the thing that Samuel had quietly dismissed only minutes ago was now his absolute truth for as long as he would live.

The large floating rock that had skidded the water suddenly breached the dull brownness of the ocean surface, surging up toward the sky like a sunken ship that had been resurrected by Poseidon. It moved forward toward the beach as it rose, angling up the slope of the land until its face was fully above the surface. In the dull light of the gloam and from the considerable distance at which they watched—there were perhaps seventy-five paces separating the boys and the creature—Samuel couldn't see the details of the beast's face. But he could sense its stare. Feel its craving.

"I told you, Samuel," Nootau said, his face awash in disbelief, fantasy. It wasn't a statement of victory, it was as if he were speaking to himself.

Samuel could only move his head back and forth, unclear that what was happening was indeed real. Was he truly witnessing the arrival of this thing on the shores of his adoptive home? He'd always feared the invaders of this land would come in the form of Spanish ships and thundering cannons, but it was instead this dark creature before him—surely an animal, Samuel presumed—flesh and blood, a being known only to him and Nootau and perhaps a few other natives. Kitchi for sure. But who else?

The dark monster's torso was now in the open air, and as dusk began to envelop the beach, the features of the figure became less distinct, a silhouette, an outline of this manlike entity that had arrived on the shores of this New World for a purpose that was yet unknown to Samuel.

The creature stepped effortlessly from the waves that broke at its feet until it had cleared the water and was positioned on the wet sand of the beach, perhaps only ten paces down from where Samuel and Nootau had been standing only moments ago.

Samuel couldn't breathe, but his eyes stayed fixed on the creature, and his mind raced for an explanation to what he was witnessing. It *was* religion, he thought, just as Nootau had explained moments ago, but this god was unlike anything found in his own theological studies. This god was incarnate, alive in this moment, its body standing so close to Samuel that he could have struck him with a stone.

"What is it doing?" Nootau whispered, and the quiver in his voice surprised Samuel. The brave warrior from moments ago seemed to be shrinking at the sight of the creature in its full form.

Samuel took the temperature of his own emotions and realized he didn't feel any fear in the moment, only awe and curiosity. "I don't know," he answered. And then, "Look!"

The black monster from the sea lifted its chin, turning its face toward the sky, as if looking there for some signal, some beacon being sent from off in the distance.

But Samuel knew what it was doing: it was smelling.

The creature lowered its chin back to its original position, and then it pivoted its head slowly from one side to the other, finally settling its direction on the clump of grass where Samuel and Nootau were hiding.

Nootau opened his mouth to speak, but Samuel put a finger to his own lips, silencing the boy before he could utter a sound. Samuel was in control now, and he pointed gently toward the creature, encouraging Nootau to watch and wait.

But the fear was growing in Nootau, and within moments it had enveloped him fully. The panic on his face was demonstrated by a paleness beneath his brown skin, and he suddenly began crawling away from the clump of grass, edging himself back toward the dunes that buttressed the sound.

"Nootau, wait," Samuel whispered, but it was too late. The Algonquin boy had risen to his feet and was now in a full sprint back toward the dunes and the awaiting canoe. Samuel kept his eyes on him for as long as he stayed in view, and then the darkness took over and the boy disappeared into the night.

Samuel took in a breath and then exhaled fully. And then a thought entered his mind: He had no fear of the creature. None at all. He could have spent all night staring at the beast, watching its movements, studying it until it too disappeared into the blackness of the evening.

Samuel's lack of fear buoyed him now. He had never felt brave in his life. Not once. He'd been as afraid of speaking with the girls in his class as he was of the natives in the village and the Spanish that were rumored to be arriving any day.

But not now, not when he should have been, and this courage sent a surge of strength through the entirety of his body. It was as if he had been injected with the antidote to all the shortcomings he had been cursed with since birth. Nootau, however, Samuel's Algonquin counterpart who had been better than Samuel at everything they had ever done together, and in whom Samuel had never noticed a trace of fear, was suddenly rendered petrified by the sight of this magical being of the sea. But Samuel was thriving on the vision, watching the emergence of this new miracle not with anxiety or terror but with reverence, idolatry.

But Samuel also recognized there was only one way for him to get back to the colony, and that was in the canoe.

And if Nootau was completely consumed with fear—as he appeared to be—he may just leave Samuel behind. Samuel wanted to continue examining the creature, but he also knew the barrier island was not a place to spend the night. Not under any circumstances, and certainly not those he currently faced.

Samuel stood and began to follow Nootau's tracks to the dunes, turning once more toward the ocean to catch a final glimpse of the creature.

It was gone.

Samuel stopped and squinted, taking one step toward the ocean, moving out of the thicket of grass and stepping back onto the sand, trying to bring it back into his vision. He stared out to the water now, considering it had, perhaps, returned to the sea. But there was only the darkness of the disinterested waves.

Samuel was torn now; he wanted to investigate further where the beast had gone, but his sense of preservation finally won over, and he raced back to the sound, arriving at the place where he and Nootau had docked the canoe. Nootau was there, standing on the bank, crying.

The canoe was gone.

"What..? What happened?" Samuel asked. "Where is the boat?"

Nootau said nothing.

"Nootau, where is the boat?"

Nootau turned to Samuel now, the pleading, desperate look in his eyes as painful a thing as Samuel had ever seen. "It must have..." Nootau only shook his head, disbelieving their fate.

"It's okay, Nootau, we'll..."

"What?"

But Samuel didn't know exactly what they would do. "We may have to stay here for the night, I suppose. But in the morning, when we haven't returned, they'll come for us. Someone will see that the boat is missing and they'll figure out that we've come to the ocean."

Nootau scoffed, and Samuel noted it was the first time he'd ever heard his friend make that particular sound. "I can't stay here, Samuel. Not with that...I can't stay here. I can't *be* here."

Samuel gave a bemused smile. "But this is what you wanted to see. You were the one who insisted we come. You knew of it, right. From Kitchi? Why are you so frightened by it now that you've seen it?"

Nootau looked at Samuel, a quizzical look on his face. "Why are you not frightened, Samuel?"

Samuel looked away, giving the question its due consideration. He frowned and shook his head. "I don't know."

Nootau turned his head up to the sky as if measuring the time, or perhaps forecasting the weather, and then he looked across the sound and inhaled deeply. "I'm going to swim it, Samuel. You can stay here. When I get back—"

"Swim it?"

"I've done it before. My people are good swimmers, Samuel; you know that. It won't be easy at this hour and with the little food that is in my stomach, but I have to try."

"No, you don't. We can build a lean-to shelter for the night and—"

"I'm going, Samuel!"

Samuel had also never heard Nootau raise his voice in anger before, and he allowed the words to ring in the air. "Okay, Nootau.

Samuel turned and walked back to the dunes, half-expecting Nootau, if not to follow him, at least to request a moment to give his apology. But Nootau said nothing.

Samuel listened as the boy slipped into the calm waters of the sound and began his smooth swimming stroke back to the colony. Samuel was alone now, left to his own survival for the night. Nootau would bring help as promised—Samuel had no doubt about that—but in the meantime, Samuel needed to find shelter.

Bwoosh!

Samuel screamed aloud at the sound, which hadn't come from the ocean this time, but from the sound, where Nootau had just begun his long, aquatic journey.

"Oh my god," Samuel whispered, and then sprinted back to the shores of the sound.

Samuel stopped frozen at the shoreline. It was as if he'd run straight into a tree, and he nearly tumbled forward into the water.

The first vision of the creature had changed Samuel's outlook on life forever, knowing now that there were beasts and monsters that were beyond his own nightmares. But now, as he witnessed the creature devouring his friend, writhing its head and arms in a fury of destruction and power, Samuel became a devoted follower.

Samuel stood silently as he watched the beast rip Nootau's limbs from his torso, and then sink its teeth into the top of the boy's head. Samuel could see only the whites of the Algonquin boy's eyes in the darkness as they filled the entirety of his sockets.

There were few screams before his life was taken completely, and as the creature dipped beneath the surface of the sound, his victim in tow, Samuel smiled.

Chapter 4

It was Thursday.

That meant Shane had seen the black and purple man—Danny's Ocean God of two years ago—only five days earlier. Danny assumed it was on the very beach where he now stood, but he couldn't be a hundred percent sure on that count. But the boy had looked out to the water when he spoke, as if considering that it might appear any moment, so Danny decided his assumption was probably a good one.

Still, there were other details that would have been useful. The time of day. How far it had come out of the water, if at all. And if anyone else had seen it. As to this last question, Danny had to assume a no; otherwise, he figured, Shane would have mentioned it, as children are usually quick to offer corroborating evidence.

Danny gathered up his light equipment and jogged back to the rental house, immediately rushing to the locked storage closet beneath the house. He fished the key from atop the jamb and opened the door, and then began to bring out the amplifiers and the rest of his sound equipment that he would be using that night. He paused a moment and looked to the ground, thinking about what had just happened. There had been a first-account sighting of the creature—albeit from a nine-year old—but it was news that was nothing short of stunning.

It also meant the morning experiments at the beach using only his iPhone were no longer sufficient. It was time to bring out the big guns.

He closed and locked the storage door, and then brought two of the four amplifiers up the steps and into the kitchen, and as he turned back for the other two, a voice from behind him asked, "Are you ready?"

Danny shrieked and spun around, knocking over one of the amps, nearly stumbling over it as he backed away.

"You've got to be kidding me," Sam chuckled, rolling her eyes and shaking her head.

Danny took two deep breaths and then gathered himself, trying to look relaxed, acting as if it he hadn't forgotten the woman was still in his house. "Kidding about what?"

"You forgot. You forgot about me and breakfast."

Danny made a face that said he was incredibly offended by the accusation. "What? That's not true. I never forget about breakfast."

"Not funny."

"I'm kidding. I haven't forgotten. I just need to get some things ready for work tonight. And I'll admit it, I was lost in thought, but I did not forget."

Sam frowned and raised her eyebrows in a look of *Yeah, sure*, and then asked, "And what kind of work do you do, Dan?"

"I'm a...songwriter. Didn't we talk about this already? Last night, maybe."

Sam shook her head. "So you got some kind of gig tonight?"

"Yeah, something like that."

"Really? Maybe I'll come by and see you. You playing over at Fat Boy Sam's? Or The Dunk Tank?"

"No, neither, it's not exactly *that* kind of thing." Danny had no intention of letting the conversation get much further along, since that would require getting into the details. He changed the subject. "You ready for breakfast?"

"I thought you'd never ask."

Danny quietly brought the rest of the equipment inside and then he and Sam drove to a diner that overlooked the ocean in the only bustling part of Wickard Beach. After a short wait, they got a perfect corner table next to the window.

Once they were seated and had finished complimenting the beautiful view, an awkward silence befell the table, and for several minutes, each took sips of water, alternating murmurings of 'just lovely,' or 'nice day,' or some such banality. Danny was praying for the waitress to come and hurry the date along; his mind was elsewhere obviously, and he and Sam were beginning to feel the embarrassment of last night more heavily. For a moment, Danny considered pretending to get a phone call—an emergency, of course—thus forcing them to have to leave immediately. He would obviously drop Sam off on the way, but things happen. Sorry.

"Why are you here, Danny?" Sam asked bluntly.

"At breakfast? I'm hungry."

But Sam didn't give even a courtesy smile at the joke. She just stared at Danny, her eyes cold and locked in. "That's not what I mean. Why did you come to Wickard Beach? You aren't from here, that's obvious, and you're not here on vacation either. You're clearly here to stay though. At least for a while. So why?"

Danny shrugged and then nodded out the window. The sun was now high and the pier that stretched out from the restaurant into the ocean was awash in its rays, the surf beneath it splashing against the A-frame pylon supports. It was a gorgeous scene, and the dunes that separated the diner and the water sprouted golden sea grass from their mounds. Danny loved dunes, always had, even in his life before the sighting. He knew a lot of people thought they were an eyesore, weed-carriers that ruined an otherwise smooth, perfect seascape. But Danny thought the dunes were perfect.

"Look at this place. Who wouldn't want to live here?"

Sam looked out the window and seemed to give an earnest assessment of the landscape before saying, "Yes, it's very beautiful. There's lots of beautiful places. Why did you pick here?"

"Hi, I'm Natalia," a voice chirped from behind them. "I'll be taking care of you today."

Danny turned to see a girl who looked barely seventeen, her eyes wide and smiling, pencil and pad positioned for the order.

"Hi, Natalia," Danny answered, the relief in his voice palpable.

"Can I start y'all off with—"

"Can we have a minute, please?" Sam interrupted, her eyes never leaving Danny's.

Natalia shifted her wide eyes over to Sam and then back to Danny.

Danny gave a painful, squinted smile. "Sorry. Just another minute."

Natalia moved to the next table and recited her welcome line and Danny sat back in the booth, staring at Sam. "Okay, Sam, if you must know, I moved here because I like the ocean. I really like the ocean. It's that simple. I like to be near the sea. Maybe I was a pirate in a past life."

"Didn't you live at the ocean before? In the last place you lived?"

Danny narrowed his look, tilting his head slightly. "I don't remember telling you that."

"Yeah, well, you also didn't remember my name this morning. What did you do, take a peek at my license?"

Danny didn't address the accusation, still suspicious of the previous question. "I have some bad memories in the place where I lived before. Very bad. So I'm trying to give myself a fresh start."

"Memories like what?"

Danny snickered and shook his head, hoping to convey the signal that he was willing to put up with this line of questioning for perhaps a little longer, but that Sam was starting to push it. And that if it continued, he would shut the whole rest of the morning down, breakfast or not.

"You know, in some parts of the world, a question like that would be considered intrusive. Rude even."

"Not here in Wickard, I guess."

"No, I guess not. But then I guess my reply of 'None of your business, Sam' wouldn't be either."

Sam didn't flinch, which made Danny slightly uncomfortable.

"Why are you so interested in what I'm doing here anyway? Who cares? By all the indications I've gotten since I've been here, this is exactly the kind of place where people come for no reason. Just to retire or drop out or whatever. Why all the curiosity?"

Sam dropped her eyes now and directed them out the window. "Where the hell's the waitress?"

Danny was intrigued now by the chord he had apparently struck. "Do you know something about me?"

Sam returned her stare to Danny. "Is there something I should?"

Chapter 5

"Tell us again what happened, Samuel."

Samuel's head was as low as it would hang, his chin pressed tightly against his chest, shame emanating from him in the form of tears and spit and snot. He shook his head slowly, the mess on his face exaggerated with each turn of his neck.

"Pick your head up, boy, and answer the question," Samuel's mother hissed from behind him, shoving a handkerchief in front of her son.

Samuel cleaned himself up and then tried desperately to compose himself, trying not to draw suspicion by recovering too quickly from his hysteria. He looked up slowly at the four brown figures seated in front of him. They were seated tall and proud, with their backs pressed against the northern wall of the village's largest wigwam. The expressions they wore were as still and muted as the face of a stone mountain.

"It is okay, Samuel," the only female amongst the group offered. It was Nootau's mother, unquestionably the most beautiful woman on the island. "We don't blame you for anything, but we must know the details of what happened to Nootau."

"Nootau was a very strong swimmer," a male voice added. This was Nootau's father, and that he didn't make eye contact with the boy standing before him, Samuel took as a sign that he did, indeed, blame him for his son's death.

"Tell them, boy," Samuel's mother barked, and Samuel could almost see the clench of her teeth. Fear was dripping

42

from her with every word. She knew they were in danger here every day, even under the best of circumstances, which these times were not. And with Samuel's father now gone, perhaps forever, there were no other options but to survive here in the colony, to coexist with these natives who had magnanimously decided to allow them to stay.

But with the death of one of their own—a boy—the talented, bright son of a prominent native family, one who possessed a promising future for the tribe, the situation for the Cook family became that much more precarious, especially when his white colonialist friend was a witness to the whole thing.

Samuel steeled his expression and looked at Nootau's mother, trying to keep his eyes above her ample chest and on her face. "He said that his father encouraged adventure, that he should use his free days as a means to overcome struggles, to prepare for his encroaching manhood years."

Nootau's mother averted her eyes to the floor of the wigwam and then turned her head just a fraction in the direction of her husband. Nootau's father closed his eyes for a moment, the corners of his mouth edging down slightly.

"So, we took the canoe to the barrier island, and then we ventured further, across the dunes and down to the ocean. And there we played a game. A game we made up together." Samuel looked away again, as if the memory of he and Nootau's escapades were too painful to recall.

"What game, Samuel?" The kind voice of Nootau's mother now frightened Samuel, as if she already knew what he was about to tell her was a lie.

"We called it 'Invaders.'"

"Invaders?"

Samuel smiled weakly and nodded. "We would pretend that Spanish ships were appearing by the dozens on the horizon, and while they were approaching, we would prepare our fortifications and arsenal for the impending battles. We pretended it was just the two of us who had been assigned to protect the village, so there was much to do." Samuel smiled. "And when the Spaniards finally arrived and the fighting began, of course we were always victorious."

Nootau's mother smiled now, and Samuel felt her hand rest on his shoulder. The touch wasn't one of consolation; it was a signal that her son was doing an adequate job of keeping the natives at bay.

"And then what happened?" Nootau's mother asked.

Samuel took a deep breath and gave a long blink, opening his eyes just before exhaling. "He said we couldn't wait on the shores for the final ship of the armada; they were firing cannons from the bow and we were taking too many casualties on land. He said..." Samuel stopped and swallowed, choking on his words for a moment. "He said we had to swim out past where the waves broke. That we had to board the ship and take out the enemy from aboard. I'm not a good swimmer, I wouldn't have made it, and Nootau knew that, so..."

Samuel began to cry again, but before he went into another bout of full-on bawling, he gathered himself quickly, bravely, standing tall, mimicking the rigid look of the Algonquins.

"So he told me to defend the shoreline while he took to the water." He paused and looked Nootau's mother directly in the eye. "And that's when it took him."

"The shark?" Nootau's mother asked.

Samuel nodded.

"I only saw the fin right before it was upon him. I didn't even have a chance to call his name. He screamed and went under. I saw the blood and then..." At this point the tears came again, and in seconds Samuel was hysterical.

"It is okay, Samuel. Thank you."

Samuel nodded and went under the outstretched arm of his mother, pushing in close to her as they walked slowly from the wigwam and out to the awaiting eyes of the colony.

Samuel didn't open his eyes the entire way home, but as he walked, he envisioned the sight again of the beast that rose from the sound. And with that memory, he couldn't hold back a smile.

***

"I don't believe him."

Kitchi, now the youngest member of the four Algonquins who lived in the wigwam, was back in his bed, carried there by his brother Ahanu, who had returned to his work repairing the family's longhouse. Kitchi's back was flush against the wall in the corner of the structure; he was smoking tobacco and sipping mead from a cup made of clay.

"You don't know him, Kitchi," Nootau's mother answered, her voice dreamy, still in disbelief that her son was gone forever. "He and Nootau were friends. They were very good friends." She continued sweeping the sawdust from the home, her eyes never leaving the floor.

"I don't need to know him. He is a white man. And thus, he is a killer inside."

"He is a boy."

Kitchi waved a hand at his sister.

"What do you believe, Matunaagd?" Nootau's mother stopped her house work and stared at her husband, as if the idea that he may have thoughts had just come to her.

Nootau's father had not moved from the chair where he sat only moments earlier, listening patiently, ostensibly, to the tale of his son's death, a tale that had been spun from the mouth of a white English child. He quietly stared at the door where Samuel had exited, his eyes as distant as the land of the white man, reflecting on his own child and what role he, Matunaagd, had played in his death.

"Matunaagd?"

Matunaagd turned to his wife, a lone tear now in the middle of his cheek. He pinched his lips, trying to hold back the emotion that was bubbling beneath.

Nootau's mother, Nadie, strode slowly toward her husband and stood beside him, taking his head in her breast, stroking his hair as she took in a deep breath, holding back tears of her own. "What do you think, Matunaagd?"

Matunaagd wiped the tear from his cheek angrily, and then stood and walked to the opening of the wigwam.

Nadie followed him, placing her hand on his bicep as he reached the threshold. "Where are you going?"

At his wife's touch, Matunaagd stopped and stared out at the scene of the village square. It was a vision of solitude, a depiction of peace and cooperation.

To his left he watched Ahanu assist in repairing the long-house roof, a critical job as they prepared for the encroaching winter months. There were white men and Algonquins working in harmony, brown hands below passing long strips of bark to white hands above, or white shoulders below hoisting long poles up to another set of Algonquin shoulders that rose high atop the roof.

This scene alone was an unthinkable possibility only one year ago, Matunaagd thought, let alone the dozens of other projects and transactions that occurred daily. He had always assumed by now one of the groups would have been killed off, and, he was ashamed to say, he truly thought it would have been his own.

But a truce had been developed between his people and those from the sea—the place called England—a land at the other side of the Great Western Sea where rulers chased their own people from the land.

The Great Western Sea.

It was a moniker brought to Matunaagd's land from the white man, the name given to the *Yapam*—the sea—which had been a part of his entire life. Of course, the Yapam sat to the east of his tribe, east of every tribe in this land, but Matunaagd had grown to enjoy the majestic sound of the 'Great Western Sea,' and he had begun to refer to it the same way.

It was just one of the many things he and his people had adopted from the white man, just as they had borrowed from his people, and this mutual exchange of language and ideas—and later goods and services—had cultivated a semblance of respect amongst the two groups. Somehow, despite the unwelcomed nature of the relationship, there began the start of a road that could one day lead to lasting peace. It was a narrow road, one still obscured by a litany of differences, but the first stones had been set.

But then the hunger came.

The harvest had been a difficult one for two consecutive cycles, and though the hauls brought in by the fishermen were still moderate, the animals of the land had all but disappeared from the immediate surroundings. Hunting for deer and moose now often required trips of several days just for a chance at finding meat, instead of the late morning kills that had been so routine before. It was as if the land animals had sensed the danger of the European invaders and had fled for safer pastures.

The wisdom of the animals.

Of course, if Matunaagd was being honest with himself, he knew that scarcity was no new problem in this land, and with the failed crops of the current cycle, hunger would have been a challenge with or without the existence of these settlers. There had been at least one lean cycle every decade for as long as Matunaagd's memory went back, and with each of those cycles, his people had struggled through with grace and strength. And there was no question they would have seen it through this time around.

But with the arrival of the English—who Matunaagd had counted at a little over a hundred when they first arrived, but whose numbers were now closer to eighty, mostly due to the departure of the men who had traveled with John White back to England—the village was nearing a breaking point. Matunaagd figured in a little over a month, scarcity would turn to famine.

And the tribe had begun to look to him for answers.

"This won't last, Nadie," Matunaagd said, as if acknowledging the truth for the first time. "The harmony of this village won't last for much longer."

Nadie turned away, feeling the sting of her husband's words, and then she sighed and turned back, her chin high and sure. "You're angry, Matunaagd. I am too. And I don't know..." She caught her breath, putting her hand to her chest, panicking at the thoughts racing through her mind. "I don't know how to go on without Nootau. Perhaps I won't."

Matunaagd whipped his head toward his wife, a look of fear and abandonment glistening in his eyes.

Nadie only shrugged at the look from her husband, in no state to be reassuring. "But we have done much to bring the village to this place of peace." She nodded out toward the hard-working villagers working alongside the colonists. "And you have been a big part of it. Food is scarce, and that is a problem, but we have grown a resource even more valuable to our survival: trust."

Matunaagd allowed his wife's words to settle, considering them deeply as he resumed his surveillance out across the village, watching the setting sun as it illuminated the roofs of the wigwams like unripe kernels of corn. He wanted to tell her that none of it mattered if they all starved to death, but he kept his tongue silent on that matter. "Do you trust them?"

Nadie frowned and lowered her head, now searching for the truth herself.

"Because Kitchi doesn't," Matunaagd continued, lowering his voice further, keeping his brother-in-law out of earshot. "And I fear if rebellion comes, it will be he who leads it. He cannot walk, but his voice is as strong as any on the island."

"Kitchi," Nadie scoffed. "What merit can you put in his opinion? He doesn't trust anyone from outside the tribe."

"Perhaps that is another strength."

"No, Matunaagd, it isn't. There is no life for us without the trust of these people. How could there be? Our people have collided now, there is no turning back. More of them will come."

"So then the answer is 'yes,' you do trust them. But only because you must. That is something, I suppose, but it is not trust."

"I trust the Cooks," Nadie answered quickly, "and that is the only issue on my mind at the moment." She lowered her voice again. "They have given me no reason not to. Even if the motives of some of the others are nefarious, and they intend war at some point, I don't believe that of the Cooks. I believe it has always been their intention to live beside us. To integrate their lives with ours. Morris Cook is a good man."

"And Elyoner?"

Nadie focused her eyes into her husband's, swallowing hard before answering. "Yes, I trust her as well."

"She doesn't trust you, Nadie. You know that, right?"

"I don't believe that."

"Did you hear the way she spoke to Samuel? Did you see her face as he spoke?"

"That was fear, Matunaagd, not distrust. She is frightened to be here. She is a woman—one of only a dozen in the village to have come here from her land—and she is in a place as foreign to her as the night heavens. And with her husband gone, she is also alone. I would be frightened too."

Matunaagd shook his head. "You would not be frightened like that. There *was* fear, of course, but there was anger within her too. Rage. It was directed at her son during the questioning, but there is a more concentrated anger that bubbles beneath her. I can feel it in her, as I do in many of these settlers. You can feel it too."

Nadie nodded solemnly.

"We have structured a peace, that is true, but it is as precarious as the longhouses during the great winds."

Nadie said nothing further on the matter, instead switching back to the subject of her son's death. "Why did he go there, Matunaagd? Why did he go to the Yapam? We have told him not to go there alone. Not during this time of the cycle."

"He wasn't alone, Nadie." Matunaagd felt the burn of shame form on his face, and he could only look to the dusty ground that was just outside of the wigwam. It was his suggestion to explore the world, and though Nadie had emphasized that Nootau must always stay on the island, unless given explicit permission to leave, Matunaagd, himself, had never stressed the point during the conversations he and his son had had alone.

"I don't blame you, Matunaagd," Nadie replied, sensing the guilt flowing from her husband. "But the stories from Samuel are confusing to me." She looked away, shaking her head, trying to organize the thoughts that were scrambled inside it. "I want to believe him, and I suppose I do, but if Nootau wanted to go to the Yapam, he knew to ask us for permission. It was not a point of debate."

"He is...he was twelve, Nadie."

Nadie furrowed her brow, trying to find the point.

"I was mating fishing expeditions at that age."

"He is dead!" Nadie screamed, and then instantly settled her demeanor. "I don't care what you were doing when you were twelve. You've had forty years since. For Nootau, it is the last age he will ever experience."

Matunaagd turned his stare back to the bed where Kitchi still lay. The crippled man's head was now resting back in a drunken state against the wall. His eyes were slightly open, presumably from the sound of his sister's cry, and they shifted toward Matunaagd, catching his look just before Matunaagd looked back to his wife.

"I'm sorry, Nadie," Matunaagd whispered. "It was my fault."

Nadie shook off the apology, as if no longer able to bear the sound or her husband's voice. "It wasn't your fault, Matunaagd. I have no anger toward you."

Nadie walked back inside the main room of the wigwam and sat at a desk she had helped construct for Nootau out of chestnut and pine only months earlier. She sat straight in the chair for a few beats, staring at the wall, and then put her head in her hands and began to cry.

Matunaagd looked back to his wife and then walked out of the wigwam.

The desk beneath Nadie's cheeks had begun to form pools of tears in the crevices of the imperfect surface, and Nadie couldn't imagine the sorrow would ever end. Each sob jogged another memory of her son, each more meaningful than the last. And just as Nadie was rounding into moanful release, a voice from across the room spoke.

"Nadie."

Nadie nearly screamed at the sound of her own name. She turned to see her brother, his head in the same position as earlier, only his eyes were open now, thin and alert.

"Kitchi?"

Having seized the attention of his sister, Kitchi turned away and stared at the wall in front of him. He lit an oak leaf rolled with kinnikinnick and exhaled the smoke slowly, allowing it to dissipate before speaking. "Have you ever heard the story?"

Nadie blinked several times and shook her head, unclear about what her brother was asking. "The story? What story?"

Kitchi closed his eyes in a long blink and then turned his head toward his sister, opening his eyes slowly and softening his look upon her. "The one about the Croatoan."

Chapter 6

Danny had finished adjusting the speakers on the porch well before lunchtime, and by mid-afternoon, he had tested the sound a dozen times, positioning himself at various places on the beach, testing whether he could hear the low bass cries of the whales from a variety of places. He even waded out into chest-high water at one point, nearly becoming hypothermic, catching the confused, disapproving looks of an elderly couple taking a hearty stroll across the sands of Wickard Beach.

Danny realized his testing was largely unnecessary, since the recorded sounds of the minke whale would need to penetrate the surface of the ocean and be heard by the sea beast from beneath the water. And even at the highest volume, Danny could really only hear the feedback from the speakers, not the impossibly low sounds of the actual whales.

He had dropped Sam off immediately after breakfast, a breakfast that required him to dodge her questions, making sure never to get close to the subject of Rove Beach or the sighting.

Or his encounters with the god.

As far as Sam knew, Danny was in the throes of a mid-life crisis, the source of which was a messy divorce and a burning need to find meaning in his life. Collecting royalty checks from a hit song was a nice way to feed your belly, he had told her, but it fell far short of feeding your soul. It was a good line, he thought, one he was proud of coming up with on the spot.

Still, there was something about the woman that touched him the wrong way. She had come on strong the previous night at Mason's when they had met over flat beer and a game of darts. Danny had planned to spend the night playing alone, but Sam had sauntered over, watched for a minute, and then invited herself in to the game. Danny had pegged her as kind of ditzy, frankly, a past-her-prime bar chick with a moderate drinking problem who was looking for a string of good times to fill up her weekly calendar.

But the next morning had revealed someone a bit different. She was suddenly sharp, aware of herself, and whereas the two or three one-night stands Danny had had in his life preferred discreet mornings and silent exits, Samantha chose to stay a while.

And then came breakfast, where the questions had come fast and loose, challenging even, with a real desire to know about Danny's life. She'd asked more about him after one night than most people did in a year.

Danny sat at the edge of the faded Adirondack chair—the only piece of furniture on the porch—and methodically began to flip through the first few sections of the Washington Post, stopping when he reached the local Metro section. He tossed the rest of the paper to the floor of the porch and began scanning each of the columns, looking for any headline that might suggest the beast's appearance. This was his morning routine for the past two years, and though he was confident now that he had landed in the right place by coming to Wickard Beach, old habits died hard.

Danny found nothing unusual in the local section of the national paper, so, as was his practice, Danny moved on to the local rag—The Wickard Beach Times. Danny could read the entire paper in ten minutes, so he normally read more than just the headlines, trying to immerse himself in the local culture. He had just finished reading the first sentence of the front page, when something—he couldn't have said it was a sound, but rather the sensing of a feeling—caused him to look up and south down the beach.

Above the surface of the water, barely within the range of Danny's vision, were two figures rising just above the surface of the water.

Danny stood and walked to the railing of the porch, leaning forward as far as he could without tumbling over the rickety plank. But he'd barely narrowed the distance at all and was still well too far away to even guess what he was seeing. The figures could have been a pair of birds or simple debris.

Or the creature.

Danny blindly reached to his left, feeling for the binoculars that he had always kept beside him, but his fingers felt only splintered wood. "Dammit!"

Danny rushed back inside and immediately saw the binoculars sitting on the bar. He swiped them and then, instead of heading back to the porch for a magnified look, he rushed down the stairs and toward the water, scaling over the dunes until he was standing on the beach.

He knew the decision was a mistake even before he arrived on the sand. He had no doubt that whatever objects he had just seen floating on the water would now be gone when he looked through the lenses. The elusiveness of the god was a curse now. The binoculars weren't on the porch for a reason; they weren't where they should have been because it was the intent of the universe for him never to see the creature again.

Danny took a deep breath and then another, internalizing his feelings, noticing the manic nature of his thoughts. He closed his eyes and lifted his head slowly, turning it in the direction of the figures on the water, keeping the binoculars down by his side.

He opened his eyes again. And the figures were still there.

The two dark blobs atop the water were shaped differently from one another, he could tell that much, so it was likely that whatever the things were, they weren't birds. But it was just as unlikely they had to do with the creature either.

For a moment, Danny considered not looking through the binoculars at all, and instead turning back to the house, packing what little possessions he had brought with him, and setting off to some dry, landlocked state up in the Rocky Mountains. It would have been a safer decision for both his sanity and his life. After all, what if one of the things on the water was indeed the creature, and this new vision that Danny caught of it through the magnified lenses converted him back to the addict he had been before, instead of the hunter he had vowed to become?

But this was the moment to which Danny had committed the last two years of his life. He was confident he could see it again without falling under its spell, but if he saw it *kill* again, that was a more unknown proposition. Danny compared it to recovering alcoholics. Most could walk into a bar without succumbing to the addiction, but few could actually take a drink.

Danny took another deep breath and cleared his mind of any thoughts. He lifted the binoculars slowly and then stared out to the waves, and within seconds, he could tell at once that neither of the figures bobbing amongst the waves was the creature. They were too small, both in height and width, and there was something less secure about the way they drifted in the current, as if struggling for stability.

But Danny was right about the presence of something alive, and by the looks of it now, at least one of the figures was a person.

The object furthest out appeared to be a head, and it was just barely above the surface of the water, though still relatively close to the shoreline.

Danny lowered the binoculars and walked up to the water's edge, glancing down the beach in either direction to see if anyone else was in the vicinity. It was a cold afternoon, and there were only a handful of people as far as he could see, several of whom were fishermen who had set up in various positions well down the beach from where he stood currently.

Danny broke into a steady jog in the direction of the "swimmer," and within twenty seconds or so he was standing parallel with him. It looked as if the person was trying to wade in the same spot, to stay as far out as possible without being below the water, but he was losing his fight with the current, and it was slowly bringing him further and further from shore.

Danny flipped off his sandals and waded into the ocean, at first just up to his shins, and then waist deep. At this distance, he could see the clear shape of a head, and a full head of hair—there was no question now that this was a person. But why was he just drifting there? And what was floating behind him?

"Hey!" Danny screamed. "Do you need help?"

The figure turned instantly toward Danny's voice, and Danny noted immediately the wide, terrified eyes of the boy he had met on the beach earlier that morning.

Shane.

Danny lifted his shirt above his head and tossed it to the surf, his throw not quite making it to the sand, and then he began to swim toward the boy.

"What are you doing out here," Danny called, keeping his chin above the water with each stroke, his eyes focused on the boy. As he neared him, he could see that the other thing on the water was a bag of some sort, a backpack, a Jansport by the looks of it, and it was sitting atop a round inflatable.

The boy turned back toward the horizon, and then made a feeble effort to move south, down the beach and away from Danny. He could barely move his arms, and Danny imagined he must be close to hypothermia in these temperatures.

Danny followed him and was now within grabbing distance of him. But he restrained himself. At this distance, Danny figured he could bring the boy in, even if he fought, be he didn't want to take any unnecessary chances. Maybe he could just talk the boy into shore.

"What are you doing out here, Shane?"

Shane looked to be nearing panic now, and he glanced once out toward the horizon before looking back at Danny.

"I know he wwwants it," he said, Shane's blue lips struggling to form the words.

But the sentence, even with its lack of grace, sent a chill down Danny's already ice-cold spine. "He?"

Shane closed his eyes, and Danny thought he saw a smile appear for just a moment. "The Black and Purple Man."

Danny nodded, suddenly terrified at his position on the water. The god was here, in Wickard Beach, at least that's what he now believed. And twenty yards out from the shore was not the place to be. He looked out in the distance of the endless surface of black-green water, and envisioned the beast rising from the surface. It was the game he played as a boy, only then it was the fin of a shark he imagined.

"What does he want, Shane?"

Shane swallowed hard, and somehow his eyes grew even wider than they already were. And then he glanced toward the backpack.

"You've brought him food, Shane? It's food for The Black and Purple Man?"

Shane smiled widely now, there was no mistaking it. And then he gave a slow, confident nod. Danny recognized the spell he was under; he could see it in Shane's every movement.

"Well, why don't we go in and let him come to us? It's very cold, Shane. We won't last out here much longer."

"Not until he eats."

Danny knew he had no choice now but to grab the boy. If he didn't, he was either going to drown or freeze to death. And if he waited too long, both would meet that fate. "We'll feed him from the sand."

Danny tried one last time, moving closer to Shane as he spoke, his hands searching beneath the water for one of the boy's arms.

"I think he wants him here," Shane said. "It will be easier."

"Him?"

Danny looked again at the backpack, which looked stuffed to its limits.

And just as Danny grabbed Shane's wrist beneath the water, he heard the cries of a baby.

Chapter 7

"Of course I know of the Croatoan. They have been our neighbors for centuries. And we have existed peacefully with the tribe for as long as that."

Kitchi nodded, as if he had expected this very reply from his sister. "Yes, the Croatoan tribe. But somehow, I think you know I'm not asking about that. I think you have heard the story—the story of the Croatoan—from our Numohshomus."

Nadie stood quickly, scoffing and shaking her head as she rose, and then she strode with purpose to the doorway. She had heard many stories from their grandfather, most of which were to do with spirits and ghosts, the rising dead or some other such monstrous nonsense. "I love you, Kitchi, but I cannot see your face in this moment. I am mourning the death of my only son; I will not entertain the talk of foreign myths that were once told by grandfather."

"Sit down, Nadie," Kitchi barked.

Nadie turned in shock toward her brother, her jaw in a clench that signaled preparation for a fight. She would have fought a bear at this moment, and would have had no reservations about mixing it up with her brother as well, crippled or not.

But there was a tenor in Kitchi's voice that penetrated Nadie. It was grave, in a way he usually was not, and it completely masked the drunkenness that had certainly set into his cells. She couldn't remember another time when she had heard him speak in this way. She walked back to the chair in front of the desk and this time sat high and rigid, staring at her brother with a look of challenge and cynicism.

"I always thought the Croatoan was a myth also. You think you are the only skeptic in the family, Nadie?"

Nadie didn't answer.

"At one time, only a few generations back from ours, there were stories of people with white skin who lived across the Yapam. They were also a myth. Even though these white faces had been seen before, seen by our people, those who told their stories to others, of their encounters with these white men, were dismissed as storytellers and myth-makers."

"It is not the same, Kitchi. Those tales were of men not monsters. Most Algonquin suspected there were others in this world besides us, others beyond the tribes, beyond the Yapam that we could not reach."

Kitchi shrugged. "Perhaps. But it was still a story. Suspected but not known for sure. Just as we may believe there is life outside of this world. Beyond the depth of the sun and the night sky. We suspect but don't believe. Because we cannot see it."

"What is your point, Kitchi?" Nadie was losing patience with her brother, regretful that she had engaged him. "My husband has left in a state of dismay and I must find him before the sun sets. I must make my house right again before nightfall."

"Numohshomus lived amongst the Croatoans when he was a boy. Were you aware of that?"

Nadie shook her head reflexively, furrowing her forehead, shaken by this revelation concerning her grandfather. "Lived with them? Why?"

"His father conducted trade with the Croatoan, it was his business, and for most of the cycles, he was prosperous in trade. But not all. There came consecutive cycles of frost and drought, and at one point disease left the village depleted of men to work, and at the end of the third or fourth cycle, he was despondent, indebted."

"So?"

"He had offered his son, our Numohshomus, as collateral."

"My god."

"And when he couldn't deliver for what he had been paid by the Croatoan, he had no choice but to give over his son to them."

"Is this true?" Nadie whispered, her voice a combination of both fascination and disgust.

"It is true. I believe it is."

"But he returned to the village. It is how we came to be here now."

"His time with the Croatoan was short—he said that the village was able to pool enough resources to buy him back within a full cycle. But he spent time amongst them, as a slave in practice, and during those days, he saw the sacrifices they offered."

"Sacrifices?" Nadie scoffed. "What do you speak of, Kitchi? Sacrifices? The Croatoans are not like us, that much I will grant you, and on the few occasions when we have crossed paths, admittedly, I've been less than impressed with their demeanor. But they are not an uncivilized people. They are not like those empires to the south that fell when the white man arrived. The Croatoans don't slaughter virgins for the pleasure of their gods. They don't *sacrifice* in exchange for peace or bounty. Or whatever it is those earlier people did it for."

Kitchi nodded his head in agreement. "No, that is true, Nadie. But the Croatoan did not kill for the pleasure of their gods."

"Then what, Kitchi, what are you telling me?"

"The Croatoan. The beast of the sea. The tribe sacrificed their victims for the vision of it. For the pleasure of watching it kill."

"Pleasure of watching it kill? I don't know what that even means? Where is this coming from, Kitchi? I never heard any of these stories from Numohshomus. He did speak of a sea creature, black and awful he had said, full of brute strength and teeth. And he spoke of it in the way we speak of travelers from the stars or our own tales of the sea. With great exaggeration, in the language of cautionary tales. Those were never intended to be heard literally."

Kitchi listened to his sister speak, granting her the space to find the truth.

Nadie held her brother's eyes, and the resolute nature of them made her suddenly doubt her own recollection and the sincerity of her grandfather's tales. "He did tell me the Croatoan took their name from this creature, but...that this thing, which he never quite described fully, rose and fed every cycle and a half or so."

"Just as he told it to me."

"It was a rather nonsensical tale, really. I recall it bored me." Nadie tried to manufacture a laugh of dismissal, but it came out as nervous and fearful. "So many of his tales had such great creativity. Great metaphors that gave a tiny addition of meaning to life. But not this one. With this one, I never knew what story he was really trying to tell."

"This was no metaphor, Nadie. That is why it seemed out of place. He was telling the story as it happened. The story that he was a witness to. Numohshomus saw this creature with his own eyes. Saw it rise from the ocean like a devil from a watery hell. He saw it kill."

Nadie shook her head again, faster now, not wanting to give her brother's tale any more merit. "No, no. Just because he said he saw it, that doesn't make it so, Kitchi." Nadie's words came fast now, shaky. "He was your grandfather, he was trying to entertain his grandson. That is what grandfathers do."

Kitchi shook his head, his eyes fixed on Nadie. "No, Nadie. I heard his other stories too, just as you did. I heard all of them many times. But this one...this one always presented differently. And it was the one he told me in his last days, again and again, even in the hours just before he died. And it was on that occasion that he added more."

Nadie remembered the final days of her grandfather. The sickness and dementia. The smell of the longhouse where they kept him. She rarely went to see him during those days, and when she did, it was only when several other members of her family had already gathered.

But Kitchi was there constantly. Often lying in bed with him, stroking his grandfather's head and speaking with him as if they were on a fishing boat in the sound.

"What more?"

Kitchi closed his eyes and took in a deep breath, gathering his thoughts. Nadie could see her brother was thankful that she was willing to hear him out.

"Numohshomus was sold to the Croatoan during one of the beast's feeding cycles; it was just a coincidence. And it was during those weeks just before one of the new cycles that he remembered vividly. Even more than the feedings themselves."

Nadie turned away at the word 'feedings.'

"He spoke of an energy that arose in the village, one that he had never felt before or since. But it was no positive energy, like those felt during our Manitou ceremonies. It was an energy born of stress and..."

"And what?"

"Malevolence." Kitchi swallowed and rubbed his hands across his face before continuing. "Numohshomus said that only a few members of the tribe were permitted to gather at the beach each time. The rest of the tribe would stay behind, nervously waiting for those who had traveled to the beach to return with detailed descriptions of the events. Begging for as much detail as possible."

"Details about what?" Nadie listened without skepticism now, having decided to turn fully into the story.

"About the killing. About the feeding."

"Why...who were the chosen?"

"I asked this questions to Numohshomus as well, but he never quite knew how the witnesses were selected. At first, he thought it was to do with their status in the village, elders and such, but the more he observed, the more he saw it wasn't that at all. It seemed to be random, that perhaps they were selected based on some lottery system. And Numohshomus would always speak of that nervousness. How important those days just prior were, how the village was consumed with the selection, how they would speak of little else, other than their hopes of viewing the 'magic' of the kill."

"How did Numohshomus see it? Surely, he wasn't chosen. Not as a slave boy."

"No, of course not. But it was his slave work that brought him to the Yapam that day. He was well up the beach from where the ritual was being held that first time, cleaning the barnacles from the bottom of the fishing boats. It was a part of his weekly duties, though he normally did it earlier in the day. But that day had gotten loose from him, and it was closer to dusk when he made it to the beach. During the time of sacrifice. He was at some distance, perhaps four or five hundred paces, a detail he always admitted to me. But he could tell its size even from there."

"Who was this victim? Why did she allow to be taken?"

"It was no woman," Kitchi corrected. "Women were not the only ones to be offered. Numohshomus said the victim on his day was an older man. And that they buried his legs in the sand up to the waist. There was no struggle from the man at first, but..."

"But what?"

"After the witnesses buried him, they retreated to the dunes, taking distance from the shore, leaving no doubt as to who the creature's victim would be. And though this chosen man didn't struggle at first, Numohshomus said when the beast appeared, as it began slowly to rise from the sea, climbing the slope of the shore, that is when the screams began.

He told me the sounds of those screams never left him. That there was never a day that went by, even in his old age, that he didn't hear them."

Kitchi frowned and bowed his head, seeming to sympathize with both the victim and his grandfather's memories.

"The beast ripped the man's arms from his torso and then tore his face from his head. He was alive for several minutes until the screams finally died." Kitchi was quiet for several beats, allowing the magnitude of the story to weigh on his sister. He then said, "It is no metaphor, Nadie. The story is real."

Nadie stared at her brother silently, studying his face, and then, as if it had floated down from above her, the reason why her brother was telling her this finally struck her. She stood slowly, suspiciously, and then a surge of anger filled her, propelling her to the side of her brother's bed. She stooped down and leaned forward so that her face was only inches from Kitchi's.

"Are you saying that Nootau was killed by this creature?" Nadie asked. "By the Croatoan? Is that why you're telling me this story now?"

"I believe it is the time of the next cycle. I believe it more than the story of Morris Cook's son."

Nadie looked off to the side, considering the possibility that this tale was true, and that her son had been a victim of some ancient sea beast. She looked back to Kitchi and said, "But it was Nootau who knew of the boat at the sound. It was Nootau who would have led Samuel to the beach. There is no way Samuel Cook knew this story of Numohshomus, so it was Nootau..."

Kitchi averted his eyes from sister.

"Look at me, Kitchi."

Kitchi turned back, his sad stare locking with the defiant one of his sister's.

"How did Nootau know about this story?"

"I told him."

Chapter 8

Danny sat shivering on a fold-out chair in a crumbling parking lot that sat just beside the Wickard Beach boardwalk. He wasn't quite sure how he'd arrived here, in this exact spot, as he had been drifting in and out of sleep since the beach, internally debating whether everything that had happened that afternoon had, in fact, just been a dream.

His eyes drooped again, but he rapidly snapped them wide, and then gritted his teeth and clenched the muscles in his back to keep himself awake. He held a thick towel across his shoulders and neck, and he pressed it tightly against his skin, trying to soak up the cold of the ocean that seemed to have seeped into his blood.

He looked over at the deserted boardwalk, which was a rather lofty term to define the three or four blocks of stores of which this walk consisted. And the stores themselves were depressing: a couple of low-end restaurants, a dilapidated arcade, and dozen or so trinket and t-shirt shops that all basically sold same thing.

Had he made a mistake in coming here? Now that he was so close to it again? Danny began to re-trace the events of the afternoon one last time, trying to remember how it all had concluded.

The baby.

He had dragged Shane and the backpack from the water onto the beach, unzipping the bag to the sight of a screaming infant. He had held the baby close to his bare chest, trying to imbue it with any warmth that still remained inside of him.

Danny remembered trying to carry the baby to one of the homes along the beach, or at least devising the intention, but he simply had had no strength. Instead, he had pulled the infant into his belly and wrapped his knees around it, rubbing its back slowly. He had lain there, fetal-like, acting as a human cocoon, all the while staring over at Shane, who stood like a pillar in the sand, staring out at the water. He never once turned to Danny. He was entranced. The last thought Danny had before the EMTs arrived was that Shane was going to re-enter the water.

Perhaps he had.

When Danny awoke for the first time, he was still on the beach, but the baby was gone. He thought for a moment that Shane had extracted it from his grip, but when he saw the EMTs tucking blankets beneath his back and shoulders and draping the thick cloth across his chest, he decided it was safe with them. To think the other was unbearable.

Danny was shivering so badly when he awoke that he couldn't make out the faces of the men, so blurred were they by his quivering eyeballs. He had absently thought they looked like the fuzzy faces one sees from riders on a passing bullet train.

"Where is Shane?" Danny had asked instantly, trying to look past the EMTs for any sign of the boy. "And the baby?"

It was the last words he remembered speaking, and he realized now, as he sat alone in the open air of the parking lot, that he had not yet gotten an answer.

Danny stood and tried to take a step, but his knees buckled at once, and he nearly collapsed to the pavement. He grabbed the back of the chair and sat back down.

"For Christ's sake, take him to the hospital," a voice said from behind him.

The voice was vaguely recognizable to Danny, but he couldn't have placed it for a billion dollars.

"He won't go. Says he just needs to warm up and he'll be fine. He's groggy, fading in and out, but we can't *make* him go if he doesn't want to. We're monitoring his body temperature though, and if he passes out again, we'll load him in. Otherwise he's all yours."

Danny didn't quite register this last sentence, not the meaning of it anyway, and instead focused on the part about not wanting to go to the hospital. He didn't remember refusing, but it certainly sounded like him. It was residue of his former life. Ever since the grotto, ever since his time as the prisoner of Lynn Shields, he had become phobic of entrapment, reluctant to be anyplace where he didn't feel free to leave at any moment. Planes were out. Most boats. And he could never imagine entering a high-rise apartment building again.

"Take this, sir."

Danny turned and saw a thin hand holding a cup of what was obviously coffee, the smell of it intoxicating. He took the cup and sipped it instantly, as if he had been starved of it, basking in the warmth of the fluid as it cascaded down the back of his throat. He closed his eyes and sighed, and then re-opened them, willing himself to stay alert and focused on the scene around him.

He's all yours.

Danny scanned the parking lot, noting the Wickard Beach police cruisers, plus a few from the county, as well as a fire truck and two ambulances, including the one he sat beside currently. He turned his wrist, but his watch had been removed, so he looked to the sky, judging the height of the sun, which still hadn't risen fully. That meant the events of the morning couldn't have occurred more than a few hours ago.

An image of the baby flooded Danny's brain. And then of Shane and the purpose blazing in his eyes. The boy was bringing his brother to the god. As an offering. As food.

Danny knew the truth now: the beast was here in Wickard, and the power of its allure had already been wielded over one person. At least one.

"Hi, Danny."

The greeting came from a male standing somewhere to Danny's left. It was the same voice from a moment ago, and as Danny turned toward it, he was greeted by two pairs of black boots and the tightly pressed slacks of two uniformed Wickard police officers.

"I understand you had quite an afternoon," the man added.

Danny looked up to meet the faces of the two officers, one male, one female, standing hip to hip; they looked to be far enough apart in age that the man could have been the woman's grandfather. He had never seen these two cops in person, but he recognized their pictures from the newspaper. He couldn't remember their names, but the man's voice was familiar to Danny, probably from the couple of occasions when he had called the local precinct.

"Are you okay, Danny?"

"Where is Shane?" Danny asked, returning to the moment. "And the baby? Are they okay?"

The woman looked at her partner, a genuine concern draped across her face, and Danny could see she was looking for permission to answer.

"What were you doing down here at the beach today, Mr. Lynch?"

The officer's voice was more solemn now, and the transition from Danny to Mr. Lynch meant they were now down to business. "I live at the beach. I come here *every* day." Danny didn't mean for the answer to come across as smart-ass, but it had that ring, even in his own ears.

The male officer frowned and nodded, as if accepting this answer as brilliant, one he hadn't considered. "So you do."

The officer looked down at a small notebook, flipping through a few pages, leaving a wide space for Danny to say more. He didn't.

"You moved here recently." The officer looked up from his notebook, resting his eyes on Danny. "If I have my research correct, which I think I do." He paused. "I'm pretty sure we've not met. I've met almost everyone in Wickard Beach. At least those who have lived here for any amount of time."

Danny could see where this was leading, and he was already forming his strategy. He would decline to go down to the police station to answer any questions, as was his right. Unless they arrested him, of course.

But he didn't think they had any cause to detain him at this point, and certainly no evidence that he'd done anything wrong. He hadn't abducted or harmed those kids, he had saved them, and though there were questions that still needed to be answered, most of all by the parents, there was nothing to suggest Danny had committed any crime.

But Danny was objective enough to be able to place himself in the boots of the police officers, and he knew from that vantage point, the situation appeared weird and suspicious.

The sudden thought of prison made Danny's palms begin to sweat.

"We have some questions to ask you, Mr. Lynch, as I'm sure you can imagine. You mind?"

"As long as it's here," Danny answered, studying his coffee as he swirled the quarter-filled cup in a clockwise motion as if aerating a glass of wine.

The male officer looked around, surveying the suitability of their current location. "I suppose that will be alright."

Danny sighed and nodded, bringing his attention to the officers again. "Then yes, of course. But first, please, just give me an answer? Are the kids okay?"

"They will be," the female officer blurted, and Danny could see the wince from her senior partner. "At least we think so. You likely saved two lives today, Mr. Lynch. One for sure."

Danny sighed again, this time with twice the relief he felt at not being hauled off to jail. Thoughts of Shane pulling his baby brother out to sea were going to stay with him for a while, but knowing the child—both children—would live, would help to soften the memory.

The questions about that morning came from Officer Calazzo in quick, staccato bursts, very formally, not trying to lead Danny to any guilty confession or contrary point. And Danny basically just relayed the truth of how he came to be holding the baby of Gerald and Lori DeRose. Of course, the truth wasn't the *whole* truth, which included his theory about why Shane was in the ocean to begin with, swimming in the frigid waters of the Atlantic, by himself, with his baby brother in tow in a zippered backpack.

"Why did he do it?" Danny asked, flipping the script, wondering if the police had yet formed any theories.

Calazzo frowned and shrugged, never taking his eyes from the pad. "Who can say? But the parents tell me you came into contact with the boy this morning. That they saw you talking to him on the beach just in front of your house."

Danny nodded.

"What were you doing out there at that time?"

Danny returned the shrug and grinned, trying his best not to come off as defensive. "I was right in front of my house. It was sunrise. I go out to the beach every morning, rain or shine."

Calazzo nodded. "I see. Rain or shine? Why so devoted?"

"I just like it there at that time of day. I don't know, do you find that unusual?"

"No, not at all. But the father..." Calazzo checked his pad again. "Gerald DeRose, he says you were working with some equipment down there. Said his boy had mentioned whale sounds or something."

This was a lot closer than Danny had intended to get to his story, and it was time to shut it down. Time to lie. "I don't know what that means, officer. I had my phone. I was listening to music and humming along. And the boy—he told me his name was Shane—came out of nowhere and surprised me."

"What did you talk about?"

"What did we talk about?" Danny scoffed. "I don't know, what you talk about with most nine-year olds: you know, our trade deal with China. Instability in the Middle East. That type of thing."

The officer smiled, but Danny knew it wasn't from his joke. It was because now Danny *was* coming off as defensive, rattled.

"I have to go now, Officer Calazzo. It's been a traumatic day. Physically and emotionally. I'm sure you understand."

"Of course. You sure you don't need to go to the hospital?"

Danny shook his head and waved his open hand in the air. He then turned to the female officer. "I'm sorry, I didn't catch your name."

The woman handed Danny a card with her name printed across the top. Officer Renata Benitez. Danny held the card up and flicked his wrist, indicating he would keep the card for future reference.

"One more thing, Mr. Lynch," Calazzo said, in the matter-of-fact way TV detectives always seemed to.

Danny was standing now, rubbing his head with the towel one last time. "Sure."

"Do you think what happened here today has to do with this?" Calazzo handed Danny a folded section of a newspaper.

"What's this?"

Calazzo nodded for Danny to take a look.

Danny flipped up the fold and almost shrieked at the image at the top of the page. It was the image that had changed his life forever, the black head of the sea god that he had captured on his phone the day of the first sighting.

"Is There Something Lurking in the Waters Off Rove Beach?" read the headline from the Rove Beach Rover. Sarah's article. The one that had been written by a serious journalist and printed in a small but respected paper as real news, but which was laughed off by the town, mocked by the locals, and thus never seen by the rest of the world.

It was proof of a life form that was unknown ever to have existed, and it had simply disappeared in plain sight.

Until now.

Danny handed the paper back to Calazzo and repeated, "I have to go."

He stood and dropped the towel on the chair, and then clutched a fist in an open hand, rubbing them together, trying to keep himself warm as he prepared his walk home.

"We can give you a ride, Danny. Plenty of room in the cruiser."

"I'm good. Thanks though."

Danny was about ten yards away from the officers when they called his name again. He turned and lifted his head.

"You're not where you were," Calazzo called to him, his face calm, as if he'd just imparted some great words of wisdom to Danny.

Danny paused waiting for more, and then asked, "What the hell is that supposed to mean?"

Calazzo chuckled. "It means we don't believe in Bigfoot in Wickard Beach. Know a little bit about your story, and I'm willing to keep it at 'a little bit.' You got a chance for a fresh start here, son, and I suggest you take advantage of it."

Danny looked off to the side and scoffed lightly. "Just want my community to be safe, sheriff. Haven't you heard?" Danny turned his focus to Officer Benitez. "I saved a couple of lives today."

Calazzo gave a cold smile and a slight twist of his head, indicating that in his mind, that point was still in question.

"And from reading the paper, that's a hell of a lot more than you've done over the past few months."

Calazzo's smile fell immediately, and Danny knew he'd perhaps gone too far with this last jab.

"We'll be in touch if we have any other questions, Mr. Lynch," Officer Benitez said, and then placed her hand on her boss' shoulder, coaxing him back toward the incident scene.

Calazzo let his eyes linger on Danny for a few moments longer, and then he turned and walked away.

Chapter 9

"Samuel Cook."

Samuel heard the call of his name but kept walking, lost in the images floating through his head, a load of kindling across one shoulder and an axe across the other. The familiar sound of his name had entered Samuel's ears, there was nothing wrong with his hearing, but he didn't register them as coming from the outside world. This was the new state of being in which Samuel found himself most of the time now, this awakened state of dreaming. When he looked back on the hours of his days since Nootau's killing, Samuel found he could recall very few specifics. It was as if he had slept through them.

"I know you have heard me, Samuel Cook," the voice called again.

Samuel took two more steps and then stopped, looking around in confusion, first to his right and then back to his left. He saw nothing initially, but with another quarter turn to the left he saw Nootau's uncle—or cousin—sitting on the wooden bench that ran along the outside of Nootau's family's wigwam. The man's thin legs hung below him, and though they looked no different from any pair of functioning legs, the useless limbs captured Samuel's attention the way a lame doe triggers the urges of the wolf.

Samuel stood still for several seconds before finally lifting his head, meeting the eyes of the crippled man. The Algonquin grinned at Samuel's lack of manners, and seeing no fear in Samuel's eyes, his smile broadened. He took a long swig from a thick stone container, and the pleasant grimace that followed indicated to Samuel the vessel was filled with mead.

"Come to see me now, Samuel Cook. Son of Morris Cook, the great adventurer who has left us to return to the land of devils." Nootau's uncle or cousin patted a space next to him on the bench.

Samuel stood frozen, and he could see from the corner of his eye a pair of women move quickly away, their eyes toward the ground, clearly not wanting to become embroiled in this encounter.

Samuel swiveled his head in both directions, not moving his feet. The rest of the road was empty, as was the central square. For the moment, he was all alone with the crippled man who had invited him to sit.

"I have to get the wood back home before supper. My mother is waiting."

"You don't have a spell or two for the uncle of your best friend? Surely you do. Nootau would have wanted you to spend a little time with his favorite uncle, Kitchi." Kitchi's eyes thinned and the smile on his face grew wider.

Samuel swallowed and walked toward the entrance, trying to force his own version of a smile, the formation of which felt painful. He wasn't frightened of the man physically, obviously, since, Samuel noted, the man couldn't even shit by himself.

But Samuel knew this man was smart, and he was known to have a general dislike of anyone in the colony. He was a trouble-maker, an instigator, and had even invoked talk of rebellion and war some months back. Most in the colony dismissed him because of his limitations below the waist, but Samuel's father always spoke of him as if he were a problem to be addressed, someone who would eventually need to be dealt with. Samuel even suspected the only reason his friendship with Nootau was allowed was because of his proximity to the man now before him.

Samuel stopped a few paces short of the wigwam and was now standing directly in front of Kitchi. "Where has everyone gone?" he asked.

"It is the time of the harvest prayer," Kitchi said irreverently. "So many of these older fools in the village still believe that the squash and pumpkins are concerned with what we have to say about them." Nootau's uncle began laughing hysterically now; it was a sinister tone that Samuel immediately recognized as drunkenness.

But Samuel connected with Kitchi's irreverence. The last four days of his life had been spent reliving activities of the beautiful beast Nootau had discovered for him. There was no doubt in his mind: Samuel considered the ocean beast his new god. He would continue to speak Jesus' praises on Sunday, at least for as long as he lived in his father's home, but in his heart, he would pray to only one deity from that day forward.

Kitchi abruptly stopped laughing and then used his arms to scoot his torso forward on the bench. He raised his head, his eyes pleading. "Have you seen the Croatoan, son of Morris Cook?" he asked. "Did you see it kill my nephew?"

The words sounded as if they had been screamed from the heavens, and Samuel suddenly felt like he was back in his awakened dream.

The Croatoan.

Samuel had never heard this term before, and the name rang beautifully in his ears. He now had a name to put to his new god, since there was little doubt as to what Nootau's uncle was speaking.

"I can see the truth in your face, young Samuel Cook." Kitchi was sober now, his voice steady, awed by the truth he had just confirmed. "You have seen it?"

Samuel glanced around the grounds nervously, measuring his surroundings, searching for an escape from the accusations being hurled in his direction, some person that could act as a distraction.

But the roads and square were still clear. Most of the colony was already inside for supper, and the natives, according to Kitchi, were conducting some harvest ritual.

"I didn't think anyone would believe me," Samuel said, the tears already beginning to fall down his cheek. "There was nothing to be done for Nootau. I swear it."

Kitchi just stared at Samuel, and for a moment, Samuel thought the man was preparing his lungs to scream, to alert the village that a murderer was in their midst and that someone should come quick to take Samuel away. He would go to the gallows, or perhaps to a holding prison where he would await his death by stoning or burning, acts the Algonquin were rumored to perform. Samuel had seen no evidence of this practice occurring on the island, but that was of little concern now.

And yet, there was no scream from Kitchi, only the wide-eyed look of wonderment. "You will take me to it, Samuel. You will take me to the Croatoan."

Samuel took a deep breath of relief, but then a new fear gripped him almost immediately. He shook his head. "I couldn't go there again. I don't think I even know the way. And how could I get you there anyway?"

The steady smile of Kitchi's face slowly grew menacing, and a string of saliva begin to drip from his mouth. "You will take me there. That is if you wish to keep the skin upon your body and your mother from being sunken to the bottom of the sound."

"My mother doesn't know anything!" Samuel cried.

Kitchi closed his eyes and leaned his head back so that it was resting against the outer wall of the wigwam, a relaxed smile still on his face. He looked as if he were about to fall asleep. "I knew it was true," he said. "I always knew it was true."

Samuel stood in front of Kitchi for what must have been a full minute, staring at the man as if he were a type of human exhibit in a museum. And then, hearing nothing else from the man, Samuel turned slowly and started back to his home. Perhaps in the morning Nootau's uncle would forget any of this conversation, Samuel thought. His own father was known to be belligerent after a night of ale, and then the next day he would act as if nothing at all had happened.

But Samuel wasn't past the perimeter of the wigwam's property before Kitchi spoke again.

"You will come tonight," Kitchi instructed. "I will be in the longhouse." Without opening his eyes, Kitchi nodded in the direction of a structure about forty paces to his right.

"The longhouse? There is an unfinished roof?"

Kitchi shrugged. "They bring me there many nights due to my snoring. I don't notice the temperatures by then."

"It is far to the sound," Samuel pleaded. "Too far. How will I get you down there?"

"Lucky for you, I'm as slight as a teenage boy. And as you say, most of the way is downhill. There is a wheelbarrow in the longhouse. You will use that to take me there."

"But I could never get you back. There is far too much slope from the sound to the village. It is impossible."

Kitchi didn't respond to this latest rebuke. "Tonight," is all he said. "When all are asleep, you will come for me and we will visit the Croatoan. If you don't show, prepare for punishment in the morning."

Chapter 10

"Are you ready, Shane?"

At the sound of his father's whisper, Shane DeRose grabbed his Baltimore Orioles cap and backed out his room, holding a small pouch against his belly with one hand and flicking the light switch down with the other. He closed the door gently behind him and began adjusting the pouch on his hips, snapping the plastic buckle into place.

The light pouch was too small for him, he had had it since he was six or so, where it had sat upon a shelf in his room for years, unused, the black and orange face of another smiling oriole looking back at him all the while. And while it wasn't the ideal item for his purposes tonight, it was all he had in a pinch. If his dad asked him about why he was wearing it, Shane would just tell him he was bringing a snack for later. But he doubted his dad would notice; he had other things on his mind tonight.

Gerald DeRose met his son in the hallway after giving the same careful effort to his own bedroom door, cautious not to wake his wife. He held a finger up to his mouth and nodded for his son to move it outside, which they both did quickly.

"Are you sure about this, dad?" Shane whispered. He stood outside on the porch now, hugging his arms, averting his eyes from the direction of the sea, knowing that with the sky clear and the moon nearly full, he would be able to see the water from where he stood. "Maybe we should call the police. You know, like you wanted to do."

Shane studied his dad's reaction, praying that he was selling this lie, not overacting it, and that his dad was still too angry about Shane's story to see through the drama.

He told me to meet him at the beach, Shane had told his dad. *After he got me and Brian in from the water. He told me to come meet him at the beach tomorrow.*

Shane had been taken to the hospital within minutes of being found, sitting alone on the beach, well away from where his brother and the man had lain shivering in the fetal position. Shane thought of yesterday morning, of the water and the feeling that the beast would arrive, and how he had felt almost nothing at the time. A slight chill had come upon him a little later, but well after he had left the beach.

Shane was sure he was going to be punished for what he had done, for what he had put his brother through especially, but there was only concern about his health. Punishments would come much later, if at all.

But he and his brother were fine, released from the hospital that same morning, their mother weeping in the way she often did in times of crisis. By lunchtime, they were home. By two o'clock, Shane was asleep in his bed, dreaming of his next encounter.

Of course, his father was far less fussy than his mom and had plenty of questions, the most obvious concerning why Shane had gone to the beach that morning. And why he had nearly drowned his baby brother. *I wasn't there to drown him,* Shane remembered thinking. *I was there to offer him.*

Instead, Shane quickly thought of the man from the previous morning, and he told his father that he had gone to see him.

He told me I had to come to the beach that morning, Shand had lied. *And that I had to bring Brian.*

When Shane's parents asked how the man even knew about Brian, and why Shane had gone into the ocean with his brother in a backpack, Shane just shrugged and started crying. He had no good answer to give, it was all too much.

And that was fine. He didn't need an answer, he was only nine after all.

Later that night, Shane had listened carefully as his dad explained to his mother that he did believe Shane's story, of course he did, but there was no way to prove any of it to the police. And besides, even if he did have evidence, going to the police would just scare the man away. He looked like a drifter, and as soon as word got out that he was attracting legal trouble, he would drift on to the next town.

No. No cops. Gerald DeRose would handle this matter his own way, just like he handled all his business.

But Shane knew his dad had other reasons for not calling the police. He was afraid of the cops and had been for as far back as Shane could remember. Shane didn't know the details of his father's 'business,' but he knew it was very different from whatever his friends' dads did for work. And he was pretty sure it was illegal.

So, Shane built a new story about the man at the beach. He told his dad the guy had instructed Shane to come back the next day, to a certain spot in front of his house, that he had whispered the instruction to Shane just before the ambulances came. It was an outrageous story, of course, but why would Shane tell such a dramatic story unless it was true. And Shane knew his father would never tell his mother about it, because she would have insisted on calling the sheriff's office.

"I think this guy might just need a good old-fashioned talking to, Shane. Some guys are just like that, you know? For some guys, it's the only way they listen. You understand what I mean?"

Shane frowned and nodded trustingly, giving his dad a look which indicated he'd just been imparted with the wisest words any man had ever spoken. He then walked in silence beside his father toward the beach, and within minutes, they were standing on the sand directly in front of Danny Lynch's rental house.

Shane's dad took in the crumbling structure of Danny's house, shaking his head at the disrepair, mumbling about the crap that was bringing down property values. Shane looked in the opposite direction, studying the ocean. Absently, he moved his fingers across the bulge in his pouch, making sure he could feel the outline of both the phone and the ice chipper.

"We still have about twenty minutes until sunrise," Shane's father said, "so let's go over this one more time. It's simple, right? I'm going to be right back there." He pointed to a thick patch of shrubs that shrouded a short dune about forty yards from where they both stood currently. "When this perv...when he comes out—if he comes out—I'll be moving in right behind him. Not but a couple feet away, okay? He'll probably see me right away, and then I'll take it from there. You don't have to do anything."

Shane continued staring out into the ocean as his father spoke; he could hear the deep New Jersey accent ringing through the air, but they had no impact on him, the way the sound of the wind brushing through the trees rarely registers.

"Shane!"

Shane blinked twice and then reluctantly turned his face toward his father, fighting the urge to keep his eyes locked on the water. It was as if a magnet had been attached to the horizon now, and Shane's eyes filled with iron pellets.

"This is important, Shane. I know you're still a little bit scared about what happened yesterday. So am I. But that's why we need to handle this on our own. You get it, right?"

Shane nodded, but all the emotion he had conjured earlier to portray some frightened little boy was gone. Now that he was back here, so close to the beast again, so close to the behemoth that lived somewhere just off this coast, beneath the surface, he had lost the ability to keep up his scared kid act. All he wanted was just to see it. Just to feel its power.

Shane's dad rolled his eyes and sighed, and then lightly gripped the back of his son's neck and ushered him over to a place in the sand that was still aglow with moonlight. He stopped on the spot and then placed his hands on his son's shoulders and pushed down gently. "Just sit here, boy. That's it, just sit here. I'm going to my place on the dune, but I'll be able to see you the whole time. Just as long as you stay right here."

Shane sat obediently, only pivoting his body enough to watch his dad retreat to the brush before turning back to the ocean. With his back to the dunes, Shane unzipped the pouch and pulled out the smart phone that he had only gotten last Christmas. It's all he had wanted at the time, never realizing how important it would come to be. He touched a series of buttons on the screen and pulled up the two applications beginning with the sound booster. He adjusted the settings of the boost to ten, and then opened the recording application. He opened the first and only recording in the library.

Whale sounds.

He turned the phone outwards toward the water, resting it tall on his lap against his belly, trying both to project the sounds and hide the device from his father.

This whole concept of what the man on the beach had told him. about using whale sounds as a lure, made no sense to Shane; even at nine, he knew that whatever noises came through the tiny phone speakers would get pushed around and covered up by the beach winds and crashing waves. How could the sound of the minke whale coming off the shore ever be heard by anything that lived deep in the ocean?

But his beast was something new in the world, unknown by the books of science, not mentioned among the popular ancient myths and stories that had survived over the centuries. And, just as Shane had read of sharks smelling a drop of blood in a million gallons of water, or the ability of bats to detect the flight of a housefly in the night, it wasn't impossible that his creature had some similar extraordinary sense, only this one having to do with detecting the cries of distress.

Shane looked back over his shoulder, but he could see nothing other than a cold stretch of sand about eight feet in front of him. Beyond that was only the night, and somewhere his father lie in wait for a man that would never come.

Shane scooted forward a few feet and then dipped his hand back into the shallow nylon pouch. He felt nervous now, as if the eyes of his father were following his every move. He doubted his dad could see the details of what he was doing, but he couldn't know for sure.

He felt in the bag until he touched the first of the six sharp points of the ice chipper and began breathing rapidly. He ran his finger down the middle of the tool, which was about eight inches in length, until he reached the end of the wooden handle. He wrapped his fingers around the chipper, feeling the thickness in his palm, imagining the strike that would come soon.

Shane saw the first appearance of daylight in the sky as he stood and began to walk toward the water. It would be light in a few minutes, but no one would be on the beach for another hour or so.

Shane stopped at the edge of the shore and within seconds heard his father behind him.

"Shane, what are you doing? I told you to stay put!" The anger in his whispers was as forceful as any scream Shane had ever heard.

But Shane didn't budge. He stood tall and focused on the dark waters that spanned forever in front of him. The sounds of his dad grew closer now, and Shane knew the mission was over for the day. Tomorrow he would try something different. A new person to bring to the edge for his god.

Tomorrow was always waiting.

And then he heard the splash.

Chapter 11

For the first time in as long as he could remember, Danny Lynch slept in.

He didn't set an alarm and didn't care about the sunrise. He almost didn't care if the creature was standing on the beach at this very second. He had no desire to feel the sand in his toes this morning, no desire to stare out at the sunrise. The ocean had won yesterday, perhaps permanently, and as Danny lay in his bed staring at the ceiling, he thought seriously about starting a new life somewhere far from the salty air. In the mountains perhaps. Maybe Arizona. The desert suddenly seemed like the best place in the world.

Danny turned and checked the clock. Still twenty minutes until the sun started breaking through. The beach would get a day off today. Maybe he would go again tomorrow, he thought, and then he flipped his pillow over and fell back asleep.

Chapter 12

Samuel lifted the low handles of the wheelbarrow once more and pushed forward, rolling the solid wooden wheel over a wide, smooth road. It was a path he had never known about before today, and it was a far more sensible path than he and Nootau had taken on the day they went to the sound. And today, Samuel was grateful for it. Nootau's uncle was light for a man, that was true, but Samuel knew he would have never made it to the water taking Nootau's route from days earlier.

But Kitchi knew the path well, giving clear instructions about where to turn and when to slow at every turn and rise in the dirt.

"You think because I am crippled I don't know my own land?" Kitchi asked. "You would be wrong. I know it better than most *because* I am crippled. I listen, you see. And I learn. I drink, yes, but I listen and learn."

Samuel took several rests during the trek; clear path or not, the haul was tiring, and Kitchi had little to argue about during these stops. Samuel was still a boy wheeling a grown man in a wheelbarrow, and he was not well known for his respiratory prowess.

But what Samuel lacked in fitness, he made up for in strength. His father was a big man, one of the tallest and brawniest in the colony, and Samuel had been blessed with this trait as well. He would be an important member of the colony one day, his mother always told him, and, she said, it was his father's seed he had to thank for it.

Kitchi held the torch out in front of the wheelbarrow, and with the clarity of the sky above the two travelers, there was plenty of light to guide the way.

After returning home earlier in the day, following his initial encounter with Kitchi on the road, Samuel had spent most of his time worrying about the darkness of the night, and how he could ever make such a trip without the assistance of a bright sun. It seemed impossible. But when the time came to sneak from his house, almost immediately he formed the opposite concern. The veil of darkness that would blind him, but that would also keep this adventure secret, was lacking. The moon shone bright on the colony, as if marking it for some higher purpose, and the stillness of the night left every sound he made hanging in the air for all to hear.

But Samuel had made it to the longhouse unseen, and there he had found Kitchi sitting in his makeshift bed of bark and cornstalks, his face as awake and sober as a newborn fox. The wheelbarrow he had promised was also there, resting against the back wall, and Samuel wondered how he had managed to position the tool so conveniently and who he had gotten to place it there. Or perhaps he had known it would be there and chose the longhouse for just that purpose. Whichever the case, Samuel had thought it wiser not to ask.

Samuel came to a small but steady slope rising in the path along a shallow ridge that wove through the forest. Kitchi immediately barked for him to put his weight behind it and start running; otherwise they would never make it. Samuel followed the order, driving his feet into the dirt, feeling the burn in his arms and thighs as he dug his heels back, dipping his head low as he heaved his body into the one-wheeled cart.

And with a power he was sure could only have come from his new god, they made it to the top, and as Samuel crested the slope, he could now see the shoreline of the sound below.

He had made it. It was all downhill from that point, and he needed only to keep the wheelbarrow slightly angled as they descended the path to keep it from getting away from him.

Still though, he thought, there was no way he could ever get Kitchi back to the village. The rise from the sound back to this point was simply too steep. Both he and Kitchi knew the truth of this, but the subject remained unspoken during their journey, though Samuel sensed the puzzle was always lingering in the space between them.

"When we get across the sound, you will have to carry me to the Yapam," Kitchi said. "You know this, right? You must drag me to the ocean."

There was a lilt of wonderment in Kitchi's words, almost disbelief that he had arrived even to this point in the journey. Samuel could only imagine the last time the man had ever seen the big waters of the sound, let alone the Great Western Sea.

"A wheelbarrow in the sand is like a woman in battle," he continued. "It will only slow us down."

With this last sentence, Kitchi erupted into a full-throated laugh, but Samuel knew it had little to do with his joke. He was in the land of Samuel's new god now—The Croatoan—and that was nothing short of euphoric.

Samuel couldn't help but smile himself at the thought of the creature. For the first time since this quest began, he realized he, too, may be seeing it again shortly. All his work and worry to get Nootau's uncle to the beach had kept his mind occupied, but now that the job was nearing completion, he could take a moment to relish his position. And he was suddenly flooded with energy.

Samuel heaved the wheelbarrow up to the side of the canoe, the same one that had been swept away the night Nootau was taken by the Croatoan. Samuel had spotted the canoe shortly after Nootau was killed, floating just down the shoreline from where they had left it originally. It hadn't been swept away at all, it seemed, only moved temporarily by the tide and breeze. Samuel had wondered if that, too, had been the work of his new god, or the heavens, perhaps, playing its role in presenting the deity to him. It didn't much matter to Samuel which; for him, it all ended in the same place.

Kitchi crawled inside the narrow opening of the boat with sneaky deftness and within moments, Samuel launched the boat into the water. In a few short minutes, they were across the sound.

"Get on my back," Samuel ordered.

Samuel stooped in front of Kitchi, who was sitting upright and eager in the canoe, and the thin Algonquin grabbed Samuel around the neck, clutching his fingers at the boy's throat. Samuel grunted and stood tall and then began the heavy slog toward the ocean.

Helpless, Kitchi could only drag his toes across the surface of the sand, making the journey through the thick powder all the more difficult. But Samuel was in a place of joy and strength now, knowing where he was headed, and the calm smile that extended above his chin never left his face. By the time he reached the top of the first dune and looked down on the shimmering waters of the Great Western Ocean, he was nearly delirious with glee.

Kitchi released his grip from Samuel's neck and collapsed to the sand, and immediately positioned himself on his elbows so that he was facing the ocean. "When does it come?" he asked, almost giggling. "What do we have to do to bring it from the sea?"

The questions were those of a child, Samuel thought, as was the pitch of the man's voice. "It is your story," he replied. "You should know these answers better than anyone."

Samuel looked down at Kitchi, challenging him for some form of reprimand, and, at first, he could see in Kitchi's eyes that the man was eager to offer one. But Samuel was a temple of confidence now, standing atop the dune like a king, shoulders and jaw high against the horizon, engorged with the power of his deity. Samuel was in control now, and he knew his face reflected the feeling.

Kitchi swallowed and lowered his gaze back to the crashing waves of the ocean.

"We wait now," Samuel said, "just as Nootau and I did. It will come or it won't. All we can do now is wait."

Chapter 13

"Shane, what are you doing? I told you to stay put."

Shane pulled the ice chipper from the pouch and gripped it with a strength that felt foreign to him. He felt a ripple in his undeveloped bicep and forearm that suggested there was more to his form than what he saw in the mirror each morning. It could be a false sense of strength, Shane recognized this possibility; after all, he wouldn't reach puberty for another three or four years. But there was a new power inside of him. A new belief in his life that filled him with vigor, and he was at a point now, both in life and at that very moment, that the only way he could see to move forward was to believe in this power.

He closed his eyes and focused on the approaching sound of his father's footsteps, feeling the grains of sand at his feet as they pushed through the narrow cracks of his toes.

"Shane!"

Shane opened his eyes to see the top of the sun pushing through to the horizon, and rising in front of the star, a dark shadow was being born from the sea.

The dark mass moved quickly upward, rising so that its shoulders breached the sea like two mountains, pushing forward through the water as it rose, encroaching the shoreline with a speed Shane would never have believed possible.

"Oh my god!"

Shane heard his father's voice directly behind him—he could almost feel the breath on the back of his neck—and without allowing another thought to enter his mind, Shane spun around and dropped to his knees, and then plunged the six prongs of the ice chipper into the top of his father's left foot.

Gerald DeRose screamed in agony, the sound rattling the dawn air like a gunshot. People would come, Shane thought, certainly the man in the house above them.

But it was a secondary thought to Shane now. All he could think about now was the Black and Purple man.

Shane looked up at his father's face, measuring his level of incapacitation by the grimace of pain. But there was only disbelief in his father's eyes as he stared down at his son, and Shane imagined how difficult that must have been for him to avert his gaze from the majesty of the approaching giant.

"Shane? What are..?"

They were the final three words Shane would ever hear his father say. With both hands around the handle of the ice chipper now, Shane lifted the weapon from the top of his father's foot and then spun it deftly in his hands so that the daggers were pointing straight to the sky. Shane shot himself upward like a rocket ship, feeling a similar strength that he had felt in his biceps now in his thighs, and he thrust the ice chipper into his father's throat. He twisted it once, hoping to lodge it there tightly, but it was barely hanging on when he let go.

Gerald DeRose grabbed at the kitchen tool with his hands and pulled it from his larynx, only making the damage worse. The opening in his jugular vein was wide, severe, and blood erupted from the wound like lava from a volcano.

Shane watched in astonishment, his neck and face twitching in a combination of fear and horror and wonder, both at what he was seeing and at what he had just done. But the feeling lasted only a moment; his god was coming, preparing to devour, and there was nothing else in the world right now but that.

Shane walked slowly backward toward the dunes where his father had lain in wait only moments earlier, and as he retreated, he fixated on the gashing mouth of the sea god approaching.

Shane looked down to his father now who was writhing on his back, attempting desperately to keep the blood that still remained in his head from escaping through the awful wound in his neck. But there was no stopping the flood, and Shane prayed he wouldn't die before the god reached him. He couldn't know for sure, but he assumed the struggle of the prey would enhance the scene he was only moments away from witnessing.

The giant beast didn't hesitate as it stood over Shane's father, showing no desire to taunt or admire its victim. It was all animal as it reached down with its massive arms and grabbed Gerald DeRose by the sides of his head, lifting him high, seeming to take just a moment to study his eyes before sinking his teeth into his neck at the wound site.

Shane reveled in the glory of the scene as he sat behind the thicket of sea grass, knees pulled tightly to his chest, never blinking as he watched the Croatoan devour his father, wondering which was greater, the sight of the event, or the sound.

Chapter 14

The night was growing lighter, and sleep was inevitable for both Kitchi and Samuel. But Samuel knew he wouldn't be the first to fall. He had seen the god already, and this fact alone was enough to see him through for a few more hours. He looked over at the Algonquin uncle of his best friend, Nootau, and could see the man was beginning to drift.

"You won't see it if you're sleeping," Samuel warned, teasing the man, knowing there was little Kitchi could do now to will himself to consciousness.

Kitchi blinked and grunted himself awake. "I wasn't sleeping," he replied. But within a few seconds, his eyelids began to quiver again until finally coming to rest tight and still.

Samuel looked out to the dark churn of the sea and smiled, and then gave a silent prayer that it would come tonight, on this evening where he had expended so much work and which had culminated in the perfect climate.

He looked back at Kitchi, making sure he was still asleep, and then stood and walked toward the water, searching. The creature had risen from the sea when he was last here with Nootau, but it had not stayed there. It had followed the boys to the sound, hunted them, finally settling on the panicking Nootau.

But had it stayed in the sound or retreated to the ocean? It was a question he hadn't considered until this moment, now with his thoughts clear in the tranquility of the barrier

103

island, far away from the distrustful eyes of the natives and the equally frightened ones of his countrymen.

Samuel knew his life here in this new world wouldn't reach the days of his manhood. And it wasn't to do with any demon animal from beneath the sea. Things were too fragile here. There was too much darkness. Darkness not only in the hearts of the men that passed by him every day, both native and domestic, but literal darkness as well. When night fell on the colony, it was as if a black shell had been placed over its top. It was suffocating. Portending of bleakness, death.

But not on this night. On this night, Samuel was in the arms of the Great Western Ocean, a full moon above him, the light and stars of the dark heavens beaming down upon him, signaling for him to summon his god, to let live the myth of these ancient people and make it his own. There were opportunities tonight. And they were his alone.

Samuel closed his eyes and breathed in the cool air, and then stooped at the shoreline, filling his cupped hands with the salty water of the sea and splashing his face with it. He smoothed back his long, shaggy brown hair and then stood and turned back to the dunes, his eyes narrow with hate and hunger. He could see only the dark outlines of the sea grass, but he knew within the cover of it was a sleeping cripple who was ready for sacrifice.

Samuel stalked back to the dunes but did not stop at the sleeping Kitchi. Instead, he retraced his steps back down to the sound and the awaiting canoe, which, this time, he had made sure to secure well up on the beach, pulling it far enough so the hull was well buried in the dry sand, far from the greedy waters of the sound.

He stepped inside and reached beneath the stern seat until his fingers touched the thick twine of rope. He gathered the coil and trekked back to the dune until he was standing over the helpless Indian beneath him.

Samuel rolled Kitchi to his stomach and then grabbed his left arm, swinging it behind the man's back. He repeated the same motion with his right hand until both were resting on his back, the tips of Kitchi's index fingers touching. Kitchi grunted once and shifted his shoulders, but he didn't wake.

Next, Samuel grabbed one end of the thick rope and began to wrap it around Kitchi's wrists, making several passes, pulling it tight with each revolution until it was four or five layers thick. He then tied the rope off with a bowline knot and stood quickly, satisfied with the procedure and efficiency of his work.

Kitchi raised his face from the sandy dune. "What are you..? No." It didn't take long for the Algonquin to figure out what was happening. "You cannot do this, Samuel. You are visitors to our land." His voice was calm, but there was desperation attached to every word. "We have welcomed you. And I have spared you from death by keeping this secret I know of you."

Samuel heard every word but felt not the slightest pull of persuasion. Instead, he stooped low in front of Kitchi and grabbed him at the ankles, one in each hand, and then began to drag him off the slope of the dune and toward the beach.

Kitchi's tied hands were creating a bit of drag in the sand, and Samuel realized now that he should have tied them in front of his body instead of at his back. But it didn't much matter; there wasn't far to go. Forty paces maybe. That should be plenty of distance for him to both witness the approach of the beast and take in all its power and ferocity. Of course, Samuel had to be sure not to give the prize up too early and cheat himself of the vision. The advance of the monster on the beach was as magnificent as the kill itself, and this anticipation brought tears to his eyes.

"Okay, Samuel, I will make this deal with you." Kitchi spoke with a clear head now, temperately. "You take me back to the dune and you let me see the Croatoan as you have promised." He paused. "And for that, I will give to you Jania. You like Jania, yes? I have that power within my family. In my village. I can ensure she is yours. You like the girls now, yes?"

Jania was almost seventeen and quite beautiful, and Samuel knew that her marriage had been arranged for many years, as was custom for the native girls. Kitchi was a troublemaker in the colony, that was true, but Samuel knew he didn't have the power to call off marriages, much less make new arrangements involving the children of colonists. It was an absurd attempt.

Besides, Samuel would have been far more interested in a deal for Jania's sister, Sokwa, who was the same age as Samuel, and with whom he had shared a classroom for a time last month. She had been in love with Nootau, Samuel was sure of that, but she was kind to Samuel, and he fantasized about marrying her one day.

But there were no deals to be struck on this day or any other. There was only one subject he gave his mind to anymore. One thing that consumed him wholly. The Croatoan.

Samuel dragged Kitchi further onto the beach, turning his head every few paces, measuring the landscape to ensure he left the correct distance between the water, Kitchi, and the dunes. It was all perfect. There was no need for Samuel to dig a hole or even sever the man's feet. He was incapacitated, and nature had done the work for him.

"It is an intriguing offer, Kitchi, but not one I am interested in."

"You tell me, then," Kitchi retorted quickly. "You make the deal."

Samuel stopped for a moment, considering this challenge. He knew there was no way he would allow Kitchi to ever leave the beach alive, regardless of whether or not the black beast came, but perhaps he could extract something additional from the man, something that had been weighing on Samuel since the moment Nootau had spoken of it.

And who was Kitchi to deny him what he asked? He was, at the moment, a living example of vulnerability. "Okay, Kitchi," Samuel said, dropping the man's legs to the sand. "Perhaps there is a deal to be struck."

Kitchi's eyes were wide and hopeful. He licked his lips and nodded. "Yes! Yes, anything."

"I want to hear the story from the beginning. The full story."

"What story?"

"The story of the Croatoan. The story you told to Nootau."

Kitchi closed his eyes regretfully. "It is a story now that I wish I had never known."

Samuel gave a sad smile at this statement, realizing how different everything would be at this moment. His friend Nootau would still be alive, and Samuel would be home resting in his bed, preparing for another day of chores, pining for some future moment when his father would return to the colony.

This thought of his father suddenly sobered Samuel. What would happen when he returned? Would the colony still be here? Would war have broken out and all of the colonists savagely murdered and scalped by the natives?

It was more likely that they would all have starved by that point, but it all came to the same conclusion.

Samuel focused back on Kitchi, his eyes signaling that he was waiting for an answer to his proposition.

"I know only of the story as told to me by my grandfather."

"What does that mean?"

"That story I told to Nootau, much of it was told in the style of allegory, as it was told to me. It was a ghost story for children."

"But..."

"I always knew the tale was true, I could see it in my grandfather's eyes. Of course, he sprinkled the tale with exaggerations, hoping to mislead me from the truth, but I always knew it had happened. Though..." Kitchi now wore a look of pleading, uncertainty.

"What is it?

"If you are looking for the origin, Samuel, for the secret to summon and control the Croatoan, that I do not know. But I know of one who may."

Samuel didn't recognize the tactic of his prisoner at first, but it came to him within a few seconds. Kitchi was smart, smarter than Samuel—Samuel had no delusions about that—and he was creating value in himself for survival. It was now Samuel's purpose to learn if Kitchi was bluffing. "Who knows this tale if not you?"

"She is a half-day's walk from here, on the far side of the island."

"Where exactly?"

Kitchi smiled and cocked his head. "Well, that detail must be an addendum to our deal, Samuel."

"Perhaps I don't believe you, Kitchi. In fact, I'm sure I don't."

"I could easily make up a story, Samuel," Kitchi shot back, "tell you an invented origin of the Croatoan that would be a true myth. Give you some ancient incantation to speak into the water that would bring the creature to you each time you spoke the words to the crashing waves. I could do these things and you would never know whether it was truth or lie. But I wish to know the truth as you do. I yearn for it, now that I know for a fact it is real."

Samuel stayed silent, implying the next question with his eyes.

"I can tell you she does not live in the village. Not in my village or your colony. She is on the western side of the island, to the south, across from the Big Island. She was banished there a lifetime ago from the tribe that gave name to the being we both seek."

"Why did she flee north to our island?"

"She couldn't stay on the island of the Croatoan, but she couldn't come to our village either. My people would never have accepted her there. So she had no home there or here."

"I have never heard of such a woman," Samuel said, feeling agitated that this news had somehow evaded him.

"You and yours are strangers in this land, Samuel. There are few with white faces who know of her. And she makes little demonstration of her existence. There are many of my own people who don't know of her either. And there is a chance she could be dead by now."

Samuel frowned at this last part, but accepted the overall theme of Kitchi's story as true. At least for the moment. There was no doubt the man was a mason with words, so the chance remained he was attempting to fool Samuel. "How is it that you are sure she knows about it? About the god...the Croatoan?"

Kitchi dipped his head and raised his eyebrows at the word 'God,' but did not explore it. Instead he only shrugged and said, "She is old. And, I am told, learned in the craft of witchery. Necromancy, perhaps. Ancient women such as this always know the dark stories of the land."

Samuel was truly intrigued now. "Told by who?"

"What?"

"You said you were told she held these powers. Who told you?"

"My grandfather lived with these people when he was a boy. He knew the woman then, when she was a girl herself. He remembered her well and was still alive when she was banished to the western woods. It is how I know so much more than most about the woman."

"And you know where she lives? Where her house is?"

Kitchi hesitated, and Samuel could see the man was measuring how much more he should tell without giving away his advantage. "I have never been to her shelter. But what I know of it, it is no house, but rather a cave. It is shrouded in the dark woods of the island, but I remember enough from what my Numohshomus told me that I've little doubt I could find her. There is much treachery on the western shores, particularly in the south, and there is little light to guide you there. But the shoreline caves can be—"

The explosion from behind Samuel nearly knocked him from his feet and on top of Kitchi, and he felt the thick spray of water across his head and neck. He turned toward the ocean; there was only the emptiness of the water, but beyond the break of the waves he saw a giant ripple of foam.

Samuel looked down to Kitchi, whose face looked as if it had been frozen in ice. *Had he seen it?* Samuel wondered. He felt the compulsion to ask but was too shaken to speak. Instead, he moved behind Kitchi, careful not to trip over the stranded man, and then Samuel slowly began to walk backward, keeping his eyes fixed on the shoreline all the while.

It was happening.

Not a sound came from Kitchi at first, but then, finally recognizing the finality of his circumstances and the intentions of Samuel, a thick blanket of panic enveloped him. "Samuel," he croaked, his words dry and powerless, like those of a dying elder. "Samuel, you must help me! It was our deal!"

But Samuel was lost in his own focus now, continuing to scan the ocean's edge for the rise of the god. He was suddenly lightheaded with expectation and realized he wasn't breathing and in danger of collapsing. He had an absent thought what a comedy it would be to fall victim to his own god this way, so overcome in the presence of his majesty that he lost consciousness and was then devoured by the animal. But if he were to die on this beach tonight, in that way, that would be as fitting and acceptable a way as any to pass.

But Samuel steadied his breathing and fought off the dizziness, picking up the pace of his retreat to the dunes. The sun was not yet visible, but a red hue now painted the sky above the horizon, marking the beginning of morning.

Kitchi continued his pleas, the words beginning hoarse and dry and then quickly evolving to full screams. Samuel's only thought now was how perfectly the cries would act as a lure.

Kitchi must have seen it, Samuel thought. Perhaps not the details of the form, but at least the bold strokes of the thing that had made the powerful splash. But Samuel could still see nothing other than the eerie stillness of the sea, and he hadn't figured out how such a creature, large though it was, could make the sound that announced its appearance.

Samuel thought back to the first time he saw the god with Nootau and recalled the calm following the crashing sound. And just as then, he could almost feel the presence of the beast approaching the beach. And he thought he detected a growing smell.

"You will never find the woman!" Kitchi screamed now. "If you ever want to meet the Witch of the Western Shores, if you ever want to know where the beast comes from, I am the only one who can tell you?"

This thought startled Samuel, and for the first time he considered the challenge of finding this woman on his own. He knew it would be nearly impossible, but he was no longer afraid of such an exploration. Not anymore. Not after tonight. He knew when he witnessed the ferocity a second time, he would never fear anything again.

But that didn't change the difficulty that lie ahead. He could find the western shores, he figured. He knew of the Big Island and the general direction of it. It wasn't far; Samuel figured he could make it there in less than three hours. But how would he find the cave? And even if he accomplished that much, he would never be able to communicate with the woman. The natives in the colony had learned English over the years, as many of the colonists had learned the native tongue. This was a skill that was almost essential for survival. But this hermit woman from the Croatoan tribe would no more know Samuel's language than he would hers.

But all that was a problem for another day. Tonight, he would soak in the glorious killing of the struggling man before him.

The light was improving, and Samuel could see Kitchi digging his fingers into the moist sand, trying hopelessly to pull himself up the slope. He looked like a crab whose back legs had been removed, instinctively looking for the safety of cover.

But there was none to be found on the open beach, and even if there had been, Samuel would never let him reach it.

Samuel knelt behind the tall grass now, sensing the imminence of the beast, reciting soft prayers to the wind.

Within minutes, his prayers were answered.

As if Samuel, himself, had summoned the vision, a wide, black dome breached the water, and seconds later the giant began its steady march to the beach.

Chapter 15

Danny felt the long fingers of the monster close loosely around his foot, and he could only watch in horror, helpless, his back pressed against the wall, the thick rope tied tightly around his arms and chest. He opened his mouth to scream, and instead dry heaved, his tongue unfolding from his mouth like a fleshy carpet.

He couldn't see the body of the creature in the darkness of the cave opening—he could never see it in these dreams—it was only the clawed hand that appeared to him, glowing next to the fire that burned brightly beside him.

The hand grabbed Danny's foot and then the fingers crept slowly up to his ankle like a giant tarantula before finally gripping him above the heel. At that point, the creature began to pull Danny forward, sliding his back down the wall toward the wild, rapid snapping motion of its eager jaws.

And that was always the point at which Danny awoke, just before his toes crossed the threshold of the beast's black lips.

He gasped and blasted his eyelids as far apart as they would go, and then whipped his head toward the nightstand, squinting at the clock. Only twelve minutes had passed since he'd last looked at it. This wasn't surprising; Danny had been waking up before dawn for a few years now, so taking in the morning with leisure wasn't going to come easily.

He lay in bed and closed his eyes, reflecting on the dream once again. It didn't come every night, but enough that it was becoming an item of anxiety at bedtime. And now, with the possibility that he had located the creature, he feared it would recur nightly from this day forward.

He kept his eyes closed and soon felt the drift of sleep again. He let it take him, and a second later he heard the screams.

For a moment, he thought they were coming from his psyche, and that he was picking up the dream at the point where he left off. But when he opened his eyes and the screams continued, he knew they were occurring in reality.

Danny threw off the covers and swung his legs toward the floor and then sat on his bed and listened, not breathing. The screams were distant, as if coming from some old movie playing on a television in a far-off room. He got up and walked from his bedroom and then opened the door to the guest room that sat just to the right down the hall. For a moment, he wondered if, perhaps, Sam had gone in the room the other morning to watch a little television just before deciding to stay and torment him with her extended company. Maybe it had been on this whole time, and he was just now hearing it in the quiet of the morning.

But the television was off, and as he moved back down the hall of the small beach house, the sound quickly fell silent.

Danny stood motionless in the kitchen now, trying to position himself centrally in his house, hoping to find the best angle at which to locate the sound. But there was only silence now.

He slipped on his flipflops and moved to the porch door, and as he was one step out the entrance, his aim toward the beach, the phone rang. It sounded like a fire alarm in Danny's ears; if he were twenty years older, he thought, he would have had a coronary.

He held the screen door open and looked off to the sand, an ear to the wind, listening for the continuation of the screams. It was still too dark on the beach to see any detail from that distance, but he thought he could just make out the figure of someone walking on the sand, away from his house, south down the beach. It was unusual for anyone to be out at that hour, in this stretch of the beach especially, but it wasn't impossible.

Still though, had he picked the wrong morning to skip his surveillance? Was this the morning the sea god would show himself once again, basking in the sand in all its grandeur?

He let the door fall and then reached inside for the phone.

"Hello," he said, a ping of irritation in his voice.

"Don't sound so happy to hear from me," the voice chirped on the other end.

"Hi, Tracy. You're up early."

Tracy was unemployed, and as for long as Danny had known her often slept until well past noon. *Must be nice not to have to make the rent like every other person in the world*, Danny thought. He also knew that was going to be an uncomfortable conversation, the one where he had to tell Tracy their arrangement would soon be ending. He could make the payments for a few more months, maybe even a year if he stretched his money in other places. After that, though, he would have to sell. But that was a conversation for another day.

"Yeah, I'm trying something new," Tracy replied.

"What's that? Daytime?"

"Very funny."

Danny thought so.

"Listen, Danny, the reason I'm calling is one, to see how you are, and two, because I found something...I don't know, weird, I guess. Something I thought you might be interested in."

Danny knew instantly it had to do with the creature, though he couldn't have said how he knew. He continued to stare out at the beach as he talked, watching the sun coming up over the water, searching for the figure that was there only moments ago. "What is it?" Danny asked.

"I don't know, really. But I was going through some old stuff in Aunt Lynn's attic and I found something."

Danny had a faint notion to correct Tracy and inform her that it was, in fact, *his* attic now. Instead he listened.

"It's a book, like a journal, and it's really old looking. Like, *really* old. It was in a Ziploc bag and buried in one of her chests, but the pages are really faded and falling apart."

"A book? What is it called? What is it about?" Danny knew Tracy well enough that she wouldn't have brought up this find if she didn't think it was significant.

"I don't know. I didn't want to take it out of the bag, but..."

"But what?"

"I don't know, I just think it has to do with...the thing. It must, right?"

Danny felt the familiar tightening of his chest at the thought of the creature, and his face quickly flooded white with fear and eagerness. Tracy had made a connection between the book and the creature without even looking inside, and that was all Danny needed to hear. "I'll come for it," Danny blurted. "I'll come tomorrow."

"Okay, settle down, Danny. I don't know if it is about Lynn's sea creature or not, it's just a guess."

"Of course it is, Tracy. You know it is."

Tracy was quiet for a moment. "Yes, I think so too."

"Then I'll come for it."

"Actually, if it's okay with you, I was thinking I needed to get away from here for a while. I need a new start or something. And that was the last thing I was calling about. Would you mind if I came to stay with you for a few days? Maybe even a week?"

A 'new start' didn't sound like 'a few days' to Danny, but he kind of liked the idea of Tracy coming to visit. And he wanted to see the book. She knew about the creature, of course, and she knew the reasons why Danny had left Rove Beach. What she didn't know, however, was how close she had come to being a victim of the god.

Danny calmed his breathing and put a smile on his face, grateful that Tracy was still alive and that he hadn't become the murderer he had set out to be two years ago. And maybe if she visited, during her time there, he could find an opening to confess this part of their past. It was a catharsis he needed in his life.

"Do you think you're close to finding it?" Tracy asked.

Danny was caught off guard. "Why did you ask that? What made you think to ask that?"

"I don't know. I just kind of got that feeling. Something in your voice sounds different today. But why aren't you out at the beach? Isn't this your time of the day to be down on the ocean with your Meineke whales?"

"*Minke*. And yeah, well, I had kind of a long day yesterday, so I took the morning off."

There was a pause on the other end, and then, "So, can I come stay with you for a few days? I promise I'll bring the book."

Danny closed his eyes and sighed. "Sure, Tracy, whenever you want. I'll email you the address. It's no palace, but there's plenty of room. And you can stay as long as you want."

"Thanks Danny, I really appreciate it. I'll see you soon. And stay careful."

Danny hung up the phone and stepped out to the porch, placing his belly against the railing as he peered down to the coast. The beach was caped in a purple shadow, and the dark blue water of the tide was easing back and forth from the shore, in no hurry either way.

He let his eyes drift up the beach and noticed the tide had brought a lone piece of driftwood in from the sea and had placed it neatly in the middle of the sand, about halfway from the dunes to the water. The log was only a silhouette to Danny, but he was struck by the unique angle of it, as well as its distance from the shore.

"What is that?"

He pulled the binoculars from beside him and lifted them to his eyes, immediately finding the object in the lenses. It was no log, that was for certain, and if he was seeing things correctly, he was pretty sure the thing was an arm. A left arm to be exact.

"Jesus!"

Danny dropped the binoculars to the porch, where they bounced once on the wooden planks before diving out through the bottom opening in the railing. He rushed back inside and grabbed the phone again, dialing the '9' and then stopping before pressing the first '1'.

He was already a pretty bright blip on the radar of the Wickard Beach Police Department, and calling in another incident on the beach—one directly in front of his house, no less—was probably not the first step he should take. At least not as it concerned his own preservation. Besides, the thing in the sand *looked* like an arm, but it could have been a fake, the arm of a mannequin perhaps.

But if it was a human arm, he needed to get to it first. The beachcombers would be down soon, and the shrieks from the first woman who saw it would mean the police would be arriving at Danny's door within minutes.

The screams from his dream.

They were real, and Danny could only assume they had come from the mouth of whomever the arm belonged to.

And who had he seen walking away?

Danny descended the steps and within moments was standing next to the severed limb of a man, which he concluded based on the thick fingers and abundance of hair on

the hand and forearm. The arm was torn off just above the el-
bow, in the middle of the bicep, and the bone of the victim's
humerus shone brightly amongst the deep red strings of flesh
and muscle that surrounded it. Sand caked most of the site,
in some way adding to the gruesomeness of the scene.

There was nothing to do now; Danny had to call it in.
He reached for his cell phone, but his pocket was empty. In
his rush to reach the beach, he'd forgotten to grab his phone
first. "Dammit," he whispered and dipped his head, turning
toward the water as he put his hands over his face in a show
of shame and exhaustion. Another person was dead now, and
unlike the previous 'drowning' victims he had read about before he came here, there was little doubt in Danny's mind
that it was his former god that was to blame for this one.

But what about Danny? Was he also to blame? Should
he have tried harder to convince Calazzo and Benitez of his
theories, told them that he suspected the creature, who they
believed was a myth, was responsible for the string of deaths
on their beaches? Maybe they would have laughed him off,
or even threatened to lock Danny up, but still, he would have
been doing his due diligence.

Danny steadied his thoughts, leaving the possibility that
the arm lying at his feet had nothing to do with the beast.
He slid his hands to his chin and opened his eyes, and immediately saw the trail of enormous footprints leading to the
water. They were well up from where he was standing, and
the high tide was lapping over them, but there was no doubt
about what he was seeing.

Danny walked to the shore, his eyes locked on the sand
now so that he wouldn't lose the fading outlines of the prints,

and in seconds, he could see the remnants of two prints that were facing the other direction, leading from the ocean to the arm.

There was the proof. There was no longer any doubt.

He stopped at the edge of the tide line and then, as it ebbed, he stooped to get a better measure of the print, studying the foot size of the beast for the first time. He needed to get a photo of it, but, again, his phone was sitting on the bar in his kitchen.

"You okay, buddy?"

The words sounded as if they were only a foot or two away, and Danny turned to see the approaching figures of two men. The sun was risen now, and Danny could see the men were probably in their mid-seventies, fit and alert. Probably took this walk quite often, he thought, though Danny didn't recognize them. By this time of the morning, he was already back inside skimming the papers for the latest evidence.

"Yeah, sure," Danny replied, rising to his feet. "How you doing?"

"Just saw you stooped there, thought you was hurt or something."

"Nope, just studying something." *Really, Danny?* he thought. He knew better than to throw out such a vague line, especially to men of a certain age. They almost never took into account that privacy was implied with those types of statements.

"Studying? Whatcha got there?"

Danny snickered and shook his head, letting the gentleman know it wasn't anything they would find too interesting.

"Just a—"

"What is that over there?"

One of the men began walking toward the arm, and Danny felt the blood rush to his head, his heart now in his chest. "I don't—"

"Holy shit, Ralph. Come look at this!"

Within moments Ralph and the other man were standing over the arm, staring down at it. Danny noted how unafraid they were, and speculated they were either military men or physicians—perhaps both—and not prone to squeamishness.

Danny walked up on them and stood beside them. "I saw it from my porch this morning. Was going to call the police but I forgot my phone, and then..." He paused.

"Then what?" Ralph asked, intrigued.

"I saw some prints and—"

"Prints?" the other man asked. "Show us."

Danny and the two men walked back to the shoreline, and as they did, Ralph dialed 911.

And when they reached the place where Danny had been stooping, the prints had become shallow indentations, indistinguishable as footprints.

"I don't see it, son," the man not named Ralph said. "You see it, Ralph?"

Ralph held the phone to his ear and shook his head, and then said, "I need the police. Got a situation out on the beach. Maybe a murder."

Danny swallowed at the sound of the word murder.

"Not sure the mile marker," the man continued, "but it's right in front of the house where that new fellow moved in."

Chapter 16

Samuel slipped into the door of his home with the stealth of a prairie mouse, holding his breath and tiptoeing through the tiny kitchen until he reached the threshold of his bedroom. From there, he could see into his mother's room. She was asleep on her side with her back facing the opening of her door, in the same position she was when Samuel left. Thankfully, his mother had always been a heavy sleeper; it was one reason among many that this night had been possible.

Samuel eased himself into his bed, feeling a desire for sleep that was almost painful. He was hungry and nauseous, and his feet and thighs burned with exhaustion. But despite the encroaching morning—only an hour or so away, he estimated—and the grueling, sleepless day that lie ahead of him, Samuel couldn't fall under just yet. He had too much to reflect on, too many recent memories to relive.

After a few minutes though, the draw of sleep was too strong, and Samuel closed his eyes, accepting the inevitable. He could only pray the images in his dreams were as beautiful as those he'd seen in the bake of the moonlight.

But the promise of his dreams would have to wait for another night. Samuel had barely a moment to embrace unconsciousness when the first sounds of anxiety began drifting in from the outside. The words were foreign, distant, but he knew they were to do with Kitchi.

Samuel opened his eyes and listened, shifting his eyes, searching for meaning in the low tones of the Algonquin language. He hadn't been asleep long enough to feel groggy, and a new energy was flowing through him, activated by the milling from outside. He got up slowly and stepped tepidly from his room into the front of the house, stopping before he reached the opening of the main room window. He then dropped to his hands and knees, and then crawled over until he was positioned beneath the bottom frame of the window, listening. Slowly, he raised his head until his eyes were just above the jamb, and he peered into the village square where the new day's sunlight shone on a group of five Algonquin, Nootau's parents among them. They were huddled no more than twenty paces from the longhouse where Kitchi slept, not far from the center of the square. The postures and movements of the group were agitated, signaling concern, and Samuel could hear Nootau's mother crying.

"What is it, Samuel?"

Samuel ducked beneath the window and placed his back against the wall, scrunching in his shoulders tight, as if the words were arrows that had started flying in from the square. But they had come from behind him, and he turned to see his mother standing just inside the kitchen, her arms folded, a look of weary confusion across her forehead.

Samuel's eyes were wide and crazed, searching for the lie that would explain this scene. "I...nothing. There is some conversation from the Indians. They...they woke me up."

Elyoner Cook said nothing for several beats, and instead studied her son with a look that contained both suspicion and sadness. She could see the change occurring in him, Samuel was sure of it. She couldn't have known the source or impetus for the change, though he suspected she thought it had to do with Nootau's death. That was true, of course, but not in the way she would have suspected.

But there was more to his mother's look than just concern and sadness. Samuel had noted it during their meeting with Nootau's parents. Beyond the fear and anger that his actions had caused her, they had triggered a new emotion: Dread. And she seemed to sense that whatever terrible thing was headed toward them, it was somehow caused by her son.

"Well, you're up at least," she said finally. "And dressed, I see. So, let's get breakfast started. We've a long day ahead of us and a lot to do."

Samuel stood now, in the full view of the outside, and as he did, the faces from the village square all turned in unison toward him. He couldn't see their eyes from his position, but he could feel the distrust in them as clearly as if he'd been standing on their feet.

Kitchi was missing, and Samuel knew it wouldn't be long before he was asked about it. After all, he had stopped to talk to Kitchi in front of their wigwam yesterday, an encounter that had been witnessed by two of the colony's women. There hadn't been anything unusual about it on the surface—they hadn't been engaged in any sharp-tongued debate at the time—but still, it was an unusual pairing.

But Samuel had spent time on this problem on his journey back from the sound. The disappearance of Kitchi was an inevitable issue that he would have to face, and he had talked through a solution. Nootau had died, and though Samuel had spoken with his friend's parents, Kitchi, himself, had not been part of the conversation. Samuel would simply tell whoever asked that Kitchi had stopped him on his way home, asking for any other details that he may have forgotten to tell earlier. That story was reasonable, particularly since it was fairly close to the truth.

The mystery would deepen with the missing wheelbarrow; that detail would not go unnoticed, since there weren't more than three or four in the village. Samuel had considered bringing it back with him from the beach, but time had become an issue, and so, instead, he had dumped the tool into the waters of the sound before rowing back across to the island. Someone was likely to discover the wheelbarrow's tracks leading from the longhouse into the woods, but at that point, they would disappear, forever lost in the leaf litter of the dry forest floor.

Elyoner walked across the room and stood next to her son, and both looked out to the huddle of Indians in the distance. It was a standoff of stares, as the natives continued their surveillance of the house, and the Cooks measured their reluctant hosts.

"They'll not need much reason to kill us, Samuel. You know that, don't you?"

Samuel suddenly felt a surge of power flood inside of him. It was a feeling not unlike that he felt only a few hours earlier as he watched the sea beast rip apart the crippled man on the beach. He thought of Kitchi flailing and twisting his arms and torso, screaming with a terror Samuel hadn't known possible in a man, his legs hanging below him like the impotent limbs of a dead squid.

His death had come too quickly for Samuel's pleasure, but unlike with Nootau, this time he could enjoy the full spectacle of his god, its power on open display. The exposure of the beach was like a canvas for the creature, and Samuel had viewed its work with reverence. It had reminded him of the ancient Greek plays he'd read in school, and the magnificent amphitheaters that had staged the tales for all to see.

Except Samuel was the only audience to this tragedy, the lone witness to the magical destruction of the ocean demon. "What do you mean?" Samuel asked, his words knowing, confident.

Elyoner continued her stare on the open village. "They don't want us here, and we have nowhere else to go. I don't know what really happened with Nootau, but I will not sentence the entire colony to death for your wrongs. Do you understand what I mean, Samuel?"

Samuel did. If it came to it, his mother would sacrifice him for the sake of the colony. It was fair, he thought; sacrifice was how civilizations had survived since the first presence of Adam in the Garden. And it would be how he survived as well. He needed his god. Needed to learn how to summon it. Control it. Use its power for his own.

"I understand, mother. I'll not make trouble for you again."

Samuel finally turned from the window and walked past his mother, stopping for a moment in the doorway to his room. "I'm not feeling well today," he said. "I'll be staying in bed until I'm better."

There was no argument from his mother. "That's probably for the best," she said.

Samuel walked into his room and lay on his bed, and then, just before he went to sleep for the rest of the day, he thought of a plan to find the Woman of the Western Shores.

Chapter 17

"Funny seeing you here," Calazzo said.

"Hysterical," Danny agreed, matching the sarcasm of the portly sheriff. He sat back casually in the metal chair that had been folded out for him in front of Sheriff Calazzo's desk, looking much more relaxed than he felt. He had come to the station voluntarily, but really, he had little choice this time. There was a body found—at least a part of one—directly in front of his house, so if he had put up any reluctance, he felt arrest would have been a certainty. And, he thought now, it still might be.

"Do you want a lawyer?" Calazzo asked, shifting his tone into one of a more formal nature, leaving all the passive banter that he and Danny had developed behind.

"I don't know anything about what happened, sheriff, so no, I suppose I'll pass on a lawyer for the moment."

Calazzo pursed his lips and nodded. "I appreciate that, Danny. And I also believe you. But I also don't."

"What the hell does that mean?"

"It means I believe you when you say you don't know what happened to that poor soul who was in possession of that arm you found on the beach. But I also think you *think* you know what happened, and that part I don't believe."

"You think *I think* I know?"

"I think you got some ideas about a sea monster terrorizing our little beach town here. Like some kind of Bigfoot *Jaws* situation or something." Calazzo paused, sparing any mocking looks. "I think you believe in that story I showed

131

you yesterday. The one written by your friend. What was her name? Sarah, I think it was. Yes, that's it."

Danny didn't reply, and he suddenly felt the situation was nearing the point of him needing a lawyer. "Did you have any questions for me, Sheriff?"

Calazzo let his eyes linger on Danny for a moment and then said, "Did you hear anything last night or this morning?"

Danny nodded and said calmly, "I thought I heard a scream. Screaming. But I was sleeping at the time, so my first thought was that they were coming from my dreams."

"You have nightmares, Danny?"

"Who doesn't?"

"Where is your wife?"

"What?"

"Your wife. I did a little research on you. I know you're a married man—at least you were back in Rove Beach—but I don't recall seeing a wife on your arm since you've been here in Wickard."

"Maybe she's back at the house frying up some bacon."

"Is she?"

"If she is or she isn't, what does this have to do with th—"

"Sheriff." Officer Benitez appeared in the doorway, her light brown face now a pale shade of pink.

"What do you got, deputy?"

"The prints came back. We know who it is?" Benitez swallowed hard, shifting her eyes from Danny and then back to the sheriff.

"You gonna make me guess, Benitez?"

"It's Gerald DeRose. The father of those kids from yesterday."

"What?" Danny blurted, his throat constricting as the news registered in his mind. He stared in disbelief at Officer Benitez, trying to meet her eyes, but she was vigilantly focused on Calazzo now, avoiding him.

"Shit." Calazzo closed his eyes and sighed, as if his suspicions had been revealed as true. "Have you contacted Mrs. DeRose yet?"

"Not yet."

"Okay then, I suppose that should be my duty. I'll head out there now."

"Yes sir."

"And Benitez?"

"Yes, Sheriff?"

Calazzo stood and walked to the door of his office. "Place this man under arrest."

"What?" Benitez asked. "But sir?"

Calazzo shook his head and crinkled his face, confused. "What's the problem, officer?"

"I...I just don't think—"

"When I need your thoughts on something, I will explicitly ask for them."

"Well, great, then I guess—"

"I saw something on my porch," Danny interrupted, steering the growing tension between the two officers toward himself.

Calazzo dipped his head and stared at Danny, a thin smile on his face. "Did you now? How convenient?"

"You never asked me if I saw anything. Too busy with my marital history, remember?"

Calazzo chuckled. "What did you see, Mr. Lynch?"

"It was dark still, so I couldn't see any detail from my porch, but before I went down to the beach, I saw, I don't know, a figure there. It was walking away from the spot where I found the arm."

"In which direction was it walking?"

"South. I thought it was just an early riser; I didn't think much of it at the time, but now..."

Calazzo let the information linger and then said, "No description? That's not too helpful."

"Well, I guess that's not entirely true."

"Well, then why don't you go ahead and just give me the whole truth, Danny. I thought that was the point we were at now."

Danny swallowed and took a deep breath. "The figure was short, thin. It looked like a child."

"A child?" It was Benitez this time.

Danny nodded. "I can't be sure, but the more I think about it, it might have been the DeRose kid, Shane."

Calazzo stared hard at Danny now. "You saying you think that little nine-year old boy killed his father at the beach in front of your house in the middle of the night? Is that what you're theorizing, Mr. Lynch?"

It wasn't exactly Danny's theory, but the other one was no longer suitable to be put on the table, at least not according to Sheriff Calazzo. "I don't know, sheriff, I'm just telling you what I saw."

"Okay, Mr. Lynch, thank you for the information. We appreciate it." Calazzo turned back to Benitez. "I'm headed over to the DeRose house. In the meantime, like I told you, lock him up."

Chapter 18

"Sokwa!"

Samuel crept from the darkness of the thick loblolly pines that grew like giant asparagus just outside the window under which Sokwa slept. The night was as clear as the one before, and Samuel could see the window—which was wide and low and easily accessible to Samuel, even from the ground—clearly from the forest.

Sokwa's family's wigwam was as humble as any in the village and was built on the outer edges of the community, as far from the center as any home in the colony. The geography of the wigwam was the only reason Samuel's mission to reach the girl was even plausible.

And Samuel knew the location; he and Nootau had visited twice before, both occasions upon which Sokwa had requested to meet the two boys after suppertime. She was an adventurous girl, Sokwa, causing much trouble for her father during her twelve years, often due to such things as inviting boys to her window in the evening hours while the rest of her family slept.

Of course, Sokwa had really only wanted to see Nootau on those occasions, Samuel knew that, but a request to meet Nootau alone would have revealed too obviously her feelings for the boy. Besides, even though she didn't care for Samuel in the way she did for Nootau, Samuel knew she thought of him as pleasant enough to be around.

He placed his face inside the small opening, and from there he could see Sokwa lying on her side, her back facing the window. He could have leaned in and touched her shoulder from where he stood, but he was cautious not to startle the girl, fearing she may scream and draw attention. Samuel wasn't concerned about stirring Sokwa's grandmother, who was her guardian, though it seemed Sokwa was more of the caretaker in the arrangement. It was Jania, Sokwa's sister, the girl Kitchi had 'offered' to Samuel on the beach the previous night, he was worried about. Jania slept just across from Sokwa, and a scream from her sister would certainly have triggered her awake.

"Sokwa!" Samuel whispered again, and this time the girl turned over immediately and opened her eyes, rubbing them once, trying to bring Samuel into focus through the darkness.

"Samuel?"

Samuel held a finger to his mouth. "Yes."

"What are you doing here?"

"I need your help, Sokwa."

Sokwa sat up in her bed and scooted to the edge so that her face was nearly outside the window, holding a blanket to her chest. She turned back to where her family slept inside and then again to Samuel. She lowered her voice. "You are under suspicion, Samuel. You must know that, yes?"

"That is what I am here to talk to you about."

"Then you know what happened to Kitchi?"

"Kitchi?" Samuel scrunched his face tight, shaking his head quickly, confused. "No, I am here about Nootau. What is suspicious about Kitchi?"

"He is missing, Samuel. You have not heard?"

Samuel shook his head again. "I have been sick today. I was in bed since the morning. And I heard no visits to my home regarding Kitchi? What is it about? What has happened?"

Sokwa shrugged, and Samuel could see his act of ignorance was working. "He has gone missing. That is all I know?"

"Missing? I have talked to Kitchi recently, just yesterday, in fact. On my way home from re-stocking the wood pile."

"That is the reason for the suspicion. You were seen by others during this meeting."

"Of course I was seen. Why would I take steps to avoid otherwise?"

"I don't know, Samuel, but Kitchi's whereabouts are all the village is concerned with tonight. Jania and Matwau spoke of little else today, and your name was mentioned often."

Matwau was Jania's intended husband. His father was arguably the most influential Indian in the village. Samuel swallowed and opened his eyes, hoping to express his fear at this news.

"I don't know anything about Kitchi. I swear it. I talked to him because he wanted to know more about the day Nootau died, that is true, but I had little more to say, other than what I had already told to his parents. About the games we played. And the shark attack."

Sokwa dropped her eyes for just a moment, letting Samuel's words resonate, and then she returned her gaze to him, frowning. "It is not just Kitchi."

"What else?"

"There are many who don't believe your story of Nootau's death." Sokwa lowered her eyes again at the sound of the Algonquin boy's name, and then placed a hand to her mouth, stifling a sob. "What happened, Samuel? I know the story you have told. But...it doesn't sound right to me either. It doesn't fit with the boy I knew." Two tears fell quickly from Sokwa's face, and she instinctively lifted a knuckle to her eye to catch them.

It was Samuel's turn now to bow his head, which he did slowly, dramatically. He took a deep breath as he stared at the ground and then looked off to the side, gathering his thoughts. He lifted his head and stared Sokwa in the eye. "They are correct to be suspicious of my story about him. As are you."

"What?"

"The story of Nootau's death. You're right, Sokwa, it is not how I told it."

"I don't understand, Samuel. Did you...did you kill him?"

"No! Sokwa, of course not. I loved Nootau. I do love him. I would never have done anything to bring harm to him. Please believe this about me." Samuel paused, building the effect for his lie. "And..." He stopped in mid-sentence, as if he'd said too much.

"What is it?"

Samuel took in a deep breath and opened his eyes wide, shifting them from left to right before letting them fall heavy on Sokwa. He leaned in and whispered, "I believe he is still alive."

Sokwa scoffed reflexively. "What? Alive? How is that possible? Where do you think he is?"

"It is a bit of a story, but one I am willing to tell. I fear your sister will hear us soon, though. And we'll both be in boiling water."

Sokwa turned back again to the wigwam, scoping the scene inside, and then nodded in agreement.

"I think I can find him, Sokwa, and bring him home. But I can't do it alone. I need your help."

"I...of course. What do you need me to do?" Sokwa's voice was hopeful, eager to help.

"I can't tell you all of it here. Meet me at the southwestern edge of the village just before dawn today. Just beyond the colony church." Samuel looked to the dark sky, measuring the position of the moon. "That is only a few hours from now. Will you meet me there?"

There was a look of both terror and wonderment on Sokwa's face as she shook her head. "No, not at dawn. I cannot meet you until this evening. I have duties for my father that cannot be neglected today. But I will meet you at dusk. Can you wait?"

It would be far more difficult to make the journey at night. Samuel could only pray the evening would be clear and the moon full and bright. He nodded. "Then you must get sleep now, since you'll have none tomorrow night. I will tell you more of the story on the way."

"On the way to where?"

"Be there by dusk," Samuel said, ignoring the question, intent on keeping his directions cryptic and intriguing. "And you can't speak of this to anyone, Sokwa. It is for the sake of Nootau."

Sokwa nodded.

Samuel gave his own nod in return and then disappeared from the window, far enough away that he was once again masked by the night. He stood ten paces from the wigwam and inhaled the cool aroma of the pines, closing his eyes and smiling as the air filled his lungs. He felt strong tonight, healthy, both in body and thought. He felt a divine focus within him, a clarity that was almost blinding.

He would make it to the Woman of the Western Shores. He was as sure of that now as he was of his devotion to the new god that rose from the sea only days ago.

He turned from the wigwam and began his trek into the forest. A hundred paces should be enough, he calculated, before he started on his path to the southwest border of the colony. There he would hide and sleep and wait patiently for Sokwa.

She wasn't the ideal guide and translator—a strong male with a thorough knowledge of the terrain would have been a much more suitable traveling companion—but she was vulnerable, gullible, and she had an eagerness for excitement, all traits that would serve Samuel well.

And more than anything, it was her tongue he needed most. He prayed the language of the Algonquin was close enough to that of the woman's that communication would be possible.

Samuel decided to double the paces from one hundred to two hundred. It was unnecessary, perhaps, but he wanted to ensure the necessary berth around the perimeter, to keep well outside the view of the wigwams and homes of the colonists. He was under suspicion—perhaps even wanted by now—so if he did nothing else, he had to stay as far away from the village center as possible.

In the morning, when his mother and the rest of the colony discovered Samuel was gone, he would be as good as dead to them all. His mother was now as much his adversary as any native villager. They were all his enemies now. The colony. The Indians. His countrymen back in his homeland who would be making their way to join them in this new world.

And if Samuel was able to find the secret of the Croatoan, they would all meet the same fate.

Samuel thought of his father now, and a simmer of hatred began to bubble inside of him. He had left Samuel with little more than a handshake when he departed for England, and even then, Samuel doubted his intentions ever to return.

But if he did, Samuel had plans for him as well.

There was much work to do before then, however, and for the next day or two, there was only one person he had to keep in his circle of trust. A native girl. One Samuel prayed could lead him to the Woman of the Western Shores. To the keeper of the origin of his new lord and savior.

Chapter 19

"I'm your phone call, Danny? Really?"

Danny couldn't help but laugh at the question. "I thought we were in love, Sam. Isn't that how we left it the other day at the diner?"

"No, not exactly."

"I must have misread it then."

"You're calling me from the Wickard Beach Detention Center, so let me guess, you need money?"

"Not exactly."

There was silence on the other end.

"Okay, yes, I need money. But it's just for bail, so you'll get it back."

"Yeah, that makes it so much better. You really do love me."

Danny sighed. "Listen, there isn't anyone close by I could call. You know, being new here and all. It's kind of the reason they won't just release me, I think. They know I'm renting my place and I guess they figure if they let me go, I'll flee. Just move on to some other town like some transient."

"Yeah, I don't blame them. That seems to be your M.O."

Danny's suspicions of Sam from the other morning resurfaced. She seemed to know more about him than he'd revealed to her.

"Anyway, you were the first person I thought of. But obviously I understand if you won't help me. Or can't. I don't expect you to be able to get your hands on that much cash at a moment's notice."

"Well, I don't know how much you need, Danny, but before I make a decision in either direction, I think it's fair to ask what you've been arrested for."

"Obstruction. And I'm no lawyer, but I know that charge is a joke. They had to throw something generic at me to detain me, but they'll never make it stick. It doesn't even make sense."

"So there was some other reason they wanted to lock you up then? Or are you just claiming general small-town cop harassment of the new guy in town?"

Danny paused. "The sheriff thinks I killed someone."

Sam was silent for a moment and then asked calmly, "Wow, really?"

"Yeah, but I guess he wasn't ready to go that far with the charges. Not just yet anyway."

"Who was it?"

"Who killed him?"

"Who died?"

"Well, I guess in fairness, they don't know for a fact the guy is even dead, they just...*I* found an arm on the beach outside of my house this morning. They printed the hand to the father of a kid I saved from drowning yesterday. Two kids actually."

Danny could hear how rambling he must have sounded, but all of it was the truth, and he figured the truth—as far as his arrest was concerned—was the right thing to tell at this point, especially to a relative stranger from whom he was asking for cash. He said nothing else though, waiting for Sam either to ask what the hell he was talking about or just to hang up, both of which would have been reasonable reactions.

But she didn't miss a beat in following the story, and, in fact, seemed up to speed. "Yeah, I think I heard something about that," Sam said finally. "The kids from the other morning, I mean. A friend of mind has a knickknack shop on the boardwalk and she said there was quite the to-do. I didn't realize that was you."

"Just trying to make a splash in my new city." Danny could almost see Sam roll her eyes at the pun.

"How much do you need?"

"Five-grand."

Sam chuckled. "Five grand, huh? Is that all?"

"I said I understand if you can't help."

"You don't have that much on a credit card or something? Big shot songwriter like you."

"Bail doesn't work that way. You need to have cash. Or a check. And silly me, I left my checkbook at home. Didn't think I'd be led off to a jail cell when they invited me to come down to the station and talk this morning. Again, Sam, I don't really expect you to help me with this. There's an ad for a bail bondsman staring back at me as I speak, so I have other options. I just thought—"

"I'll be there as soon as I can. I have to make a few calls first though."

"Really?"

"What the hell?"

"Thanks, Sam."

"You're welcome. Oh, and another thing."

"Sure."

"The only person whoever called me Sam was an uncle that I despised. My name is Samantha."

Danny smiled. "Samantha, it is."

"Don't go anywhere, Danny."

Danny hung up the phone and was immediately escorted back to his cell, which he entered with a new feeling of relief. He walked to the lone bed and sighed as he sat down on the thin mattress, placing his back against the cold, white, concrete wall that was in bad need of a new coat of paint. He closed his eyes and thought of what he needed to do once he was released, which, he'd been told, wouldn't be until later that evening, even if Sam arrived in the next hour.

He would need a good lawyer, he supposed, especially if he was arrested again for murder. More importantly, however, he needed to capture the beast once and for all. Not on camera, as he'd done before—there were too many modern tricks that any amateur could use to make the fake look real. No, he needed to capture it for real. And kill it.

Danny's heart started to race at the thought of a direct encounter with the creature. The black and purple man.

Danny's instincts had been sharp in bringing him to Wickard Beach. He'd learned from the drowning reports and how to analyze the trends, and he'd followed his nose as well as any big-game hunter. But now that he had tracked down his trophy, things were spiraling out of control. A man was dead; it wasn't Danny's fault, he convinced himself of that, but there was certainly more he could have done to prevent it from happening.

Danny sat with his head against the prison wall for several hours, searching for a plan that never quite materialized, whispering words of a strategy one minute, only to denounce it as absurd a minute later. The facts were, without knowing where and when the creature was going to appear, there was nothing to plan. He needed a clue. He needed help.

By sundown, his head began to bob forward, and just as he was about to fall asleep, Danny heard the clicking sound of the deputy's key.

"Danny Lynch. You've made bail."

Danny didn't rise immediately, now half-wishing he could have a couple of hours to sleep before leaving.

"You coming?"

Danny scratched his head with both hands and then rose, following the deputy to the front desk of the station where he signed out his wallet and keys, the only two possessions he had on him at the time of his arrest.

As he was leaving the station, he passed Officer Benitez who was entering. He caught her eye for a moment, but she quickly shifted her gaze forward.

Danny didn't look back as he walked out the front door, feeling the cool air of freedom fill his lungs. The things he took for granted. Thoughts of prison suddenly flooded his mind as he stood on the wide stoop of the Wickard police station. That was his fate if he didn't find the creature.

Before the fear of life in a penitentiary fully enveloped Danny, his attention was taken to an interior light from a car parked on the opposite side of the street. The door opened quickly and within seconds, Samantha was out and leaning against the fender, standing beneath the street lamp, waving ironically.

Danny descended the steps, walked to the car, and gave Samantha a tired, shame-filled smile.

"Hey there, felon," she said.

"Charged, but not convicted."

"Yeah, yeah. Details, details."

Danny took a deep breath. "Thank you, Sam. Sorry, Samantha. My court date is next Wednesday, and I have every intention of showing up."

"Well, that's very noble of you."

"I'm just saying, you trusted me enough to risk five-thousand dollars, which I'm not sure why exactly, but I'm not going to skip on it. In fact, I can get you the cash when the bank opens tomorrow morning. First thing."

"That won't be necessary. I know you aren't going anywhere, Danny."

Danny squinted and shook his head. "And how do you know that?"

Samantha shrugged. "You're here for a reason. Same as me."

Danny nodded, studying the woman. "What do you think you know, Samantha?"

Samantha dropped her look for a moment and then re-captured Danny's gaze. "Let's take a ride, Danny. Probably don't want to raise any more eyeballs than are already up and gazing around, right?"

Danny nodded and then made his way around the front of the car to the passenger door, keeping his eyes fixed on Samantha the whole time. He entered the car slowly, and sat tall in the seat, staring out the front windshield. "So what is all this about?"

Samantha shifted the car into drive and pulled away from the curb, and within a few minutes, she pulled into the large parking lot of the boardwalk, having not spoken a word the entire three miles. "It's about that thing out there. That thing you saw a little over two years ago in Rove Beach."

Chapter 20

"It is so dark, Samuel. How will we ever find the woman you are looking for?"

Samuel and Sokwa were less than a half-hour into the trek, a trek that Samuel estimated would take just under three hours, and he could see early on that the Algonquin girl's doubts were justified. The sun was down now, and with his eyes not yet adjusted, he felt nearly blind walking the single island road. And 'road' was a generous term for what it was. In truth, it was little more than a narrow footpath that had been carved through the forest decades ago and had been maintained very little. In many places, it was overgrown to the point of invisibility, and in no place was it wide enough to avoid the tickling pine needles on either side of the path.

But Samuel knew his own positivity would be key to completing his mission. Sokwa was daring, that was true, but she was also a child, a girl, and without the drive of purpose that Samuel possessed, he knew her enthusiasm for the adventure would eventually die.

But not now. It was far too early.

"We'll find her, Sokwa. We must find her for Nootau's sake. And I know we will as long as you ensure we stay on the path south. I'm depending on you for this, Sokwa."

Sokwa checked the sky again and nodded and then pointed up to the heavens just off to their left. Samuel could see only the outline of her figure, but the whites of her eyes glistened in the moonlight, and there was a devoted focus in them as she scanned the dark canvas above. She quickly found the beacon and lowered her finger. "It is the South Star," she said, almost as if to herself. "It is dim, I cannot point it out to you, but I can see it. We must continue in this direction."

For the next two hours, Samuel and Sokwa walked at a brisk pace, fighting their fears of the screaming foxes and hooting owls, shrugging off the branches that grabbed for them as they carved their bodies through the forest, each step requiring a faith that was quite literally blind.

Samuel told a story of fiction as they walked, quickly inventing parts to the story, and then backtracking on them when they contradicted, acting as if the trauma of the day had been too much for him to remember it all accurately. He gave Sokwa vague details about this western woman, whom he'd obviously never met, explaining how she had met him and Nootau at the ocean beach on the day of Nootau's disappearance, and that Samuel believed she had lured the boy to the cave they were heading toward now.

"But why did you make up the story of the shark?" Sokwa asked. "And Nootau's death?"

"He had wanted to push himself. To explore and grow as a man, the way his father had encouraged. But he was supposed to be gone for only half of the day. I told Nootau I would stay away from the village for as long as possible, so as not to be questioned about his whereabouts. And when he didn't come back, instead of admitting I was complicit in the plan, I panicked."

Samuel knew his story made little sense, but Sokwa didn't sound overly suspicious, asking only two or three more challenging questions which Samuel answered with similar confusion. And whenever he felt she was getting a bit too close to cornering him, Samuel would sway wildly off the path, forcing Sokwa's attention back to positioning them in the proper direction on the road.

But by the third hour, Samuel was the one losing faith in the mission. He was exhausted, and his head was heavy with a thumping pain, a result of not eating supper for two days. The thought of food suddenly stirred a growling in his stomach.

"I am hungry too, Samuel," Sokwa said in the darkness. "We should stop to eat."

"We're almost there," Samuel snapped. "Let us just keep going." Samuel paused and then said, "I've brought no food, Sokwa. I am sorry for that. And of my tone."

"I have," Sokwa replied.

"Have what?"

"Brought food. Not much, but there is enough for us to share."

Samuel felt the sting of a tear in his eye, both at the thought of filling his belly and from the sweetness of this young girl, a native who trusted him and whom he had lured along to serve his purpose. He had vowed to destroy all of them with his new god, but at that moment, he decided he may reconsider Sokwa.

Samuel began to agree to the idea of camping for a few moments to rest and eat, when his attention shifted back to the forest around him. "Look at that," he said.

"What is it?"

"Don't you see?" There was a new light suddenly, both around and above him, and he had a new feeling of space.

"Look!" he said, spreading his arms wide and jogging eight or ten paces down the road. He looked up at the sky. "Look!" he repeated. "The trees are thinning. I can see the whole sky." He kicked his feet. "And the ground is filled with sand."

"We are nearing the Wishalowe waters," Sokwa said, an unmistakable surprise in her voice.

Samuel was smiling. "What does that mean?"

"Wishalowe? It is our name for the western sound. The Wishalowe is what you call 'alligator.' We are certainly close now. I can smell it."

Samuel could smell it too, and he had to contain himself, tempering his desire to release the laugh he felt inside.

"But I don't know of any caves to the west. I don't know who you are looking for."

Samuel took a few more steps down the path, and could soon see the first glimmer of water, and with that sight he began to run at full speed, and when Sokwa reached him a few moments later, the laughter that Samuel had been restricting was now on full display. In front of him he could see across the western sound to the big island that Kitchi had referenced. They were in the right place; now he just needed to find the cave.

"We are at the water," Sokwa said, and Samuel could sense the pride and pleasure in her voice. "We have made it."

"Yes, we are, Sokwa," Samuel said, not taking his eyes from the sight of the large landmass that now seemed almost close enough to touch. "And you are the reason why."

"But I don't know where to go now."

The two children said nothing for a moment as they stared out at the western sound—the Wishalowe waters—and then, somewhere on the wind, a piercing sound entered their space. Samuel and Sokwa looked at each other, their eyes wide. They were statues now as they listened.

The sound came again, this time louder, shriller, off to the north.

There was no mistaking it. It was screaming.

Samuel brought his face up to Sokwa's, so close that his nose was barely a pebble's width away from hers. His eyelids were half-closed and a smile curled up his cheeks. "I will lead us from here, Sokwa. I know where to go."

Chapter 21

"How...how do you know about that?"

Samantha laughed. "It was in the newspaper, Danny. Remember?"

"Yeah, the *Rove Beach Rover*. Not exactly the *New York Times*. Who the hell knows about the *Rove Beach Rover* outside of Rove Beach?"

"Sheriff Calazzo, for one."

"How do you know about—"

"I'm following it too, Danny. That's how."

Danny was stunned, like he'd been punched in the belly. "Following it? From...where? Why? Who are you?"

"That's like twelve questions, Danny. Just slow down. Let's take a walk."

"Who are you!"

Samantha gave Danny a long stare, her eyes glaring and her mouth flat. "Let's walk, Danny. We'll get to it."

Danny didn't move, instead waiting for Samantha to exit the car entirely before he finally opened his own door and followed her reluctantly toward the beach. He kept at least three paces behind her at all times.

Samantha scoffed. "For Christ's sake, Danny, I'm not going to hurt you. We slept together the other night. If the plan was to hurt you—or kill you—which is what I'm sure you're really thinking, I could have done it then."

They walked to the edge of the boardwalk parking lot that bordered the beach and stopped just off to the side of a dimly lit street lamp. "So what is this then? You're obviously into me for more than my body."

Samantha didn't crack a smile. "You knew a woman named Lynn Shields, I presume."

Danny felt his bowels rumble at the sound of the name.

Lynn Shields.

He thought of the woman every day of his life since he first saw her on the beach at dawn on the morning of the sighting. She had been masked by the early sunlight and the tall grass of the dunes that day, staring like some predatory bird into the vastness of the ocean, a look of calm anticipation draped across her face. At first, she hadn't noticed Danny, so engrossed was she in the crashing symphony of the sea, even though he stood watching her from less than twenty yards away. Danny hadn't yet seen the Ocean God that would appear to him only minutes later, but this steady concentration by the woman had intrigued him nevertheless.

And when the Ocean God did emerge a few moments after—and the woman was suddenly nowhere to be seen—Danny quickly made the connection between the beast and the woman.

In the terrifying week that followed that first encounter, Danny would see the death of his wife and come to learn that the woman—Lynn Shields—was some type of master to this sea beast and seemed to be the only person capable of summoning it. And during his imprisonment in the woman's grotto, he would further find out that she had dedicated decades of her life to feeding this creature, and that it began a new cycle every fourteen months.

She had tried to use Danny for this same sacrificial purpose, and instead, Tammy had lost her life in the crossfire.

And ultimately, Lynn Shields fell victim to the creature as well, devoured right before Danny's eyes by the being she had sustained for so many years.

Danny rubbed his shoulder at the location where the scar from his bullet wound rose from the skin like a hill of flesh, the itchy, everlasting reminder of that deranged year of his life. "The name sounds familiar," he answered.

Samantha frowned and nodded. "Yeah, I'm sure it does."

Samantha obviously knew something about the history of his and Lynn's relationship, but Danny didn't offer anything.

"Anyway, when she disappeared a couple of years ago, it struck me that there were, what, maybe two lines devoted to her disappearance in the *Rover*? I thought that was strange, of course; grown adults vanishing into thin air is normally a thing a reporter in a small town would jump on. Even if it turned out to be nothing, I would think stories like that are hard to come by."

Danny remembered his first meeting with Sarah and how she had told him almost the exact same thing.

"So I made a few calls to the police and the paper—and I even visited the town once or twice—just trying to get some kind of handle on what might have happened, you know?"

Danny swallowed hard and felt the blood rush to his face. It felt as if this woman who was a total stranger only days ago was suddenly able to peer into his memories and read his darkest secrets. He was tempted to ask why she cared so much about the disappearance of an apparent stranger—and the lack of reporting on it—but he assumed she was coming to the point, so he listened instead.

"I even went to her house looking for her," Samantha continued, "and that's when I found out that Lynn's niece was living there. Tracy is her name. She didn't remember me; she was just a kid at the time and we only met once or twice."

"Didn't remember you?"

Samantha shook her head. "But I remembered her. I asked her about Lynn and she told me she went to visit her one day and that Lynn was just gone. Didn't know when she left or why or how long she'd been gone. Nothing. And, as luck would have it, she had left the house to Tracy free and clear. There was some type of living will that had apparently been written, and she was the only living relative."

Samantha stopped for a beat, as if considering some new point she hadn't explored, but then she shook her head and frowned as if it didn't fit with another hypothesis she had already formed.

"Anyway, the woman just split. Left town for...well, I don't know where? Do you know, Danny?"

Danny felt like he'd been smacked to attention. "What? Why would I know that? What is your interest in her anyway?"

Samantha ignored the question and studied Danny for a few beats, searching for the lie in his eyes that Danny was sure she would detect.

"It's fine, Danny, really. The truth is, I don't give a rat's ass about Lynn Shields anymore, other than I hope she's dead and died painfully."

If you only knew, Danny thought.

He kept his eyes focused on Samantha, trying to suppress the image of the Ocean God on that morning of Lynn's death. But he'd seen the events play out in his mind so often that they appeared there automatically, like the lyrics to a song from childhood that had been committed to memory.

The creature had materialized behind Lynn that night as if by magic, the darkness of the storm veiling the thing as it emerged invisibly from the water and slogged up behind the mad woman like some ancient, two-legged dinosaur. Danny could again see the rupture of Lynn's eye sockets as the god squeezed her face at the temples with its ogre-like claws. That unnatural narrowing of the woman's face, elongating like a roll of dough as the beast pulled her to the water, would live in Danny's memory forever.

Women! she had screamed to the night.

It was the last word Lynn Shields ever spoke, one that revealed her last theory about the behavior of her god, believing that it had drawn a taste for female victims and thus had reappeared during the cycle despite having already been fed.

That theory may have been true, Danny considered, but he had never gotten the chance to verify it. Thank God for that.

"So I'm not going to ask you about her, okay? I've made my peace with Lynn over the years. Or at least have come to terms with the fact that I'll never know for sure what happened. There was never any evidence that she murdered my father, and I finally stopped pursuing it a few months ago." Samantha paused and looked Danny in the eye. "And then you arrived."

Danny had followed the story up until about two sentences back, and the confusion suddenly brought him back from the reverie of the creature, sobering him to the present. "What are you talking about? Who is your father?"

"Does the name Lyle Bradford ring a bell?"

Danny recognized it immediately. It was the name of the man who died back in 2006, the one Sarah had written the article about that first captured Danny's attention. He was Lynn Shields' boyfriend at the time of his supposed drowning. Sarah had been skeptical of the drowning story at the time, and there was little doubt now that he had been offered as a sacrifice by Lynn, one of her many victims.

Danny nodded. "That was your father? Lyle Bradford?"

Samantha nodded. "Yep."

"So was Lynn Shields—"

"No! No, of course not." Samantha sighed and ran her fingers slowly through her hair, tilting her head up to the sky reflectively before setting her gaze straight again. "But she probably would have been my stepmother one day."

"What happened? With your parents, I mean."

"I don't know, really. I thought my mom and dad were fine. They always seemed that way growing up. Not madly in love, I guess, but fine. And then one day he just left her. I already had my own place by then, was in and out of junior college, doing that whole early twenties thing, and then my mom calls and says my dad met someone and was...gone. Just like that. Packed one small suitcase and walked out the door."

Samantha shook her head, as if still disbelieving the event she'd just described had actually happened.

"But the worst part, the part that pissed me off the most, was that he never called me to let me know what he was planning to do. It's irrational, I guess, to think that he would have done that, but my dad and I were best friends for most of my life, and then he just abandoned us—abandoned me—without a word."

Danny let the weight of Samantha's parental trauma settle in, giving her a moment to repel the wave of tears that was no doubt building somewhere behind her eyes. "Did you ever talk to him again?" he asked.

Samantha nodded. "Yeah. He finally called me about a month later. Said he was in some small town called Rove Beach. I'd never heard of it. He told me he was sorry about my mom but that they hadn't been in love for years and he needed someone to love again. You can imagine. Yahda yahda yahda. Anyway, he said he was still getting settled in his new place—Lynn's place—but that he would call me again soon and I could come and visit him. And I could meet Lynn." Samantha gave a hearty laugh. "Can you imagine?"

"So I'm guessing you weren't very receptive to the offer."

"I told him to fuck off. Used those exact words." Samantha chuckled. "I had never cussed *in front* of my dad, let alone *at* him." She shrugged and a wry smile drew across her face. "And then I hung up the phone. The last words I ever said to my dad were 'Fuck off.'"

Samantha's face morphed from the smile into a pressed wrinkle of despair as she tried unsuccessfully to keep her tears back. They flowed in huge, silent drops, coating her face in seconds.

Danny moved in to console her, but she put her hand up and shook him off. Instead he watched her for a moment, waiting for her to compose herself. When she settled, he asked, "So you never met Lynn?"

Samantha shook her head. "There was a funeral for dad and she wasn't there. At least I didn't see anyone who fit the profile. But I saw the story in the local paper about dad's drowning and it sounded like the reporter thought there might be more to it."

Danny knew the article almost by heart now, and the cryptic mention that '*No foul play is suspected.*'

"I saw the police report and dad's new lover's statements about the drowning, and it never sat right. Maybe I let the article sway me, but it just seemed like there might be more to it."

There was a moment of awkward quiet and then Danny said, "I'm sorry."

Samantha wiped her face with both hands, cleaning up the residue beneath her eyes, preparing her face for the stare of hate that she shot at Danny. "Are you?"

Danny raised his eyebrows and lifted his hands as he shrugged. "Yes, Samantha, I am. What does that question even mean?"

"It means I think you know what happened to my dad."

"I don't."

"Bullshit!"

Danny stayed quiet.

"You might not know *exactly* what happened to him, but you know something. More than you're telling me now.

You and your reporter friend. Sarah Needler, right? And I'm guessing Lynn's niece, Tracy. She knows too, I suppose?"

"Why do you think that? Know what exactly?" Danny was close to giving up the game, but he wanted to find out what Samantha thought she knew first.

"Oh, I don't know. Ms. Needler writes the story about my dad, which she implies is not the real story, and then ten years later she pens some item about a sea monster appearing on the beach near where my dad died. I don't think that is a coincidence, Danny, but tell me if I'm wrong. Please, I dare you to tell me that."

"Nobody believed that story about what I saw. People called it sensational. Irresponsible and gossipy. Every negative word you can think of to describe journalism. Sarah has to write under a pen name now because of that piece."

"So am I supposed to feel sorry for you? For her?"

"No, Samantha, I'm wondering why *you* believe it."

Samantha took a deep breath and frowned. She shook her head slowly and said, "I didn't at first. Of course not. The only reason I knew about the picture at all was because the day the *Rover* had their tiny report of Lynn's disappearance was the same day they had two pages of reader responses to the sea monster article."

Danny recalled the issue and section of the paper to which Samantha was referring. The responses to the photo and the story on the Ocean God had been vicious, and most of the letters ended with vows by readers to cancel their subscriptions.

"I probably would have had the same disparaging opinion most of the readers had about the article too, but when I saw it was written by the same woman who had reported so conservatively on my dad's death, I became intrigued. I followed up on her. And on you, since you were the source of the photo. And nothing about either of you seemed scammy. You never popped up on any fringe podcasts, never wrote a salacious book. You were just normal people, normal people who didn't seem to have anything to gain from espousing a hoax like that."

"Couldn't that be said of most of the people who see a Chupacabra in the desert, or claim to have been anally probed by some tiny green star traveler?

"I suppose so, yeah, but you didn't seem to belong to that class either—off your rockers, that is—which is the category I think most of the people you're talking about belong to."

"So that was it? You believed us because of our untarnished reputations?"

"I was still skeptical of the picture, but I believed *you* believed it, and that *Sarah* believed you believed it, which meant you must have been pretty convincing. Either that, or she already suspected the thing in that photograph existed. Whatever *it* is."

Danny didn't confirm or deny Samantha's inferences, and instead circled back to an earlier statement. "You said you were following it, too. Is that what you think I'm doing? Following it?"

Samantha sniggered. "Isn't that what you're doing?"

Danny looked away.

"It's not a big mystery, Danny. You came to the wrong place. From what I know of Rove Beach, the people there kept to themselves. That's not Wickard. You were on the radar the minute you signed that lease."

Danny narrowed his gaze as a new thought entered his mind. "So you just happened to be here? In this place? The town where the...where I'm living now? How could that be?"

"I told you, Danny, I'm following it, too. Ever since that photo appeared in the paper, I've done nothing but investigate this thing. I had a hunch about this place too. Guess I'm just a little quicker than you are."

"Yeah, except between the two of us, I'm the only one that's seen it."

Danny had given up the ghost and it felt good to finally reveal the secret to someone who hadn't been a part of the original story.

Samantha gave a satisfied grin. "So there we are then."

Danny pinched his lips and cocked his head once. "There we are."

"Well then, Danny, since I've already showed you mine, how about you show me yours."

Chapter 22

What started as a faint, high-pitched chirp was now the unmistakable scream of a woman. The sounds came in erratic spurts, and with each wail, Samuel and Sokwa adjusted their course, taking one step to the left, two to the right, and so on, until they were homed in on the direction.

And they were close now, frighteningly so, as they could hear that the cries were coming from just around a sharp bend in the wide shoreline of the western sound.

Along the coast, centuries of erosion had created an earthen barrier of rock and dirt, forming a short cliff wall that ran along the beach, mirroring the shape of the water. Samuel could make out the large rocks at the base of the wall, as well as the exposed roots of the trees that sat atop the cliffs. They hung like the leaves of a willow above the boulders, desperate to find the dirt that would continue giving life to them and their sprouts towering above.

"What is happening?" Sokwa asked. "Where are we?" Her voice was quivering, close to tears. "Who is that screaming, Samuel? Is it the woman you seek? Is she in pain? Dying?"

"I don't know, Sokwa." Samuel snapped, once again sounding irritable. But he was no longer concerned with placating his companion; his only purpose was to find the woman. "How could I know the answers to your inquiries? Let us just find the source of the sound. It may only be fifty paces from us now. Even less."

"But why is—"

The scream erupted again, and this time it sounded close enough to touch. It came low through the air, not in pitch, but in location, as if it had been projected from the ground just in front of their feet, maybe twenty steps or fewer.

Samuel nearly choked on his breath, and he instinctively jumped backward, as if he'd stepped on a snake. He stood as still as glass, scanning the beach, peering into the dark sand, squinting his eyelids as if the sound itself were some tiny physical form that could be identified with close enough inspection.

Sokwa froze as well, not from curiosity, but from true petrification. She had a thought to move a step backward, but her body wouldn't allow it, as if the step itself would set the ground on fire.

They were here. Samuel and Sokwa had made it to the western shore, and they were close enough to the water now that the shine of the moon on the white grains of crystal in front of them allowed them to see all the way to the next bend in the cliff wall.

"What is this place?" Samuel whispered to himself. "These cliffs of dirt and stone? The trees standing atop them like castle guards? It is so very different than the eastern side of the island. Or anywhere else I've seen in this land."

Sokwa shook her head, fear glowing in her restless eyes. "I have never been here either," she answered, her voice taking on the same sense of wonder. "I was always told it uninhabitable in this section, but I suspect now the warning was to do with this woman you seek." She paused. "And the screams."

The children remained unmoved for several moments, taking in this new, foreign landscape. It reminded Samuel of his first few weeks after arriving to this New World, when his family crossed the sound and began their colony on the small island between the Great Western Sea and the unruly continent to the west.

Yet during those first days, Samuel's feelings were laced with a constant drone of fear. It was as if his soul was constantly being stung with the nettles of a jellyfish.

But no longer. Now, in this moment, standing in this new western world of screams and fear and pain, he felt like the king of the land.

"What is that?" Sokwa said. She took a small step toward where the cliff wall began, craning forward.

"Where?"

Sokwa raised her hand slowly, barely lifting the end of her index finger in a pointing motion, as if reluctant to find out the answer to her question. "There, Samuel. Do you see? Thirty paces out from where you stand and ten from the base of the cliff. There is a...dip in the earth. And then three more dips beyond that one, each spaced equally down the length of the cliffside."

Samuel couldn't see it at first, but as he focused on the distances Sokwa described, his eyes eventually found them. "I see it."

He took a tentative first step toward the shapes, and then he picked up his pace until he was marching slowly but confidently toward the shadowy indentations in the earth, emboldened with the promise of new evidence that would help uncover the secrets of the Croatoan.

He came to the lip of the first dip and saw instantly it was the mouth of a wide hole, perhaps four paces across. The ground was silty but hard, an extension of the forest that snaked out in front of the cliffs and buffered the stone walls from the sand of the beach by about five paces. Loose sand from the beach had crept in and formed a yellow border around the hole, disguising it.

Samuel slowly went to his knees and then his stomach and, with little thought of what might have made such a hole, placed his face inside the perimeter.

And he instantly recoiled.

The smell struck his nose like a hammer, and he pulled his head from the hole and rolled to his back, sucking in the cool beach air, gasping for it as if it were only going to exist for another second or two.

"Samuel!" Sokwa called, her voice a loud, breathy whisper that carried through the night as clearly as a church bell. "What is it?"

Samuel didn't answer, and instead lay stricken with sickness and curiosity, searching his imagination for what dying thing existed beneath him.

Another scream.

Samuel rolled back to his stomach now and pushed himself to his feet. He stared at the hole again and then moved his gaze to the next one that lie just beyond it.

He walked slowly to the second hole, approaching it as if he were attempting to steal a nestling bear cub from its mother's paws. He stopped a couple of paces short of the perimeter this time, trying to lean forward without moving his feet, hoping to get a glimpse of the contents of the hole without damaging his olfactory nerves. But he could see only dark emptiness from that distance.

Reluctantly, Samuel took two steps forward until he was standing next to the rim, and then he inhaled deeply. There was an odor there, but from that distance, it wasn't nauseating, so he dropped to his belly again, placing his face near the top of this hole, a hand's width outside the perimeter.

There was a smell again, awful but less assaulting this time, and beneath this hole he thought he could now hear something. He tilted his ear toward the hole.

Yes! He could definitely hear something below. It was a shuffling noise, perhaps. Groaning, as well, maybe.

Then, suddenly, the sounds stopped.

One beat of silence. Two beats.

Samuel could feel a sense of dread arise in his chest, and his mouth watered with fear.

Then the sound of shuffling started again, low at first, erratic, and then building to a steady crescendo. Samuel wanted to pull his face away, but his eyes stared wide into the blackness, spellbound with anticipation.

The scurrying suddenly stopped again, and Samuel held his breath waiting.

Nothing.

Samuel exhaled, closing his eyes for a moment.

When he opened them again, the face of a monster was staring back at him, toothless and smiling, crusts of hair strung down across the round, wild eyes of female madness.

The woman put a hand up and grabbed Samuel by a tuft of hair at the top of his head and pulled his face to hers.

And then she screamed.

Chapter 23

Danny and Samantha sat at a round, wrought iron table on the porch of Fat Boy Sam's. An unseasonably warm breeze gave a summer feel to the night, as did the acoustic guitarist playing Buffet tunes just inside the door.

Danny told the story of the Ocean God, starting with that first day at the beach and his swim in the morning ocean. He spoke low and quickly, checking the vicinity for eavesdroppers every few moments, backtracking to certain points that he remembered along the way, careful to leave out certain incriminating details of the story.

The biggest omission from Danny's story was that of Tammy's death. As far as Samantha knew—or needed to know—his wife had simply left Danny, just as he had recounted to the police, just as women had done for centuries before her. Danny assumed Samantha still had her doubts about this convenient tying of an otherwise loose end, but she was in no real position to challenge it.

What Danny did not hide were the details of Lynn Shields and her death. He felt no need for discretion as far as she was concerned. The woman had attempted to kill Danny, after all, more than once in fact, first as a sacrifice to her deity and later with a barrage of gunshots, one of which left him lying in the rain gasping for life. It was Sarah and Tracy who had found him on the beach that day, who had saved his life, and whom he had repaid by planning several nights of unsuccessful sacrifices in which they were to be offered.

Danny was careful to leave this part of the tale untold as well.

Samantha was glued to Danny's face as he talked, her wide eyes peering over her wine glass with each sip of pinot grigio, swallowing in fear and disgust at the appropriate points and shaking her head every so often at the miracle that was Danny's story. She didn't speak a word until the last sentence of the yarn was spun, which concluded with how Danny had followed the reports of drowning deaths in Wickard Beach and wound up in her town.

When Samantha was sure Danny had finished, she asked, "So what are you going to do? You know they're going to try to pin the death of that boy's father on you."

Danny gave a half shrug and nodded. "I guess that's right. They don't really have any evidence, but I'm starting to think in this town that might not matter."

"I don't know. I think the sheriff might be okay. A hard ass maybe, but I don't think corrupt. If you can show evidence otherwise, I think he'll listen. And if not him, then his deputy. She's young but sharp, and I think he'll listen to her."

"How do you know so much about the police force?"

"I don't really, but I do make it a point to get to know people who can help me. Or who might be a problem."

"Is that why you 'got to know me?'" Danny threw out a pair of half-hearted air quotes, not really interested in the answer either way. Clearly Samantha had used him the other night, but it didn't make much difference now.

Samantha smiled weakly and looked away for a beat. When she turned back to him she began to speak and then stopped, as if considering whether the question she was about to ask was even appropriate or necessary. Instead, she addressed the elephant. "You think it was the creature, right. This Ocean God? That killed the guy on the beach."

Danny took a sip of his beer. "Of course. But..." he broke off his sentence.

"What?"

"The better question is: why was Gerald DeRose on the beach to begin with?"

Samantha shrugged. "Taking a walk?"

"In the middle of the night? No. I mean, maybe, but I don't think so."

"So what then?"

"Do you think it's a coincidence that the man whose arm I found on the beach is the father of the boy I saved in the ocean a day earlier."

"Is that not possible?"

Danny frowned. "Did you hear any of the details about what happened out there in the water?"

Samantha shook her head. "Not really. Just that some kid decided to take a polar bear swim and then someone—you, it turns out—saved his life."

Danny took a breath and leaned in. "This kid—Shane—had his baby brother with him out there. In a backpack. Towed him out into the frigid water like a chum line?"

"Jesus! What?"

"Yeah, I noticed they're not talking about that part too much."

"Wait, you think..?" Samantha didn't finish the thought, but she didn't have to.

"Of course, I think. He brought the baby out there to sacrifice it to the god. And I think he lured his father to the beach to do the same thing. Only this time it worked. He brought him to my house because he knew that I'd been attempting to lure it out, so he probably thought—correctly, it turns out—that the thing would emerge at that point on the beach." Danny paused. "And I've had some time to think about this part too: I think he set me up."

"Set you up? Come on, Danny. What's the kid, like seven?"

"He's nine or ten. And I'm telling you, he did. How else would he have gotten his dad to come out to the beach in the middle of the night?"

Danny allowed Samantha a moment to consider the question, genuinely wanting to know if he had, perhaps, overlooked something. She shrugged. "I don't know."

Danny nodded. "Exactly. I'll bet you he told his dad that I...I don't know, told him to come meet me or something. That I threatened him. That if he didn't come to my house so that I could carry on with whatever crime I promised to commit, then ...I don't know...I'd harm him. Or his mom or dad. Something like that."

"That's pretty devious thinking for a nine-year-old."

"All I know is that kid's father—his arm—was found on the beach in front of my house." Danny paused. "And there was something else."

"What? What else?"

"I saw him this morning. The boy. I saw him leaving the beach just before I went down and found the arm."

"What? Well that changes things a bit. Did you tell the police?"

Danny tilted his head back and rubbed his chin. "Okay, so I didn't *see him* see him, not his face, so I guess I can't know a hundred percent it was him. But it was him."

Danny and Samantha sat in silence for a couple of beats, taking in all that had been spoken and implied over the last few minutes. They ordered another round and listened to the singer do a double-time version of 'Why Don't We Get Drunk and Screw?' just before he took a fifteen-minute break, giving the restaurant some much needed white space of quiet.

"So, again, what are you going to do?" Samantha asked. "You've got a couple of days, I would think, before they come at you with a murder charge. So you have a little time to figure it out."

"I guess the only choice is to find this thing once and for all. Lure it out and kill it. And then hang its body in the public square for all to see. What other choice is there?"

Samantha smiled and nodded, approving of the plan. "Sounds like a plan Danny Lynch. But how the hell are we going to do that?"

Chapter 24

Samuel recoiled his head back and the thin, gnarled fingers that gripped his hair released easily. But the hand continued grasping at the air, desperate to regain its clutch, reaching as far up through the hole as it could stretch. Samuel could still see the face of the woman, but that was the only other part of her body visible in the blackness of the pit.

Samuel knew instantly what he was witnessing now. These holes weren't just pits, they were cells. The woman was a prisoner.

The mad lady continued to scream as she clutched desperately for some part of Samuel, her voice hoarse and dry, like the croak of a dying cow. Her mouth was void of all teeth, save one or two rotting remnants that somehow remained in the back of her gums, and her nose and cheeks were wrinkled and pock marked with large sores that looked to have been opened and healed a thousand times.

And she was speaking. The words were wild and shrieked, but they were words, and though Samuel couldn't understand their meaning, they sounded like the language of the Algonquin.

"Sokwa!" Samuel called, turning his head slightly at first and then fully, peering into the dark forest at the location where he had left his companion. He waited anxiously for her to appear, and when he called her name again and she still didn't come forward, he was sure she had left him.

Sokwa's abandonment would have been crippling to Samuel' plan, especially since he was counting on the girl to be able to exchange at least basic words with the woman, if not full sentences. He rued that he had never learned the Algonquin language as so many of them had learned his. There were a few colonists who were fluent, but they were either traders or preachers of the gospel. Everyone else thought it the language of savages, and this attitude was now disabling Samuel's quest.

But he had found the woman. There was at least that. And he would simply have to figure some other way to communicate with her, through drawings or hand gestures, perhaps.

But just as Samuel had begun to accept this new strategy, Sokwa emerged slowly from the darkness into the light of the beach. Her eyes shifted nervously at the sights and sounds of the screaming woman, and she moved in tentative, uncommitted steps as she neared the hole.

"Sokwa, come here! Quickly, please!"

Sokwa took a few more steps but stopped well short of Samuel, maintaining several paces from the hole that was currently producing these awful sounds of torture and panic.

"Listen!" Samuel whispered. "Listen to her words. They are yours, yes?"

The woman had modified her vocabulary so that she was now screaming the same word over and over. It was a word Samuel had heard spoken many times in the village, a word he knew. He looked at Sokwa as he confirmed it. "Water," Samuel said. "She is screaming 'water.' In your language. Am I right?"

Sokwa blinked several times and swallowed as she nodded, and then took a curious step forward as she stared into the hole.

"Look at her face, Sokwa. Is she someone you know?"

Sokwa shook her head, never taking her eyes from the screaming face and clawing hand. "Even if I knew her once," she whispered, "she looks barely human now. She is so...frail and old. The dirt and disease has brought her to a point beyond recognition."

"Ask her name?"

Sokwa licked her lips and asked Samuel's question to the woman, but the prisoner only responded with her screams of water.

"She needs to drink, Samuel. She is mad with thirst."

Samuel gave an aggravated sigh, but he nodded and reached down to the leather bladder tied around his waist. He unplugged the wooden stopper and took a small swig of his own before looking at Sokwa. "Give me your hands, Sokwa. Cup them and I'll pour the water there. And then allow her to drink from your palms."

"I'm afraid, Samuel. What if she—"

"Cup them!"

Sokwa squatted near the hole and cupped her hands as instructed, and as Samuel went to pour the water, the weather-beaten hand from the pit shot forward like the tongue of a chameleon and snatched the bladder from Samuel's hands.

"No," Samuel uttered, his voice a gasp of disbelief. "My water!"

Samuel studied the hole for several beats, his mouth hanging wide with anticipation. But there was only cold silence from the pit. Stillness. Samuel thought to call for her, but he knew there was no point. The woman was gone and not returning.

He stood up next to Sokwa and continued to stare incredulously at the hole beneath them. The opening that was a volcano of madness seconds ago was now an empty void in the ground.

"I have water, Samuel. We'll be fine. And I heard the rustle of a fresh brook on the path from the village, back by the fallen trees. We'll find more there if we must."

"I should follow her down," Samuel said. "Perhaps—"

"No! No, Samuel. You will never get back out. You see the depth."

"You can pull me. We'll use the roots from the trees."

"She is dangerous. Likely."

"She is an old woman. I should follow."

"For what purpose, Samuel? We have water and we'll find more."

"Not for the water!"

Sokwa looked away for a moment and then back to Samuel's face. "Then what? You think that crazed beast knows anything of Nootau?"

Samuel had forgotten all about his friend and the pretenses under which he had lured Sokwa. He was reaching a point in his journey where the lies he'd told to persuade her were becoming unnecessary. But he wasn't there yet. He had to keep Sokwa close, a willing participant in his quest.

"I suppose that's right," Samuel agreed. "We'll move on. But you believe me now, yes? That there is a woman who knows something about Nootau?"

"I don't know what she knows, but I believe in this place. I believe what I have seen. It is a horrible place, Samuel, and if Nootau is here, we must find him soon and bring him home."

Samuel frowned and nodded solemnly, and as he looked forward down the beach, his eye was caught by a soft glow coming from the side of the cliff, at the point where the sheer wall met the ground. It was at the point on the beach where the shoreline curved sharply around an invisible bend.

"Look there!" he said.

Sokwa was already staring in the direction. "I see it. It's a fire."

A fire.

Suddenly the thought of a burning flame ignited Samuel's desire to find the woman, as if his hunger to see the Croatoan related somehow to the heat of the fire itself. He walked alone toward the flickering light, passing the third, unexplored, hole without giving it a glance.

He had almost reached the base of the cliff, perhaps twenty paces from the entrance to the light and the dancing shadows of the fire, when he heard the ring of laughter float in from somewhere north.

Samuel stopped in his tracks and scanned the beach, searching for the sound beneath the cliff row, past the cave where the fire lived.

The laughter came again, hysterical this time, and Samuel shifted his gaze west toward the water, the direction where the sound was born. He could see the black outline of each rock extending into a long formation that jutted out into the western sound. He squinted toward the rocks, and as his eyes adjusted further to the darkness, he could just make out a thin black shadow rising from the very edge of the last rock in the sea. The shape was human, not much taller than a child, he estimated, and as Samuel studied it, it appeared the figure was facing him. Watching him.

The laughter came again, and with this laugh, Samuel could see the figure shaking with the sound, and he knew beyond a doubt it was the source of the laughter.

"I see it too, Samuel. It is a person."

"It's her. It's the woman."

The laughter and quivering of the shape gradually stopped, and as Samuel and Sokwa continued to watch the woman in frozen fascination, she suddenly began moving. The motion was slow to start as she began to make her way over the rocks and back toward the beach, but when she took the wide leap from about the fourth to the fifth rock in the thirty-rock formation, she landed in a heap, as if the impact from the fall had left her injured, dead even.

And then she stood tall. And began to run.

Samuel breathed rapidly as he watched the figure scale the jagged rocks, in awe of her ability to move so quickly across the craggy, unpredictable surface of the wet stones. She had probably traversed them a thousand times, he figured, increasing her speed with each year that passed, returning from what was certainly a daily call to the sea god. The thought of her disappointment each day that passed without a sighting frightened Samuel. He couldn't imagine a life such as this. A life where his god refused to appear to him. A life devoid of the majestic destruction it levied upon the world.

Samuel was speculating about this part, of course, that the woman's purpose at the water's edge was the same as his, but he also knew he was right. The prisoners in the ground below were lures for the creature, and Samuel was suddenly curious how she replenished her supply. Or perhaps she didn't. Perhaps whoever those poor souls were, assuming there were at least two more in the other pits, were kept just at the edge of survival and had been for decades.

Samuel turned to his right to see Sokwa still standing beside him. She hadn't run at the sight of the leaping spectral in the distance. He smiled. It appeared she was committed to his quest now, re-energized by thoughts of her missing friend and the possibility of his rescue.

The shadowy figure took one final stride, descending the last of the rocks before landing nimbly onto the sandy beach. She stared for just a moment at the two strangers who had invaded her domain, and then she walked without concern toward the point in the cliff line raging with fire. In the glow of the orange light on the wall—at what was surely the opening of a cave, Samuel figured, though he couldn't see it from where he stood—the woman watched them in a stance that was poised and steady.

The light offered a bit more of the woman's details now, illuminating the left half of her face, and from what Samuel could see, she looked to be older than the woman he had just found in the pit, at least in posture and the cursory appearances of her face. But she also looked strong, and judging by the way she scaled the boulders, she was as nimble as an ibex.

"What do we do, Samuel?" Sokwa asked.

"Wait," Samuel replied instantly, his tone hushed and hurried.

The woman stood studying the children for a moment longer, and then she raised a hand to her face and made a gesture like an inviting wave, bringing her palm toward her, before turning toward the cliff and disappearing into the light of the wall.

Samuel didn't hesitate to heed the invitation, and within moments, he had lumbered through the sand and dirt and was standing at the mouth of a small opening in the cliff wall.

He stared in wonder at the enclave of dirt and stone, focusing on the fire that burned about five paces deep inside the cave. It was beginning to wane and in need of more kindling. Samuel couldn't see the woman anywhere, and he assumed she had slunk off down some hidden catacomb that snaked elaborately throughout the cliffside.

There was movement beside him, and Samuel almost screamed when Sokwa appeared.

"I don't want to die, Samuel."

"You won't die, Sokwa. Not today. We must do this. It is the only way we'll know if Nootau is here. We've found the woman. It's why we came here. Now we must talk to her."

Sokwa looked at Samuel with slitted eyes and then answered, "I know I won't die today. I just want to announce my intentions to the spirits."

Samuel snickered and then took a step inside the cave. He paused and then took another. Then a third. A shuffling sound behind him made him stop and pivot back to the opening. At first, he saw nothing but the darkness of the rocky cave corner, but as his eyes focused in, from the darkness he saw the wild face of a witch lunging toward him.

Her mouth was wide and toothy, moving up and down in a crazed cackle, creating a louder version of the deranged sound Samuel had heard on the beach moments earlier. Her teeth were bared like a rabid wolf, and saliva fell from the incisors in wide, white strands. In her hands she held a long, thin stick which she held out in front of her face, parallel to the ground, and before Samuel could make a sound, she dropped to her knees and swung the stick like a sword at Samuel's legs, catching them both just above the foot at the base of his shins.

The lash of pain on Samuel's feet was equal to all the pain he'd ever experienced in his life combined, and he fell to the cave floor as quickly as if his legs had been severed. His face was now only inches from the laughing banshee woman who had felled him, and he immediately rolled to his back and screamed, pulling his shins toward him and bringing his knees to his chest.

The smoke from the fire invaded Samuel's nostrils, choking him, and he turned to his side so that his back was now to the fire and his face toward the cave opening.

Samuel cracked opened his eyes, which were now coated in tears of pain and soot, and he saw Sokwa standing still at the cave opening, her mouth as flat as the cave floor. There was no fear in her eyes, no alarm or confusion. "Sokwa," he uttered, coughing out the last syllable of her name. "Sokwa, help me!"

Samuel looked now at the twisted face of the woman who had disabled him. She was still in her deadly stoop, the stick still clutched tightly in her hands, her eyes alert and twitchy, as if expecting that Samuel might make another run at her.

But he was incapacitated. His legs were on fire with pain.

The woman lifted her chin up slightly and tilted her head back toward Sokwa. And then she spoke in a tongue both foreign and familiar to Samuel.

"Matta," Sokwa replied, never taking her eyes from Samuel. The word meant 'No' in the language of the natives.

"Sokwa, help me," Samuel repeated, making one last desperate attempt for her aide, hoping that perhaps he was misreading something about the situation, and that Sokwa was only stalling, waiting for her moment to act.

But she looked like a pillar of oak in the doorway to the cave, her eyes those of a hunter. "You killed him, Samuel," she said plainly, not a drop of emotion in her words. "You killed the boy I loved."

Samuel closed his eyes and shook his head. "I didn't. You're wrong, Sokwa."

The woman turned back to Sokwa again and hissed another question, and this time Sokwa stepped to the woman and put her face so that her forehead was nearly touching the wrinkled brow of the hermit.

"Matta!" Sokwa screamed in the woman's face, causing the cave dweller to scurry to the far end of the cave behind the fire. Sokwa then turned back to Samuel. "I didn't believe it at first. Not of you, Samuel. I saw the way you cared for Nootau, and how he cared for you. You were true friends, unconcerned with differences in your native tongues or shades of skin."

Sokwa looked to the roof of the cave and then closed her eyes. She held her face that way for a few beats and then focused back on the boy beneath her.

"And I loved *you*, too. In a way different from the way I loved Nootau, but it was love. You were of a different mind than your parents and their ilk, and you gave me, and even some of the elders of my village, hope that we could coexist one day. A day not so far from this one, perhaps, once our guardians relinquished their grip on the land and passed it on to you and me. We would inherit the land and make it our own community."

"We can still, Sokwa. We can make the colony and the village as we used to talk about it with Nootau. But you must help me first." Samuel made a move to get to his feet, but the pain in his left leg was debilitating.

"Stay where you lie, Samuel, or your death will come sooner than you would like."

"I didn't kill him! Believe me."

"Then where is he?"

Samuel looked down at the ground and then did a cursory search of the cave around him, as if Nootau might be hiding there somewhere.

"He is not here, Samuel; you know he is not. You were truthful about seeking this woman." Sokwa nodded toward the woman who sat cowering against the far earthen wall, watching with the same crazed expression, hanging on every word, none of which she could understand. "But you lied about your motives. Nootau is dead, as is Kitchi, and you are responsible for both."

Samuel stayed quiet, now intrigued by Sokwa's words and what she knew.

"Why have you come all this way? What are you really seeking? This myth of the Croatoan?"

"Croatoan!" the woman hissed from behind Samuel, and he cringed at the vile, liquid sound of her voice. Sokwa turned and gave what Samuel thought was a disbelieving grin at the woman.

"How can you know this?" Samuel asked. "How can you know of the Croatoan?"

"Nadie and Matunaagd, Nootau's parents. They came to visit my family—to visit me—to find out if I knew of your whereabouts. You had gone missing." Sokwa raised her eyebrows and scoffed. "As you know. And it was then they told me the myth of this creature. That you have become...enraptured with it."

"You said you would keep our meeting secret, Sokwa. You betrayed me."

"I did keep it secret!" Sokwa snapped.

She took three long strides into the cave until she was only a pace from Samuel, who continued to lie in a fetal position on the dirt ground.

"Until they told me of the tracks they found. Tracks that you left."

"Tracks?"

"Boot prints. Outside the longhouse and on each side of the thin tracks left by a wheelbarrow."

Samuel gave a painful scoff. "You can't believe them. How could they know the tracks were mine? I'm not the only boy in the colony with soled boots."

"My people have been tracking animals smaller than tree squirrels for as long as our history extends to the past. We know tracks. We know what they mean and where they lead. It was you, Samuel. You took Kitchi down to the sound. And likely to the Yapam. Somehow, in the wheelbarrow, you took him."

Samuel shook his head, trying desperately to keep the lie alive. "No," he whispered.

"And besides, your mother confirmed the boots were yours."

"My mother?"

"She came with Nootau's parents to see me. It would seem the Algonquin are not the only people seeking your head."

Samuel looked up at Sokwa with begging eyes. "It was Kitchi's idea, Sokwa. You must believe me about that. He insisted. He knew the story of the Croatoan. He was the one who told Nootau about it, and he knew—somehow—that Nootau had fallen victim to it. I didn't take him against his will. He insisted on seeing it."

Sokwa studied Samuel's face as he spoke, a wrinkle of sympathy above her brow. "I don't disbelieve you on that. I know how he was. Who he was. But that point does not change your fate. You took him, a cripple, and thus he was at your mercy. He was your responsibility to protect. His blood stains your hands, Samuel."

Samuel frowned, resigned to his position. He let several beats pass and then asked, "If this is your belief, why did you not tell your people where I was waiting for you? Before we left for this place? You knew where we were meeting. And when. If this was your plan all along, to punish me, why come all this way to do it? Why not just have your people take me and kill me then?"

"I asked them to allow me this journey. That you had told me the story of Nootau's taking and...and that he may yet be alive. I could see in their eyes that they knew there was no hope of this, that you were lying, but I couldn't not make the attempt. You convinced me, and I them. And thus, they allowed it." Sokwa's eyes softened. "Was it all a lie, Samuel? Is there any truth about Nootau? And if not, the better question is: why have you brought me here?"

Samuel couldn't look at Sokwa's face. "I needed your help to find the woman behind me. It was for the reason I told you back at your house."

"Look at me, Samuel. Where is Nootau? Why have you brought me here?"

Samuel's eyes narrowed as he thought again of the sea god, and the familiar surge of confidence began to build in his belly. He raised himself to a sitting position and leaned back on his hands, casually, as if he were taking in the rays of the sun next to the sound on a bright spring morning.

"That is enough movement, Samuel. No further. She is prepared for another strike and will do so at my command."

Samuel turned back to the woman and cocked his head suspiciously. "How is it that you can control her? And speak to her? It's as if she knew of our arrival. How could she?"

Sokwa laughed genuinely now, and after the last of her chuckles dissipated, she looked contemptuously at Samuel and said, "You don't know this land, Samuel. You don't know my people or any of the people in this world. And it's why you will never survive here. Why your people are destined for death." She looked to the woman. "You entered her home without a formal invitation. That is why she attacked you."

"She waved us in."

"That was not an invitation as much as it was a trap. Why would she want us to come here? For what purpose? You don't understand our ways." Sokwa shot a look to the woman. "And I cannot control her. She is old and mad, and this type of woman responds only to authority."

Samuel smiled slowly as he listened to Sokwa's analysis of the situation, impressed by her in a way he had never experienced from any person before. He was breath-taken suddenly, in love, perhaps, though he couldn't be sure what that feeling meant precisely.

"And you can speak to her?" he asked. "You can understand her language?"

Sokwa looked to the woman for a moment and then back to Samuel. "No. But she speaks my tongue."

"How? Where did she learn it?"

"I don't know. If she has been here for as long as I was told, I don't know how it could be possible."

"Ask her?"

"You haven't answered my questions, Samuel! You don't demand things from me!"

Sokwa's patience was running short, and Samuel knew he had only the tiniest of opportunities with which to turn her toward his needs. "Yes, Sokwa, I will answer what you have asked. I will tell you everything. I just need to know if you can speak to her in full conversations. And how she came to know your language."

Sokwa seethed for a moment and then called back to the woman in tones loud and harsh. She spoke several words—one or two sentences—and the woman answered in an even longer string of phrases. Sokwa put her hand to her mouth and then turned away, a look of disgust blazing in her eyes. She shook her head frantically, as if trying to rid herself of the words.

"What did you ask her, Sokwa? What did she say?"

Sokwa swallowed slowly. "I asked the questions you posed. And about how she came to learn my tongue."

"Yes?"

Sokwa took her hand away from her lips. "It was the prisoners."

Samuel looked to the ceiling of the cave. "In the pits. Of course."

"She says there are only two left now, and they have been her only company for so many cycles that she cannot remember when it first began."

"Who are they? Where did they come from?"

"Why are we here, Samuel!" Sokwa screamed. "Why have we come to this land of madness! Who is that woman in the hole!"

Samuel could see Sokwa was losing control of her emotions, panicking. It was a dangerous place for him to be, perhaps, in the midst of Sokwa, whose mind was slipping into a state of anger and fury; but somehow Samuel also knew that anger and fury were necessary to achieve his purposes.

He grimaced and pushed himself to one knee, and then hopped up to his less damaged foot.

He could hear the woman rise behind him, and he spun on one leg, keeping his other leg dangling beneath him, almost toppling back into the fire. Sokwa grabbed his arm to keep him from falling, and her assistance gave Samuel a flash of hope.

He put his hand up and pointed at the woman. "No!" he screamed, and then turned his hand into a fist and punched it forward into the air.

The woman stopped and then cowered backward, keeping her distrustful eyes on Samuel as she crept back toward the wall.

Sokwa stepped away from Samuel, leaving him to stand on his own, and she moved to the mouth of the cave.

"I won't hurt you, Sokwa. Even if I wanted to, I can't. I'm hurt." Samuel could feel the pain steadily diminishing from his leg, and he knew now there was nothing broken, but he played up the injury for the moment. "And if I try, you can tell the woman I am feeble and command her to bash me in the head with her stick."

"I can," she agreed. "I won't hesitate to do it."

"I know."

The two children, one white, one brown, stood in silence for a beat, letting the rules of the situation set in. Finally, Samuel said, "Why do you think they let you come, Sokwa. If they didn't believe Nootau was alive, why did they let you come with me?"

"I told you: I insisted."

Samuel shook his head. "I don't think that is it. I think they believe what I know to be true. That the Croatoan is real. And they want to learn the secrets for themselves, to draw it from the Yapam for themselves."

Sokwa looked to the ground, a grimace of confusion on her face. "But this woman, why would she know these secrets?"

"She knows. She is of the tribe that named the beast. It's the reason for the prisoners buried on the beach. They are there as sacrifices. And why she was out far on the rocks. Surely, she was calling for the god, hoping to lure it from the water."

Sokwa shook her head, the confusion of Samuel's words coming frantically, rattling her. "I thought the legend tells of this monster coming from the Yapam—your Great Western Sea. Why would she be holding prisoners on a beach on the western sound?"

"She is mad, as you say, and she is desperate for her god. Her will to see it again has never left. She knows it comes from the Yapam, of course, but she cannot resist the urge to summon it, even in waters where it does not dwell."

This realization both thrilled and frightened Samuel, and he had a momentary glimpse of his future, naked on a beach by a lake or river, banished somewhere, perhaps on the big lands to the west, biting the heads off of fish to survive, screaming at the water for his god to return.

"She is as Kitchi described her," Samuel said to himself now. "The woman who can tell the origin of the Croatoan."

The woman repeated the word again, and Sokwa snapped at her in English. "Quiet!"

Sokwa stared at Samuel and then her pain and confusion suddenly turned to laughter again, but this time the chortle was laced with hysteria and disbelief. "The Croatoan? This story Nootau's parents told? Of sea monsters rising from the Yapam to feed on human blood? These are tales for children and simpletons. Who can believe such nonsense?"

"It is true, Sokwa. I have seen it with my own eyes. Nootau believed it too. He was the one who showed me. It is how he..." Samuel stopped, realizing he'd just answered Sokwa's only real question.

Sokwa bowed her head. "So he is gone? Nootau is dead?"

"Yes."

She took a giant breath, coughing out the exhale with sadness and panic. "At the hands of this sea beast? You saw this happen?"

"Yes."

Sokwa's sadness slipped quickly into anger, twisted with disdain. "Why did you not tell the story as it happened? Why did you lie? Were you to blame for his death? Did you leave him to die without helping him?"

"There was nothing to be done. The Croatoan is larger than any man and a half. And I did lie, but only because I knew the truth would label me a liar. By your people and mine. And then I would be banished. Or killed. My father is gone, Sokwa, you know this, and...and my mother would have offered for me to suffer either punishment before I ever had the chance to tell the story twice. She has told me as much."

Sokwa didn't argue with this excuse, and Samuel knew his mother's reputation was consistent with his story.

But his mother had nothing to do with his lie. Elyoner Cook was simply the perfect stooge to disguise Samuel's real purpose for the fabricated story.

He wanted to keep his god secret. He wanted it all for himself.

Chapter 25

"Have we done the right thing, Matunaagd?" Nadie stared out the opening in the side of the wigwam, gazing out over the pre-dawn village square, a pensive look of guilt in her stare. "We have put the life of a young girl in the path of death and terror."

"She was a willing participant in this quest, Nadie," Matunaagd replied. "She was aware of the dangers and insisted."

"But she does not know the real danger. She could not."

Matunaagd paused for a moment, considering his wife's declaration. "She loved Nootau. They would have been married if not for...that boy. And we were honest about the danger."

"Not all of the danger." Nadie repeated and then spun toward her husband, her eyes now wide with doubt and anger. "The Croatoan is real. I believe it now, Matunaagd."

Matunaagd paused "Maybe."

"Then you believe it too?"

Matunaagd dipped his chin slightly and turned away.

"What do you know, Matunaagd? What have you not told me?"

He shook his head and closed his eyes, fending off any beliefs that some ground-shaking admission was about to be unfolded. "It is nothing. There was a similar story that drifted through the generations of my family when I was a boy. That is all."

"That is not nothing. Why did you never tell me of this?"

"It was a spirit story, Nadie. Who reveals such things to his wife? Revealed as if it were some dark familial secret?"

Nadie ignored this excuse. "And why did we not tell Sokwa the truth of the Croatoan's existence? If we knew it to be so?"

"We don't know it. Not for sure. We told her what we believed. That Samuel was in search of the woman from the west to learn more about the story, not because he thought Nootau was still alive. She knows the story of the Croatoan now. We told her enough."

"She should have been told the whole story. The story Numohshomus told. About what he saw as a boy. She should have been told that we now believe those stories to be true. Then she could have made her decision based on that. Once all of the information had been revealed to her."

"And what makes you think the boy Samuel hasn't told her of it already? Hmm? About what he has seen? They are headed to the Wishalowe waters on the western shores. To find the banished Croatoan woman for the purposes of learning the creature's secrets. If he has seen it for himself—the Croatoan beast of the sea—as we suspect he has, then he will tell her of it too. Do you not think he would have told her by now?"

Nadie shook her head. "No, I don't. You saw the way he lied to us, Matunaagd. I knew his story of Nootau's death wasn't as it truly happened, not the way he told it. The story of sharks is always a convenient tale, one only a boy would tell, and much of his story was not feasible." She hesitated. "But I thought perhaps him innocent, too."

Nadie frowned and turned away, lowering her voice ruefully as she spoke.

"I thought, perhaps, he was a witness to some tragic accident, one of which he was even complicit. That some dare or game between Samuel and Nootau had turned dark, and that it became some terrifying secret in his mind he thought too incriminating to reveal." She took in a deep sigh. "But now I think it differently. I think Kitchi was right. I know it in my bones. He watched him die, Matunaagd. And he took pleasure in it."

A tear fell from Nadie's eye at the thought of the young English boy smiling as he watched her son scream in terror and pain. Not struggling in the jaws of some shore-dwelling shark, but in the claws and teeth of a beast she believed her whole life to be only a myth.

But it was real. And wherever it had slogged back to for the last ten, twenty, fifty years, it had now returned from that depth, this time to their own location on the Yapam, and perhaps into the sound itself.

She hadn't believed in Kitchi's rantings about her grandfather's tale, not entirely at least, but his disappearance from the village—combined with the death of her only son—left little doubt in her now. Only a combination of obsession and evil—the latter part played by Samuel Cook—could have moved Kitchi from the village in the middle of the night. And only a creature such as the one described in the tale of the Croatoan could have taken two of her own in less than seven moons.

"It matters little, Nadie," Matunaagd said, "they have gone to the western sound. And the Croatoan, if it is real—"

"It is," Nadie spat instinctively.

Matunaagd nodded. "It is of no danger to them there."

"That is not my worry, Matunaagd. That is not the part of the story that makes me fear for Sokwa's life."

"What then?"

Nadie stared into her husband's eyes. "It is the craving. It took only the idea of the beast to lead Kitchi away. Knowing what it had done to his nephew, believing it to be true, and he went anyway."

"You can't know that, Nadie. Perhaps he was taken by the Cook boy against his wishes. He is...was a cripple."

"No, Matunaagd, you know that is not true. It was the reason he wanted to be taken to the longhouse long before sleep was coming for him. And if Samuel Cook arrived without invitation and tried to take him, Kitchi would have screamed like the foxes of the deep woods, waking not only us but half the village as well. Not to mention that boy wouldn't have had the strength to take Kitchi unless Kitchi offered what assistance he could."

Matunaagd nodded and offered even more. "And I can't figure a reason Samuel Cook would have had to take Kitchi through the forest and down to the sound. What effort that must have been."

"The reason was Kitchi's insistence, I'm sure. He almost certainly threatened the boy. Told him that he would be blamed for Nootau's death. And it was this greed that cost him his life. And I fear our son possessed the beginnings of this craving as well."

Matunaagd frowned and looked to the floor of the wigwam. "I never want to see it, Nadie. I never want to see the Croatoan."

Nadie knew it wasn't fear of the creature's strength that her husband dreaded, but rather its ability to govern his heart. "Nor do I, Matunaagd," she concurred, leaving a thread of ambiguity in her wake. "Nor do I."

Chapter 26

Danny and Samantha walked up the front steps of Danny's porch, with the ostensible plan of coming back to his place to hatch a plan for the destruction of the sea god. But it was almost one o'clock in the morning by the time they entered the front door, and Danny could barely keep his eyes open at that point. The chance that some great idea for killing the beast was going to be born on this night was pure folly.

If roads led in other directions, however—toward the bedroom, for instance—Danny was willing to explore them. Sleeping with Samantha wasn't his goal on this night, but given the stress of his day and the impulses that four Fat Boy Sam's IPAs were providing in his loins, sex would have been the perfect ending to the night.

But any prospects of a little late-night romp were put to rest the moment Danny flicked on the kitchen light and saw Tracy sitting on his couch thumbing through one of the dozen newspapers that were scattered about the floor beneath her. Her back was to them, propped against one of the arms of the sofa, her bare feet stretched out across the cushions.

"And you used to get on me for staying up too late," Tracy said without turning around. "Must have been a good night."

She turned her neck now to see Danny and Samantha standing inside the door. They both wore the combined looks of surprise and exhaustion on their faces. Samantha blushed.

"And it looks like it's about to get even better."

"I used to get on you for *sleeping* late," Danny answered, not acknowledging the innuendo. "That's different than staying up late."

Samantha turned toward the door, clearly embarrassed to have walked in at this hour, a little drunk, to find a young woman sitting on Danny's sofa. "I'll just go then. I'm sorry."

Danny was confused for a moment but soon arrived at the reason for Samantha's brusque announcement. He frowned. "This is Tracy, Samantha."

Tracy flipped the paper to the side and sat up, swinging her feet around to the floor. "Hi."

Samantha gave Tracy the once over, and then tilted her head up in recognition. "Tracy, of course." She looked at Danny. "I didn't realize you two knew each other so well."

Danny wasn't sure how to reply to the implication, so he shrugged.

"I just rent his house back in Rove Beach," Tracy chimed in, now narrowing her stare at Samantha. "Do we know each other? You look really familiar."

The part about rent wasn't technically true, Danny thought. Tracy lived in his house, but 'rent' implied money was given in exchange for her living there.

Samantha shrugged and shook her head slowly. She was tired, exhausted, and not yet ready to dive back into her story again or describe the circumstances under which she and Tracy had met.

"I don't know, but it'll come to me. Anyway, the reason I'm here is because I found a book in Danny's house that I thought he might be interested in. He knew I was coming."

In all the drama of the day, Danny had forgotten about Tracy's earlier call or her purpose for being there now. Thoughts of the mysterious book she'd found now had him nearly salivating.

"Wow, Tracy, you drove all the way from Rove Beach to deliver a book?" Samantha said with a detectable lilt of sarcasm. "That's pretty generous. Why not just mail it or something?"

"Oh, yeah, well...it seemed...*seems* pretty delicate, so...so, I just wanted to bring it in person. I don't mind driving. I needed to get out of that place anyway."

Danny knew Tracy's stammering was brought on by a concern that she had said too much already, and that she was on the verge of spilling their mutual, mortal secret about the sea god. But Samantha already knew the story, was intimately connected to it, in fact, so Danny let Tracy off the hook before things got too uncomfortable. "It's fine, Tracy. Samantha knows."

Tracy looked at Samantha, one eyebrow raised, as if impressed that she'd been thought highly enough to have been brought into the club. "Wow, he must really be into you. That's a big thing to know about someone, don't you think? You guys getting married?"

"Yes, Tracy," Danny responded, not missing a beat. "We're getting married. The wedding is tomorrow, and you're not invited."

"I'm coming anyway."

Danny smiled at Tracy's sass, and he was suddenly invigorated now that she was here with the book. The sleep—or perhaps sex—that had seemed inevitable only a moment ago was suddenly brushed to the side, replaced by a more desperate longing.

The book.

Danny didn't know how at the moment, but it was important, and he had little doubt it would be crucial for discovering the secret to destroying the creature, or at least banishing it to some dark corner of the ocean. This was the way things worked. Tracy had called for a reason. Everything was something, and it all played at least a small part in the development of the universe. Of life. There was meaning to all things. He believed this now as much as he believed in the pull of gravity. Nothing was superfluous.

"So let's take a look at this book of yours," Danny said, trying not to sound too eager, though he couldn't have given a reason for his moderation.

"Wait a minute!" Tracy suddenly stood and stared at Samantha. "I *do* know you!"

Tracy strode quickly toward Samantha, and for a minute Danny thought she was going to hit her.

"You came to my house that day. Looking for Lynn. You're...oh my god, you're Lyle's daughter." Tracy looked at Danny now, fear in her eyes. "Did she tell you—"

"Yes, Tracy, she did. That's why she knows about it. We're all on the same team here. Now we're just trying to figure out how to win the game."

Tracy turned back to Samantha and stared at her for a few seconds longer, still a bit suspicious at her presence. Then, as if the words just registered, she looked back to Danny. "What the hell does that mean?"

"There's been some trouble in this place. This town. It's happening again."

"What?" Tracy's face flushed.

"Yes. It's here, Tracy. I found it. I tracked it down. People have died again. I don't know how many, but it's responsible for at least one and probably several more. We have to stop it. I have to, at least. It's what I've dedicated the last two years of my life to doing, and I finally have a chance. That's why Samantha came back here tonight. And that's why I'm hoping this book you found can help us."

The energy Danny had drawn from Tracy's arrival suddenly waned, and the draw of sleep hit him hard again. The temporary shot of adrenaline was gone, leaving him with an overwhelming need to close his eyes.

"But we're not going to find it tonight," he said, "and, honestly, I don't think I can say another thing about it until I get a few hours. I'm spent. We'll take a look at the book tomorrow, with fresh eyes, and if there's something in there of use, we'll figure out how to put it into action."

"Hopefully we have that long," Samantha prodded. "None of this is going to work without you, and if you're in jail—"

"Jail? What is going on, Danny? You didn't say anything about jail. Why are you going to jail?"

"I can't tonight, Tracy. Please. Just trust me that it's going to be okay."

"Promise?" Tracy's eyes lost their jocularity and turned dejected.

Danny gave a single, weary nod. "Samantha, you can have my room, and Tracy, the guest room is already made up. I'll take the couch."

"Okay," Tracy conceded, and then held the book up to show she was laying it on the bar. "But we're going to get to this tomorrow, first thing. I can't have you going to jail, Danny."

"We'll look at it first thing, but not to keep me out of jail. It's our responsibility now. Too much damage has been done by this monster, and people like Lynn and me, and god only knows how many other people over the years have allowed it...encouraged it to continue. We have to find it before it moves on and terrorizes some other town." Danny's smile turned weary. "And yes, before I go to jail."

Chapter 27

Samuel listened to Sokwa's translation of the story in a state he had never experienced before. It was happiness, yes, but it was more than that. He felt—light—like someone had lifted a heavy weight from his chest, allowing him to breathe the air more fully than he knew possible.

The story was riveting, of course, but Samuel could also sense the texture of truth in it. It wasn't like the Greek stories of Zeus and Poseidon, where nonsensical explanations were attributed to the world around them, conveniently filling in gaps that otherwise lacked any scientific depth at all. There was too much about the god's origin the woman didn't know for it to be a simple legend.

According to the lore of her people, the first sighting of the sea god was by a group of Croatoan fishermen, seining at the shore of the Yapam decades before the woman's birth, perhaps pre-dating her parents and grandparents as well, though Sokwa either couldn't quite grasp the time span or the woman couldn't communicate it.

But it mattered little to him. The tale was simply an earlier version of the one he already knew. The god had appeared to the fisherman from the sea, rising like some phantom of the water before standing in cold stillness in its watching, menacing way, exploring the land like a hungry dragon, its eyes hunting for only a minute or two before returning to the sea. There had been no record of attack during that first incident, the woman said, but Samuel knew for sure it had been surveying the shore, measuring the beach for its potential as a feeding ground.

The woman relayed a few more of the sightings that had been passed down verbally throughout the years, most of which seemed unconnected to the one before, and each of which concluded similarly, with only a sighting and the Croatoan retreating without incident to the sea. Samuel remained engaged in these separate tales, but as Sokwa's translations dragged on in similar fashion—without her speaking of any of the beast's killings—Samuel became frustrated, eventually interrupting the delicate revelations with questions.

"When did the sacrifices begin?" Samuel asked, speaking to the woman directly. "When was the first killing by the beast?" He looked at Sokwa. "Ask her. Please, Sokwa."

Sokwa reluctantly translated the question, and the woman gave a thin smile and a knowing nod.

"Diahwa," she said, and then rose quickly and scuttled back to a dark corner of the cave where she disappeared for several minutes. For a moment, Samuel thought the old hag had fled the cave through some secret back exit, but ultimately she re-emerged, creeping back into the light of the fire like a giant crab, her arms raised above her head, in her hands she held a thin stack of what looked to be a form of primitive paper, animal parchment perhaps.

The woman waved the stack in the air, the same smile still traced across her face, and then she pattered back over to where Samuel and Sokwa sat apprehensively by the flame.

She spoke quickly to Sokwa as she found a space to sit, telling the girl how her people's stories had been passed down from one generation to the next through speech alone, but finally, during her years as a young girl, she recalled how the elders of the village began to record the sightings on page.

The old hermit sat cross-legged by the fire as she folded the pages of the book one over the other, steady and careful with each leaf of parchment, finally arriving at a crinkled page that looked to be nothing more than a crusted-over rectangle of skin that was smeared with ash and dirt.

Samuel reached for the page, almost instinctively, and the woman snatched it back toward her, opening her mouth wide as she gave a growl from somewhere deep in her chest.

"No, Samuel," Sokwa warned, shaking her head slowly. "You've not been permitted to touch her belongings."

Samuel put his arms up and blinked several times as he nodded, showing he had no more interest in touching the book, only in seeing the contents of what it contained. He leaned in slowly, his hands behind him, signaling to the woman he wanted only to look. Reluctantly, she held the book out and the page steady, and as she did, Samuel craned his neck forward and studied the page closer.

He couldn't see it at first, the grime was too thick, the coverage too complete; but then, through the soot of neglect and the creases of time, Samuel's eyes began focusing, filtering, and soon he could make out what appeared to be a man's screaming face.

Samuel recoiled at the faded outline, and the woman smiled more widely now, satisfied at this white boy's appropriate reaction to her god.

The depiction of pain by the man on the parchment was undeniable, one Samuel knew intimately now, and as he continued to take in the drawing, his eyes found another figure, fainter and less detailed than the face of the man but undoubtedly there. This depiction was also of a face, and there was no question in Samuel's mind it was the Croatoan.

He formed his finger into a slow point, and then said the word under his breath, phrasing it as a question. "Croatoan?"

The woman nodded. "Croatoan."

According to Sokwa's translation, this scene was a depiction of the first slaughter by the Croatoan, and the man in the picture was not one of her own people, but a people that had been extinguished from the world at some point during the previous century. It was the first story transcribed from the oral record to the pages of the ancient text.

"What else?" Samuel asked.

"What else of what, Samuel. This is the story. This is what you came to know. The origin of the creature."

"There is more to this text. There are more pages. What else is revealed within."

"They're pictures. Many of which are hardly recognizable."

Samuel frowned and gave a look of confession. "It's not only the origin I wish to know. I want to know more. Her people called it from the sea as a protector. It destroyed a whole tribe of people."

"That is not what she said."

"I want to know how to call it from the sea. She knows this secret. I know she does. And I want to learn it for myself. It is the only reason I wanted to come here, Sokwa."

Sokwa paused and stared at Samuel, a look mixed with disgust and disappointment across her lips and eyes. "To learn to summon it? That is what you want to know? Why would you want such a thing, Samuel? Why would you want to bring such destruction to the island?"

"I don't want to bring destruction at all," Samuel lied. "I want only to kill it. I want only to avenge Nootau."

Sokwa looked suspiciously at Samuel. "And Kitchi?"

Samuel looked to the ground for a moment, considering the question. "Kitchi brought on his own death. I do not feel responsible for that." He paused. "But yes, for Kitchi, as well. And for the protection of the colony. And your village."

Sokwa's face was filled with questioning, an expression that fell well short of satisfaction at Samuel's answers.

But he held her stare firmly, knowing that if he dropped his eyes for even a moment, she would see the lie in them. Finally, she turned from him and said something to the woman, which Samuel prayed was the question he wanted to have answered more than all questions that had been raised by The Bible for the past decade, since he heard the first story of Adam and Eve recited.

Samuel sat anxiously as the woman thumbed through several more pages of the book while she spoke. Her words were very tempered now, serious, as she pointed to more unclear pictures on pages that looked to have been pulled from the sand at the bottom of the sea.

Samuel tried not to appear too eager for Sokwa's pending translation, but his throat was thick with anticipation and he wished he had his water bladder.

The woman finally stopped talking and then nodded, as if that was all she could tell.

Sokwa looked at Samuel and said, "She says she cannot know for sure exactly when the Croatoan emerges, or if it still comes at all anymore. It has never come to her in all the years she has been in this place."

Samuel wanted to remind the woman that, of course it hadn't come, she had been searching in the wrong waters the whole time. But there was nothing to be gained by this reminder, and it may have only angered the woman.

"But the record does give hints as to its arrival. It tells how the Croatoan comes at only certain times of the cycle, but again, she has lost all track of the duration or star cycle. She has lost her sense of time, Samuel. She has no calendar of when we are."

"It's okay. It's here now. The cycle is now. But can it be called, Sokwa? Lured? That is what I need to know."

Sokwa nodded, indicating the answer had been given already. "The legend tells how it can be brought from the sea with particular sounds, though it seems there is not one in particular. Her people lured it first with the conch, similar to this one." Sokwa moved her hand toward the shell the woman had used out on the rocks. "But over time, the Croatoan was drawn by other sounds as well."

Samuel's eyes were wild and flickering now. "What sounds?"

Sokwa shook her head and closed her eyes, struggling to continue the translation. But she continued. "Legend tells that the creature became attracted to the sound of voices on the shores. The voices of the natives who took to the beaches for fishing and recreation. And at one point, the creature took a young boy from the beach as his father sat in helpless terror. And once this story was told, how no conch was needed to bring the creature, but merely the screams of joy or pains, the Croatoan took to a new practice."

"Yes. What was it?"

"She says she bore witness to this as a small girl. She saw how the creature would arise from the water, drawn by the screams of..." She stopped.

"What is it, Sokwa? What did she say?"

Sokwa gathered herself and continued. "When she was a girl, her people would bring chosen victims for sacrifices. They would stand at the beach and summon the creature, screaming words of religion that they had concocted, incantations, begging for it to rise and take their offerings. The Croatoan is attracted by sounds of the conch, like the sounds she was producing on the rocks, but it responds to the beckoning of other sounds too. The sounds of its prey. It is as you said, Samuel. She was calling for it. You were right about all of it. About Nootau's death. And Kitchi's. I can't believe this is true. But it is."

Sokwa was both fascinated and terrified, and Samuel recalled the similar feelings he had on the shores of the Great Western Sea, when the Croatoan began its newest cycle on the beaches of this New World. It was a world that Samuel had never felt a part of. Until that day, when the terror and awe had turned to wonder and destiny. He needed to bring Sokwa to this same place, not because he needed her for any specific purpose or task, but because he now wanted someone else to share the glory with him, someone who could appreciate the magnificence of the carnage the god would unleash on their people.

"What else did she say?" he asked. "She must have said more."

Sokwa looked wide-eyed at Samuel and nodded. "She did. A bit."

Samuel gave a comforting smile to Sokwa, and she grinned weakly back at him. It was a look that told him he was making progress.

"As the years went on, a new generation of the Croatoan people outlawed the use of human sacrifice as a way to lure the creature, but the desire to view it remained strong in the tribe. So, as a way to keep the beast fed and away from the village, while still having the joy—it was the word she used—they began to desecrate the seas with the blood and entrails of their farm animals, hoping that this blood of the land would simultaneously lure it from the Yapam depths and satisfy its hunger."

"What about the calls for it. How would it be summoned?"

"They began to use sounds other than the distressful cries of humans, learning to mimic the calls of the whales, for instance, to draw it to the blood and flesh that had been offered to the waters. The woman says the beast added these sounds to its memory, along with the cries of man and the sound of the conch."

It was the knowledge Samuel sought. The secret to calling the god forth on command. The conch. The cries. Whales. It was bizarre and wonderful at the same time. "What time of day does it come nearest the shore? Is it at regular daily intervals?"

Sokwa took a breath of relief and shrugged. "She says the record is unclear on that. As I said, she has been here too long, Samuel. She can't know any longer when it comes and goes."

Samuel nodded and blinked furiously, thinking of the next appropriate question. But his mind could devise nothing further. He had all the information he needed now to make the Croatoan his own. To use it for his bidding the way Lucifer used the serpent of The Garden.

But he had a bit more work to do with Sokwa. Just a bit. He was so close to his god, and soon Sokwa would be the newest member of his religion.

Chapter 28

Danny fell asleep almost instantly, but by 4:30, he was rustling on the sofa, trying to find a spot comfortable enough to prevent him from having to face the morning. But it was no use; he was awake for good, and his early rising habit, which had been stuck with him for years, was unwilling to release him from its clutches.

He slipped on his shirt from the previous day and walked out to the porch where he stood alone in the cool, dark morning, listening to the crash of the waves on the sand, wondering if the god was standing on the shoreline at that moment, watching him like a stalker, the backlight of Danny's kitchen light showcasing his silhouette to the beast below.

But it no longer mattered to Danny anymore. The creature was going to die soon, he could feel it as powerfully as he felt the addiction of the beast only two short years ago. It had to die, there was no choice. It had taken too much from Danny already, and now that Tracy had arrived, he felt more obligated than ever to destroy it for good.

Later, perhaps that same day, he would confess to Tracy the things he had done to her and Sarah, about those nights soon after his own ordeal when he had drugged them and attempted to sacrifice them, an offering to the black and purple man. And he would reveal that it wasn't his own restraint that had saved their lives, but rather some quirk in the beast's cycle, some change that had brought them all to this house now.

He stepped back inside the kitchen and spotted the book, still sealed inside its plastic cocoon, isolated on the bar top, situated directly under one of the recessed flood lamps. It looked like an ancient artifact that had been placed there with purpose, as on an altar in some Egyptian tomb.

Danny examined the details of the book's cover and binding for the first time now, examining it through the bag with the curiosity of an archaeologist. It was thin, the document, perhaps only a half-inch in thickness, and its cover was dark brown with faded veins of yellow and beige spidered across the cover, a tell-tale sign of age and weathering.

There was no doubt the book was old—over a hundred years, at least—and Danny could tell that Tracy wasn't just excusing herself when she said she feared the delicacy of it. Mailing it would have been a catastrophe. The spine was cracked and frayed, barely holding the covers together with thin strands of cloth or leather—Danny couldn't tell which—causing both ends of the book to slip offline from the pages between them.

Danny stood over the book and stared at it, not ready to open the bag and touch it just yet. He had told Tammy and Samantha they would wait until morning to explore the contents, but technically it *was* morning, and he felt he needed to view the text now.

He was cautious as he took another step toward the book, though for what reason he could not have said, and then he unclasped the jaws of the Ziploc and slowly slid the contents to the bar. He ran his finger across the cover, feeling the broken leather, which was surprisingly cool and smooth to the touch.

Danny then used the tip of his index finger and pulled the cover up, guiding it down gently to the laminated counter. He stared at the first page, and to Danny's surprise, there was a clearly printed title on it, with proper publishing credentials, as well as a date typed out in Roman numerals at the bottom of the thick paper. He couldn't translate the date immediately, but he could see by the first two letters it was printed sometime in the nineteenth century.

But his eyes were drawn back the title.

Algonquin Stories of Roanoke Island and the Disappearance of an English Colony.

Danny felt his heartbeat accelerate upon reading the word 'Roanoke,' and a bead of sweat quickly appeared and rolled down his face. Instinctively, he dodged to the side to avoid staining the book with his perspiration, and the droplet landed harmlessly on the bar top next to the book.

He touched his lips curiously as he took a step backward, leaving the volume open to the first page, and then he stared at the tome with a new fascination, a new fear, as if it were a book of magic spells that had mistakenly fallen into his hands.

He stood pondering what might be in the pages for several moments, thinking back on what he knew of the legend of Roanoke and the Lost Colony. It wasn't much, other than what he had seen on a tour as a kid one summer during a vacation to the Outer Banks. Colonists from England had come and settled in what was now North Carolina, west of Nags Head in the Roanoke sound on an island of the same name.

And then they had disappeared. All of them. If he re-called, one or more members of the colony had gone back to England, and when they returned, everyone was gone. Almost without a trace. Danny couldn't remember how many, but it was somewhere in the hundreds, he thought. And to this day, there was no explanation for the disappearance.

There was a word written on a tree or cabin, if he remembered correctly. Maybe somewhere else in the settlement, too. It started with a 'C,' but Danny couldn't place it.

The book.

He stepped to it again, ready to begin the research that would hopefully fill in the gaps of his Lost Colony education and bring him closer to finding the sea god.

Dok! Dok! Dok!

Three solid raps landed on his front door, loudly, as if it had been struck with a rubber mallet. He gasped and felt his heart seize, but he quickly placed the sound and suppressed the scream that was eager to be released.

He stared curiously at the front door of his rented beach house, wondering if he had ever used it beyond the first day he arrived.

Three more raps.

Danny took several steps until he was within a few inches of the door. "Who is it?" he demanded.

"Danny, it's Sheriff Calazzo."

Crap Danny thought. Not yet. Not now. He just needed another day. Maybe two. Enough time to find the answers in the book and put them to use, neither of which he could do from a jail cell.

He turned and walked quickly back to the bar and gently closed the book before placing it into one of a dozen unused drawers that lined his kitchen. He walked back to the door and tried to put on an expression that would make sense at this hour, and then he thought, *Screw it*; this was his house, he could look however he damn well pleased. Especially at five in the morning.

"What can I do for you officer?" he called through the door.

"Can you open up for me, Danny. Let me come in for a minute or two? I just need to talk to you for a moment. Obviously, I would have waited for a more decent hour, but I saw your light on and thought I'd take a chance and call on you."

Shit! Danny thought as he turned the knob and opened the door, trusting his instincts, believing that refusing the request of an officer wasn't going to improve his situation as it concerned Gerald DeRose.

"Sheriff," Danny said cordially. "What brings you out so late? Or early, I guess, depending on what kind of person you are."

"I'd say I'm the kind of person for whom this hour would be early, though not especially."

Danny nodded, not sure what that meant exactly. "This is to do with Mr. DeRose, I take it? I'll say this, you guys must put in some long days, because it's been what, a whole eight hours since I left the station?"

"We do put in long hours, Mr. Lynch, but fortunately for you, Gerald DeRose is not the reason for my visit. Not exactly."

"'Not exactly?' What does that mean?"

Calazzo cocked his head and looked off ruefully to the side. "It means that we have another problem, similar to Mr. DeRose, which I suppose is good news for you, because after what I heard tonight, I'm pretty certain you'll be in the clear."

Danny felt a buoyancy well inside of him, hopefulness, his legal issues suddenly dwindling. But there was a new pressure now, a different type of anxiety as he waited for the other shoe to drop.

"There's been another death, Mr. Lynch. Right now we're calling it a homicide."

"What?"

Calazzo nodded. "And we know you had nothing to do with this one. And I no longer think the first one either."

"Why is that?" Danny was slightly in shock, and the question sounded as if someone other than he had asked it.

"Because every instinct in my body tells me it's the same person...the same man who killed Mr. DeRose."

"Oh no," Danny whispered, his mind beginning to make automatic calculations.

Calazzo smirked "Thought you'd be a bit more pleased."

"That someone died?"

"Believe it or not, in a case like this, for most people, the answer would be 'yes.'"

"What part of the beach?"

"What's that?"

"This killing, where on the beach did it happen?"

"Well that's just it, Danny, it was at the beach, but it wasn't on the ocean."

"What?" Danny could barely breathe now.

"Like I said. It was two high schoolers. Out late. Young lovers walking the bay front, I guess. Tippin's Point. The girl says something...someone appeared from behind them and grabbed her boyfriend. Picked him up by his neck and strangled him. A sixteen-year old boy, can you believe that?"

Calazzo shook his head, as if not quite able to picture the story he was describing.

Danny could picture it perfectly.

"And then it dragged him that way back to the water. Girl says her boyfriend barely made a sound. His neck was crushed, flopped off to the side within moments. What the hell kind of man has that kind of strength?"

Danny didn't give him the answer, though he sensed Calazzo was looking to him for the explanation. Instead he asked, "Well, the girl was there. She saw him. What kind of man was it?"

"That's just it. She says it wasn't no man at all. What do you make of that?"

"So a woman then?"

Calazzo chuckled. "No, Danny, not a woman. To hear her describe it, sounds a bit like that thing you saw a few years ago. That thing in the paper."

Danny was quiet.

"Anyways, she was hysterical, of course, and luckily she had the sense to run away. It was dark though—no moon tonight—and she was terrified, which tends to alter your perception. So who knows what she actually saw. But she's sticking to her story."

"And what story is that?"

Calazzo shrugged. "That it was some kind of a...creature. I don't know. Her description was pretty detailed though."

Danny didn't need to hear the description, he already knew exactly what the sea god looked like. His only interest now was in the location. "The bay, you said?"

Calazzo nodded. "Yep." He paused and stared at Danny for a beat. "There something you can help us with, Danny? Because goddamn, I hate to admit this, but I guess everything is on the table now."

Danny felt a surge of adrenaline run through him, knowing that the confrontation was coming soon, feeling that his nightmare was about to end forever one way or the other.

"I think I can, sheriff, but I'll need half the day to figure some things out."

"Half a day? Hell, I guess I can wait half a day for a murder to get sorted out."

"And if I were you, I would try to keep everyone away from the bay for the time being."

"That deal's been sealed already."

"And I guess the ocean too, just to be safe. Put up whatever signs you need to, just keep the beaches clear. I know that won't be easy, but I'll be there by this afternoon. Bayside at Tippin's Point. I'll let you know when I'm coming."

Calazzo gave a moment's thought to all Danny had said and then nodded, and Danny could tell he wasn't used to being in this position, taking orders from a civilian about how his job should be carried out. But he had little choice now. The stakes had been raised to a point Sheriff Calazzo and his ragtag band of officers couldn't reach alone.

"Sounds fair to me, Danny," he said. "You have a good night, sir." He turned for the door and then stopped, pivoting back to Danny. "And I am sorry about all you went through yesterday. I should have listened to my deputy on this one. She said you were a good egg. Said it was that boy who was the rotten one."

Shane. Danny had momentarily forgotten about the kid. The boy who had offered his father to the god for a few seconds of terrifying, sickening glory.

"He's not bad, sheriff," Danny replied. "He's sick. And God willing, I'm gonna find the cure."

Chapter 29

Samuel and Sokwa stood atop the shallow hill that over-looked the southern border of the village and colony, well back from the tree line so that the leaves of the oaks shrouded them in darkness. As they stared down on the peaceful arrangement of wigwams and longhouses, gardens and worksites, Samuel couldn't help but smile as he clutched the woman's book in his arms, pressing it tightly against his chest. He looked at Sokwa who stood beside him, and though she didn't look nearly as joyous or confident as Samuel, there was an aspect of resolve in her eyes, one that Samuel now took pride in having built over the course of the day's journey.

"We'll take a passage through the forest," he said, "around the perimeter, until we meet the path that leads down to the sound. It is the same course I took yesterday to reach your house. If we're quiet, no one will know we are here. Once down the path, we'll sleep on the shores of the sound, and then tomorrow at dawn, we'll take the boat to the Yapam and make the first call."

Sokwa looked to the ground as her eyes bled to sadness. "I don't want my family hurt, Samuel. Or any of my people. Can you promise that?" Her tone was doubtful, her face contorted with confusion and distrust. "How do you know when we call it, if it comes, that they won't all be taken by the Croatoan?"

"I know it, Sokwa. Just as I know the Croatoan will come. I believe it and thus I know it. Once we call the god from sea and beckon it across the sound to the island, just as the stories in the book described, we will have time to warn whoever you wish. And if they heed your warnings, they will have ample opportunity to flee. You tell them why you have done what you've done—what we have done—with vigor and purpose, and they will believe you. Nootau's parents already know the creature to be real. It won't be difficult, Sokwa. We're saving them in the end. I will have saved your people by summoning the Croatoan."

Samuel had no feelings or concern about Sokwa's family or any of the Algonquin people on the island. He only wanted to put to test the lessons in the woman's book. To see if he could still use the sounds of the conch to draw the creature from the depths of the Great Western Sea, on command, and then watch it make its way across the beaches to the sound. From there he would take the boat back across, just as he and Nootau had planned that first day, when the boat had been pulled by the tide and Nootau had tried to swim across only to be caught and torn into fragments.

But Samuel would be quicker this time. He would have Sokwa ready to go with the boat as soon as the creature had locked them in its sights. And once they were across to the island, Samuel would sound the conch again, drawing it further toward him, to the shores of the island and then up the path to the village. "You believe me, yes?"

Sokwa nodded, her eyes pleading, imploring Samuel to instill in her the belief that every word of what he said was true. "But how, Samuel? If we can draw it to the village, how will we keep it from destroying everything in its path. From destroying my people?"

"If we can draw it to us, we can draw it away. We need only see the death of my mother, and once that is complete—and you have seen the majesty of it for yourself—we'll lead it back to the sound and destroy it, if that is your wish. I've stashed weapons from my father's armory in the brush by the beach."

None of this was true, but Samuel knew it wouldn't come to matter. He had captured the imagination of Sokwa, using most of the walk back from the woman's cave to re-tell the story of his two encounters with the creature, first describing his day with Nootau, and later his night on the beach during Kitchi's death. The truth of what happened in both instances was barely existent in his words, but Samuel gave no thought to his lack of sincerity. He had accomplished his goals with Sokwa, and the girl hung on every word as if each was a bar of gold, asking him to re-tell the tale of Kitchi's death twice more before they reached the village. And with each re-telling, Samuel added some detail that was more intimate, more grotesque, illuminating the butchery of the killing with images that left Sokwa wonderstruck.

And by the time they had trekked to within an hour of the colony, Sokwa was nearly salivating at the thought of seeing the Croatoan. Her manner was reminiscent of Nootau's on that first day by the dunes, so driven by his uncle's story was he that he ran without concern to the canoe that would take them to the beach. The consequences of disobeying his parents or the danger of the creature itself were secondary to Nootau that morning.

But there was more to Samuel's plan than painting images of the creature; that alone wouldn't have been enough to convince Sokwa to agree to his plan of death and destruction. He added sordid stories of his mother's abuses toward him—some of which were true—as well as the more twisted lie that his mother had murdered his infant sister by smothering her in her cradle in order to suppress her crying and screaming.

But the real hook of Samuel's plan came from the lie about how he had overheard his parents in conversation just before his father left for England. 'He has not gone there for food or supplies' Samuel had lied to Sokwa, 'he has gone for soldiers. And iron tools which he is bringing back to build gallows for every member of your tribe. They're all going to hang, Sokwa. All of your tribe has been sentenced to torture and death.'

This last part of the fable was true—her tribe was going to die—but it would not come as a result of Samuel's father or any English reinforcements. Once the Croatoan was released upon the village, once it had been led through the forest and to the colony, Samuel knew there was little he could do to stop it. There was no reversal of the call that could end the slaughter of the people there.

Samuel's lies had also done well to lead Sokwa away from the cave. When the opportunity had arisen, during the point in their visit when the old hermit had gone to the perimeter of the cliffs to check on her crazed prisoner, Samuel convinced Sokwa that they were both destined to end up in one of the vacant sand holes, just like the woman who stole Samuel's bladder.

After much debate, she had agreed, but not to taking the book, fearing that stealing it would lead to some curse or bad luck. But Samuel insisted the book would be important to the history of her people, and that if they allowed it to stay buried in the beachside caves, it would never be found, and all of the knowledge of the Croatoan and its destruction would die with it.

And Samuel insisted Sokwa add to the book, as well. And during one of their rests, using only the flint of a rock, she marvelously re-created the woman's call on the rocks and the Croatoan's rise from the sea, Samuel describing the creature to her with all the detail he could muster.

Samuel had also taken the conch, which Sokwa did not notice. And as Samuel thought about it now, he could only imagine the fury and panic the woman would feel when she noticed it was gone. Surely, she had thought it special in some way, despite that it had never drawn the creature, and there was a new conch to be found on the beach every day.

Sokwa followed Samuel through the trees around the perimeter of the village until they reached the path that led down to the sound. From there they descended the gradual slope, winding around the corners and up the inclines where Samuel had pushed Kitchi in a wheelbarrow only days ago. At the bottom of the hill, they found a thick clump of bushes behind which they would camp for the night.

Samuel was hungry now, extraordinarily, and he knew that once tomorrow arrived, he would need a proper meal from somewhere, though he couldn't at that moment imagine where it would be gained.

He took a deep breath of the beach air and thought about his plan once daylight came, constructing it over in his mind again and again, trying to locate the flaw.

But it felt right in his mind. It was all meant to happen just as it was.

"You believe me, right, Sokwa?"

Samuel looked to the girl, hoping to garner more confidence through her assurances, but Sokwa was already sleeping. He closed his eyes and lay down beside her, and as he lay, drifting to sleep, he conjured once more the image of the Croatoan ripping out the heart of his mother.

Chapter 30

Danny and Samantha stood on one side of the bar and Tracy the other, each staring at the pages of the open book in his or her own unique way, squinting or cocking a head or neck, trying to find the string of words or an image that would provide the answer to a question that had not yet been asked. But Danny knew the gist of the question: how could they draw the monster from the sea and into an awaiting trap?

The trap part was an additional question, of course, one Danny hadn't thought much about to this point, but he figured if they could answer the first question, the answer to the second one would fall into place.

But that they had to kill it was no longer up for debate. There was no other option; it had killed again, and this time the victim was a teenager. Thankfully, it sounded as if the witness had resisted getting mesmerized by the sea god and had not fallen under its spell the way Danny had.

And Shane.

And Lynn.

Danny supposed that had this young girl seen her boyfriend slaughtered from a distance—from the safety of the dunes or a porch, perhaps—she would not have had the same restraint. But according to Sheriff Calazzo, the god was upon them before either realized what was happening, and her natural survival instincts had won the day.

Thank god for that.

"Roanoke," Samantha said shaking her head. "Christ. That was like five hundred years ago."

Danny had awakened both women minutes after the sheriff left, much earlier than he had anticipated when they went off to bed only a few hours earlier; but given the visit by Calazzo and the dire news he'd brought with him, there was precious little time to waste.

Samantha and Tracy had both gathered naturally at the bar, circling around the mysterious book as if drawn by a magnet, and there Danny had shown them the title page, getting similar reactions to the one he had expressed upon seeing it.

"Where the hell did it come from do you think?" Tracy asked. "And where did Aunt Lynn get it?"

"Five hundred years ago," Samantha repeated, not addressing Tracy's questions. "This book is that old?"

"No," Danny answered, "look." He ran his finger under the Roman numerals at the bottom of the title page. "It was published in 1874. But I do think there are things in here that are that old. Some of these drawings were copied from originals of that time. At least according to the captions. And from what I've read so far, much of the text in here was translated directly from an earlier book, one that was supposedly found on the site of the Lost Colony after it was abandoned."

Samantha shook her head. "I never heard about any book found there. All they found were those carvings on the trees. 'Croatoan.' I think it was the name of a tribe that lived near there."

Croatoan. It was the word Danny was searching for earlier—one that he had already read in several places throughout Lynn Shield's book—and now that the curious term had finally breached the air, it sent a shiver across his back.

"Most people think the colonists were killed by the tribe, and...I don't know...someone carved the word on a tree as a clue or something. A warning for the settlers coming from England, I guess."

Danny nodded as Samantha spoke, having gathered this same data from his memory bank during his scan of the text thirty minutes earlier. "That's right," he said. "That's pretty good."

Samantha gave a self-satisfied smile.

"But," Danny paused for effect, "what if it wasn't a warning about the *tribe*?"

"Who then?" Tracy asked.

But Samantha had already arrived at the answer. "The creature. The warning was about the creature. Our sea beast. 'Croatoan' was the name of a tribe, but maybe it was also the name the natives gave to the creature."

"Wait, what?" Tracy shook her head. "You're telling me this thing is five hundred years old? How could that be?"

Danny frowned and shrugged. "I'm not telling you that, but I do think Samantha may be right. There are things in this book that...I don't know. I guess there's no way to know how accurate any of this is. It could all just be a fairy tale made to look like reality. But Lynn had the book at her home, and I can't believe that is a coincidence." Danny opened his eyes wide and looked at each of the women for a long moment. "And the pictures inside...you have to see them."

Danny thumbed open to the first page, about a quarter of the way in, and there, in what the caption below described as a retracing of an earlier drawing, the smooth, black head of the sea god was rising just above the water line, its massive shoulders spread like mountains, its expressionless eyes contrasting with the huge teeth that lined the bottom of its face.

"Holy shit," Tracy whispered.

It was the third time Danny had looked at the picture since Calazzo left. The first time he had stared at it for more than twenty minutes, studying the similarities between the picture in the book and the one in his mind—the one that had been etched there forever by his first sighting at Rove Beach.

He took a deep breath and swallowed as he viewed the depiction again, nodding reflexively at the accuracy of the drawing.

"That is unbelievable, Danny," Tracy announced. "That's it, isn't it? That's the sea god."

"But how can it be?" Samantha asked, "What Tracy just said is true: how could it still be alive after all this time? Are there more of these things out there? Is this some species that just hasn't been discovered yet? Except that we *have* discovered it, just not in the universal, scientific way?"

Danny flipped a hand up and gave a weary shake of his head. "I don't know. All I know is that's it. That's the same animal that killed my wife."

Samantha popped her eyes up toward Danny, a follow up question to this admission puckered on the edge of her lips. But she refrained, seeming to understand that, at this point, she had no real claim to any of Danny's secrets, no matter how shadowy.

"The same creature that killed a boy on the bay only hours ago, and God knows how many other innocent people. Including your father. And I agree, maybe it isn't the exact one from this picture, that seems unlikely, but it is the same animal. I have no doubt about that. And I have a feeling this book can show us how to fish it out."

"I thought you already knew how to do that," Tracy reminded. "The whale sounds or whatever."

Danny took a deep breath and frowned, shaking his head as he closed his eyes. "I don't think those are doing anything at this point. I'm not sure they ever did. Or maybe they did at one time, but now it's some other sound that has its attention. The whale sounds were what Lynn did, so I copied her." He paused. "Or maybe it's to do with the migration patterns of the whales and this thing, and now they're no longer in sync. With the sea god moving this far up the coast, it may have moved outside the range of the minke whales. But that's just a guess, I don't really know anymore."

"So then we just have to wait it out?"

"No, I don't think so. It's coming to shore for a reason. It's looking to kill. To eat. And I do think it's drawn there by sound. It could be the sounds of people on the beach, or…I don't really know. But something. And from what I've read in this book so far, I think the answer could be inside."

The three stood staring at the book for several minutes, Danny flipping to the next page at erratic intervals, depending on how much text was written on the page. Most of the pages contained faded pictures of the beast or the surrounding habitat, and few were easy to decipher, other than the one Danny had shown first.

What text the book contained was either of translated Croatoan poems, which the author claimed were about the

sea god and gave sound analysis as support; or it was specu-
lative theories by the author about who killed the colonists,
always coming back to the thesis that the three monster
hunters in the kitchen now agreed to be true.

It was the Croatoan that wiped out the first English
colony at Roanoke.

Danny flipped back to the page with the rising Croatoan, allowing his companions to take in the picture one last
time.

"What is this?" Samantha asked, pointing at the page.
Her finger hovered just above the image of the creature and
slightly to the right.

Danny leaned in closer, squinting at the object of
Samantha's focus. "Yeah, I noticed that too. It looks like a
person, maybe out on a pier or a rock formation."

"What is she doing?"

"It looks like she's...calling someone. Calling out to the
sea."

"Yes, it does. That is wild. It definitely looks like she's
calling out, and the beast is rising from the water at the same
time."

"But what is in his hand?" Tracy asked.

"What?" Danny put his face closer, seeing for the first
time what Tracy was noting. "You're right. I hadn't noticed
that before. What is that?"

Samantha leaned in closer now and then said, "It looks
like a horn. A goat's horn or something."

Danny stared at the picture for another moment, and
then, as if he'd been hit in the back of his legs with a baseball
bat, he collapsed onto the stool beside him. He looked back

to the book for another couple seconds, and then stared toward the wall of the kitchen, gathering the final components of what he now knew was the answer to the underlying question.

"What's wrong, Danny?" Tracy asked. "What did you see?"

"I know what to do," he answered. "I know how to bring it to shore."

Chapter 31

Samuel stood at the shoreline and gripped the large conch shell with his left hand as he stared out over the endless gray waves of the Yapam.

Samuel had instructed Sokwa to position herself on the bank of the eastern sound, with the canoe secured and prepared to launch on his command. When the creature finally emerged, he would take in its magnificence for only a moment, and then he would concentrate on luring it to the sound.

Samuel looked back in the direction of where Sokwa was waiting, but the dunes were too high to spot the sound shore from where he stood, so he focused again on the bigger waters in front of him. She would be there when he came back. She wouldn't betray him at this point. If she had wanted him dead, her opportunity was back at the cave. She trusted him now, or if it wasn't trust, it was at least a belief in Samuel's sincerity about the Croatoan. She knew it was real, and once its glory was revealed to her, she would know then it was a sight more splendid than all the stars of heaven.

Samuel was almost melancholy now as he stood poised to trumpet the call from the stone shell, knowing that after today, after the village and colony were devoured by his new savior, he had no ideas about where his next victims would come from. Or even if he, himself, would survive the feast.

But those were questions for another day. Or perhaps not. All that mattered now was the summoning.

He placed his hand in the wide opening of the shell and barely touched his lips to the bored-out end of the conch where the spiral tip had been removed. He then inhaled to his lungs capacity, closed his eyes, and then pressed his mouth hard against the small hole.

And he blew.

The sound rang in Samuel's ears like Gabriel's horn, catching the still air of the beach unprepared, penetrating it like a knife as the low bellow exploded out toward the water. Samuel imagined his father being awakened by the sound, sitting up in his quarters somewhere out on the sea. Or perhaps the sound had extended even further, detectable by his cousins and uncles and friends whom Samuel had left behind as he was whisked away unconsulted, abducted by Morris and Elyoner Cook who were beckoned to this New World just as Samuel was beckoning his sea god this very moment.

He blew the conch again, one last blare for the earth to enjoy, and then he sat on the sand and began to cry, thinking of all he had lost and gained over the past few months. His father. The love of his mother. His best friend. It was all gone now, as was his chance at existence in this place of brown enemies and monstrous beasts of the sea.

But on this last note, this was a gain. He had found his calling in life, to serve the Croatoan. He would serve it well today, in fact, giving to it all that Samuel had in his life. All there was now to do was wait.

And he didn't have to wait long.

Chapter 32

"What did you see, Danny? What do we do?"

Danny almost had the plan fully organized, but he hadn't yet decided whether to bring Calazzo into the fold yet. The sheriff seemed earnest in his plea for help, but Danny also knew that accepting his theory would not come without questions, and any resistance from the sheriff could be a critical failure in luring the Croatoan from the bay. He didn't have time for bureaucracy, so he decided to keep the man in the dark for the time being.

"Samantha, you said you have a friend with a store on the boardwalk, right? 'Knickknacks,' you said." Danny was calm now, measured, but his speech was quick and focused.

Samantha nodded. "I do."

"Does she sell beach items, shells and stuff?"

"You mean does she sell seashells by the seashore?"

Tracy chuckled at Samantha's joke, but Danny missed it and just nodded, indicating 'yes, that was indeed the question he was asking.'

Samantha frowned. "Yes, of course. All sorts of crap like that."

"I need you to go there and find the biggest conch shell you can find. And if she doesn't have one, ask her if she knows another place that would. Meet me at Tippin's Point as soon as you find one. I'll be there when you get there."

Samantha put a hand to her chin and nodded, beginning to understand the theory. "A conch shell. Of course that's what it is."

Danny looked at Tracy. "Listen, what I need from you is going to be a bit more difficult. I need you to get Sheriff Calazzo away from the bay somehow. And keep him there for a while."

"How am I supposed to do that? The sheriff? I don't even know who that is. And wasn't a boy just killed there last night? I think there might be a little bit of action down there today."

"I don't know how, Tracy. That's why it's difficult. Can you just try to do this for me?"

Tracy gave a gentle smirk that was not reflected in her eyes.

"Look, there isn't much of a police force in this town, so maybe if you can invent some emergency that will lure him away from the bay or something. Just enough time for me to test my theory. Just put in a call, something serious. Say it's at the beach here, in front of this house. Maybe another body part or something. Just make it considerable, something that he'll respond to."

"And what if he doesn't respond? What if he sends a deputy?"

"Just do your best. Please." Danny was growing exasperated with Tracy's resistance, but each of her questions was more poignant than the last.

"And what happens when he gets here and there's no severed head?"

"I don't know, Tracy, I'm sure you'll think of something."

Tracy stared at Danny for a few seconds and then finally nodded, giving him a playful, squinty stare. "Fine, Mr.

Lynch, but only because you've been so cool about me living in your house for free. I guess I owe you this much."

Danny sighed. "Thank you. You do this, and we'll call it square."

He looked at both women one last time and nodded, feeling as if he may have a handle on things, and then he grabbed his keys and phone and headed for the door.

"So are you going to tell us your part in the plan?" Samantha asked.

"I'm going to the bay," he answered. "Unfortunately—at least in this moment—I've always been kind of a gun-control guy. So I need a weapon, and the only person I think I can get one from in a moment's notice is already at the beach."

"Who is that? What do you mean?"

"I don't have time to get into it. I've got a little convincing to do." He pointed at Samantha. "Get the shell." And then at Tracy, "Make the call. We finish this today."

Chapter 33

The booming sound of the splash came not from the ocean, but from behind Samuel, in the direction of the sound, and it was immediately followed by Sokwa's screams.

"Samuel!" Her cry could barely be heard on the wind. "Samuel, hurry!"

Samuel stood and stared back toward the dunes rising above the sound, just high enough to guard the beach from his sightline. Samuel's face was a sheet of disbelief, his mouth hanging like a harvest wreath, and he was paralyzed for several moments as he shifted his gaze back and forth between the two bodies of water, trying to understand the current vista and the sounds coming from beyond it.

Finally, Samuel made his decision and turned his body toward the sound, moving slowly at first, lifting his first foot from the heavy sand, and then more quickly as he broke into a clumsy run toward the dunes.

The dunes were fairly close, but Samuel was wheezing by the time he reached the bottom, and the pain in his foot from the cave woman's stick still throbbed. He stopped to gaze up the slope before climbing, and then he took two deep breaths, willing his lungs and legs to carry him just a bit further. The short ascent was grueling, but Samuel finally reached the top before collapsing into a sitting position, his legs splayed out in front of him.

Samuel rested for only a moment before a thought made his heart skip a beat. He stood and frantically began clutching his hands, instinctively searching for his most valuable possession. But his hands were empty, and Samuel began to scramble, spinning and looking toward the ground around him, suddenly in a panic. He had left the conch back at the beach. The source of the signal that could control his god was no longer with him.

He closed his eyes and slowed his breathing. It was fine. The conch would be back at the beach, he was confident, and he would simply go back for it.

He looked down to the bank of the sound expecting—hoping even—to see Sokwa writhing in the grips of the beast's arms, her eyes unprepared for the pain that now accompanied the tearing apart of her body.

But Sokwa was simply standing and staring out across the water, her arms by her sides, her body as still as if it had been encased in ice.

"Sokwa!" Samuel called down, still winded from the climb. "What is it?"

She turned her head slowly in Samuel's direction, the terror in her eyes noticeable even from a distance, and she stared at him and swallowed. She looked as if she wanted to speak, but she said nothing, instead turning back toward the water. And then she pointed.

Samuel had a panoramic view of the sound from this vantage, but he hadn't yet looked out to the waters, and when he finally lifted his eyes and scanned the surface, he saw it immediately.

He put his hand to his mouth and gasped, taking one step backward. And then, slowly, as if suddenly drawn by some giant, planetary magnet, he began to march forward down the far side of the dune toward Sokwa, his legs like wet reeds as he hiked, never taking his eyes from the still waters in front of him.

The Croatoan was there, knee-deep in the water, nearly all the way across to the far side of the sound. It was approaching the eastern bank of the island, just beginning its rise up the gradual slope leading to the shoreline.

It was already in the sound, Samuel thought; *it had been there this whole time*. And now it was so far ahead of Samuel and Sokwa, already making its way up to the village, that even if they left at that moment, they would never reach it in time to witness its destruction.

Samuel was rattled and confused when he finally reached the shore and stood next to Sokwa, watching.

"Oh god, Samuel," Sokwa said, still recovering from her own dazed state. "What are we going to do?"

Samuel was unable to speak. It was as if he were watching a scene from his wickedest nightmare being played out in the distance. The only reason he had to continue living was now walking away from him, perhaps forever, and there was nothing he could do to stop it.

Another frightening thought arrived: What if they killed it? The creature would surely bring ruin to the village and the colony by the time it had finished its rampage, but eventually the arrows of the natives and axes of the colonists would slay it.

Samuel quickly came back to the moment. "We have to go!" he cried toward Sokwa. "We have to get back before...It's going to destroy it and we'll never see it."

Sokwa remained motionless, but soon the realization of what Samuel was saying triggered her consciousness. She turned to Samuel. "See it? But my family. My people. You said we could call it back." She looked to his hands. "Where is the shell, Samuel? You must sound it again. You said you could call it back!"

"I left it by the ocean," Samuel pled, still slightly confused by the ruination of his plan. "I couldn't have known it was in the sound. How could it be in—"

"It will kill them all! It will kill them all if you don't sound it!"

Samuel's tears were ready to fall now, hearing Sokwa announce the massacre that he would no longer be allowed to witness.

Unless he left now. Perhaps there was a chance that if he cast out the sound again, he could bring the Croatoan back, or stall it at least. just until he had positioned himself to watch the slaughter.

"Get the boat ready," Samuel instructed. "Row it out to waist-deep water and keep the oars ready. I'm going back for the shell. There is still a chance."

Samuel used what was left of his stamina and plodded up the dune and back down the other side, and then he jogged flailingly back to the shoreline, where he instantly saw the Woman of the Western Shores' conch sitting impotently in the sand, just as he'd left it. It looked simple lying on the flat brown silt, just another piece of the ocean's discarded waste. Samuel grabbed the shell and turned back to the dunes, and as he took his first step toward them, he heard another roaring splash, this time from behind him, oceanside.

He knew at once what the splash signified, though rationally it was an impossibility. The Croatoan had already emerged from the sound; by now, it was inside the tree line of the woods, and soon it would be breaching the perimeter of the colony.

And yet, as Samuel turned toward the Great Western Ocean, there it was, the Croatoan, its head blossoming from the green waves like a desecrated rose.

It emerged rapidly now, its straight, wide shoulders rising high as its chest lunged forward. It stood fixed for just a beat, and then it came at Samuel in giant, eager steps.

Samuel was bewitched by the creature again, immobilized but for his irises and pupils. He saw the Croatoan's face clearly for the first time, noting it was nearly expressionless save for some dormant hunger that showed only in the curl of its mouth.

The creature was faster than Samuel remembered as it continued to move forward, but perhaps it only seemed so because Samuel was now its target. He backpedaled three or four steps as he basked in the miracle of the sea for one last time.

And then he turned and ran.

Samuel's steps were arduous, the sand like thick mud beneath his feet, and after twenty paces or so he turned to measure the Croatoan's distance from him. It had gained slightly, though not as much as Samuel had feared. But it was coming, quickly, in large, lumbering steps, and though it was only walking, Samuel was unable to create any significant gap. And he was nearly exhausted.

Samuel reached the base of the dunes and then turned once more to watch the approaching monster, still unsure how he was seeing it at all.

And then it came to him in a flash. It was obvious.

There were two.

At least two, Samuel thought. Perhaps there were many more. His god was no single god, at all, but a race of beings, one surely destined to devour the earth the way gods had done for eternity.

Rejuvenated, Samuel began his second ascent up the dunes, sliding backward several times as his depleted, injured legs offered little in the form of thrust. But he found one last surge of strength to reach the summit, and by the time he did, the beast was fewer than fifty paces behind him, marching steadily up the dunes, unencumbered by the slope or loose sediment.

Samuel looked down to the beach of the sound and saw Sokwa in the boat, as instructed, still staring out to the eastern shore of the island where the first Croatoan had appeared minutes before. Samuel looked toward the object of her stare, but the Croatoan of the sound was gone, ostensibly on its way to the feeding ground of the colony.

Perhaps, Samuel thought now, it would be better if that creature *were* killed by his people. If the village and colony were able to fend off the first Croatoan before it extinguished them completely, there would be offerings remaining for this second god, which was now only steps behind Samuel.

Samuel cupped his hands to his mouth, preparing to alert Sokwa of this new beast that was trudging toward them, but as he readied his shout, he couldn't bring himself to announce the danger. His sinister mind seized in the moment, and instead of calling for Sokwa to prepare the oars,

Samuel began a light trot down the hill, as stealthily as possible, with the intention of leading the beast toward the shore of the sound unseen.

When Samuel reached the bottom, he sprinted quietly toward the tall reeds that bordered the shoreline and hid there, watching.

And his plan worked perfectly.

The Croatoan had reached the opposite side of the dunes by the time Sokwa finally turned to see it, and by then it was too late. The Algonquin girl opened her mouth in a hollow scream, remaining stuck in that position for several crucial seconds before she finally began to stroke the oars outward, frantically.

But the beast had already entered the water, and Samuel watched from the safety of the tall, clustered stalks as the Croatoan descended beneath the tranquil waters and disappeared into the murkiness.

Sokwa's eyes scanned the water and then drifted over the bundle of swamp grass where Samuel stood, spotting him immediately. "Samuel," she called in a loud whisper. "Samuel, help me. Call it now. If you have the shell. Call it!"

Samuel was incapacitated with anticipation, his eyes searching the surface for any sign of the Croatoan's emergence. He had no intention of using the shell to save her or her people, and he knew it would do little good now anyway. The god had found its offering. And it was hungry.

"Samuel, why?" Sokwa cried, continuing to pull the oars toward her furiously.

Samuel knew this movement by Sokwa was a mistake. She was giving her location to the monster, signaling exactly where she was on the water.

"I helped you! I believed you back at the cave. I could have killed you then. I could have unleashed that mad woman upon your neck. But I let you live. And you gave me lies in exchange! My people have always been right about you. About all of you. It is not the Croatoan who is to be feared; it is you. We have always known you were the *Manitoosh*!"

Samuel recognized the Algonquin word for 'Devil,' and he had no grounds on which to argue the label. What else could be thought of him? Of his father and mother and the rest of the colonists? They had invaded this land without warning or permission, and in doing so, had sold themselves as a peaceful people, gift-bringers, teachers of modernity.

But the men who had come brought little more than death and disease, not only to the Algonquins, but to the women and children of England—like Samuel, himself, he rationalized—that were dragged along without consultation from a distance too far to measure.

But in this ungodly land, Samuel had found something new. Or at least he had discovered it for himself, just as the explorer Columbus had discovered this world for Europe.

But Samuel's discovery was a thing different from anything civilization had ever known. And it was now as precious to him as any god in any book, as important to the world as the God Mary had delivered from her womb in the stables in Bethlehem. Samuel would never believe differently; his devotion was resounding.

The Croatoan suddenly breached the water on the far side of Sokwa's boat, several canoe lengths ahead of her, facing the direction of the island bank. Sokwa stopped rowing and held still, and Samuel could see her watching the monster, his back to them both.

Samuel couldn't see the smile on her face, but he could feel it there, smug, thinking she had dodged the danger of the monster, who was now following the first Croatoan toward the village.

But then it was Samuel's turn to smile as the Croatoan twisted slowly, rotating its torso until it was facing Sokwa.

Sokwa began to shake her head, slowly at first and then in vibratory twitches of confused astonishment. And then cries of panic followed.

She dropped the blades of the oars back into the water and immediately started rowing back toward the beach, but it was too late. The Croatoan had begun its familiar lumber toward the boat, its eyes fixed on the young captain at the helm. Within seconds, it was standing above the boat, its hands reaching down toward Sokwa's head.

Samuel smiled wider now as he waited for the final crush of the girl's skull.

And then Sokwa did the last thing Samuel would ever have expected. She stood tall in the hull and lifted one oar from the water, and then swung it with fury at the monster above her, smashing the wooden tool across the black creature's face. Splinters exploded into the air, and Sokwa screamed with a cry Samuel knew could only be made by an Algonquin. She reached for the other oar almost instantly, swinging the second one with as much ferocity as the first, catching the Croatoan with similar weight on the same side of the beast's mouth.

The blade of the second oar stayed intact, but this time the handle broke off in Sokwa's hands sending the oar behind her to the bottom of the canoe.

But there was too much torque behind Sokwa's second smash, and upon completing her swing, she toppled over the side of the canoe and splashed headfirst into the water.

Samuel watched the spectacle in stationary fascination, all the while fending off a nagging feeling that he should be playing a more active part in the tragedy. It was his play, after all, and he was but a spectator in the drama.

He scanned the water again, and, for several moments when Sokwa didn't appear, he thought she had drowned, perhaps as a result of never learning to swim.

But then the dark sphere of a small head suddenly burst from beneath the water, well beyond the perimeter of the Croatoan, and it began moving quickly in the direction of the island.

It was Sokwa, swimming as quickly as any person Samuel had ever seen, stretching her arms and pulling the water toward her as if she'd been born of the water. There was even a moment, just for a second or two, when Samuel was yearning for her to make it to the other side, just for the sake of her own survival.

The Croatoan stood unaware for several beats, but then the splashing sound of Sokwa's arms resonated through the sound and the Croatoan turned its head toward the commotion, steadying the huge skull directly in line with the fleeing girl. It then ducked its head and shoulders beneath the waters.

"Go Sokwa," Samuel said beneath his breath, "you'll make it." There was no longer any interest in Sokwa's life; Samuel was simply hoping to have the chance to see her victimized on the land, just as Nootau and Kitchi had been ripped apart in front of his eyes.

Sokwa never stopped stroking and never looked back. She simply drove one hand over the other, pushing the brackish waters behind her as she strode for shore.

Samuel made certain the Croatoan was beyond the range that it might turn back for him, and then he entered the water, apprehensively at first, and then more quickly, recognizing time was critical. He clutched the conch as he swam clumsily toward the boat, finding the edge of the canoe with his fingers and tossing the shell inside. He then pulled himself over and into the hull and immediately grabbed the broken oar and began paddling toward the island bank, desperate.

But several strokes in Samuel knew it was hopeless. He would never be able to generate enough power to get himself back to the shore in time to catch up to Sokwa or the Croatoan.

Several minutes passed and Sokwa was now standing in the waters near the eastern shore of the island, just as the first Croatoan had done only moments earlier. She had made it to the bank, and Samuel would never witness her death or any of the colonists or villagers.

The Croatoan that had ducked beneath the water was nowhere to be seen.

Samuel made two more meek sculls and then stood in the boat, and without another thought, he brought the conch to his mouth and blew into the hole that had been carved at the top. The vibration felt good on his lips as the sounding of the call of the Croatoan rang out once again, though for what purpose the alarm served this time he could not have said.

There was a stillness in the air, as the birds and insects seemed to have frozen with the signal, and then the splash of water erupted like Vesuvius as the Croatoan rose from the water, not twenty paces from where Sokwa stood. She was still a few paces from dry land, with little chance of escaping the monster's clutches now.

The Croatoan took one lumbering step toward Sokwa and then stopped, turning now so that its focus was back to Samuel.

For a moment, the two beings—Samuel and the Croatoan—stared unblinking at one another, though the distance was too great for Samuel to see the beast's eyes, and he assumed the same was true of the monster. But Samuel could feel the danger of the Croatoan's stillness, the threat that coiled in each of its stiffening muscles.

It took a step toward him, reversing its sure path toward Sokwa from only moments earlier.

Samuel watched Sokwa look back at the beast, no doubt amazed at her luck—at her miracle—and then she focused back on the land in front of her, toiling the last few steps from the water to the beach before disappearing onto the forest path.

The Croatoan stood for what seemed to Samuel like several minutes, but was probably not more than twenty seconds, as it measured the call of the conch, appearing to debate its next move. Samuel prepared for his death as he stared back at it, knowing his fate was always going to come at the hands of his god.

The Croatoan then turned its back toward Samuel and took the final three or four steps so that it was now standing on the shores, and never looked back as it followed Sokwa through the forest toward the colony.

Chapter 34

Danny stood next to Renata Benitez, mimicking her posture as they stared out toward the sound. A heavy fog sat low on the water, making visibility almost non-existent.

Danny had never held a shotgun before—he was honest with the officer about that—and he couldn't blame her for laughing when he made the request of her.

"Weren't you in my jail cell not twenty-four hours ago?" she asked, a droll tone in her voice, amazed that she was even having the conversation.

"Oh, it wasn't quite that long ago." Danny replied, keeping a straight face.

Benitez gave another incredulous chuckle. "I haven't checked the manual in a while, but I'm going to go out on a limb and guess that arming a suspect to a murder with a police-issued weapon, within twenty-four hours of his release, mind you, is top five on the list of things cops aren't supposed do."

Danny nodded. "I'll bet it's even top three. But I'm not a suspect anymore, remember? I'm sure your boss told you about that."

Benitez smiled and shook her head, saying nothing for several beats as she took in the crime scene. Finally, she turned to Danny, softening her stare upon him. "I know the story, you know? Your story. At least as much of it as you've told publicly."

Danny said nothing.

"The first time I looked at that picture, *I* believed it was real. And after I read the article, there was no doubt in my mind. I never really understood what the debate was about. I don't know what that thing is in the picture exactly, but whatever it is, it looks real to me. And it doesn't look human."

"Thank you!" Danny blurted out, and was immediately embarrassed by his outburst. He blushed, but he didn't care. He was glad to have someone acknowledge what he had always seen as obvious. Someone with authority. Maybe the picture of his sighting had never been conclusive, per se, not with today's technology and so forth; but with Sarah's accompanying article in the *Rover*, he always thought the story should have gotten more consideration.

Danny looked to the other four officers investigating the beach—the two from Wickard Beach and a couple of county cops—but they were grimly focused on their duties, unconcerned even with Danny's presence, let alone his emotions.

Calazzo was no longer at the beach. A call had come in minutes ago—something urgent down by Danny's house. "You want me to go, chief," Benitez had asked, but the gods were on Danny's side today, and Calazzo had insisted on taking the call. It had come a bit earlier than Danny would have liked, especially since Samantha hadn't yet returned with the shell, but there was nothing he could do about it now except pray that Tracy could stall the sheriff for as long as necessary.

Benitez smiled. "You're welcome. And I'm glad Calazzo asked you to help us. I told him you were telling the truth. I don't know what's been happening in this town over the last few months—with the drownings, and now this arm you found on the beach—but I'm not going to be the one who could have stopped it and didn't."

The truth.

Danny felt the urge to offer up the rest of his story to the officer, the full story, including Tammy and Lynn's death at the hands of the creature and his own obsession with keeping it fed.

But the story was a long one, and he couldn't risk being detained at this point. When it was over, in whatever form that ending took, and if Danny was still alive, he would lay the truth on the floor for everyone to see. Let the chips fall in a landslide. What else was there to do? If Tracy decided not to forgive him, then that would be that. He hoped she would find the mercy in her heart, of course, but either way, she deserved to know what he had done to her. What he was prepared to do to her and Sarah.

If Calazzo decided to arrest him for the murder of his wife—and possibly Lynn—he would lawyer up and tell the story exactly as it happened. And if the case went to trial, a jury would either believe him or not. Or, if he was to be charged and punished for the crimes of not reporting the deaths at the time—crimes for which he was indeed guilty—than he would serve his sentence with a clear conscience.

"Are you right about this, Lynch? Do you know how to bring this...what is it that you call this thing anyway?"

Danny thought about how at one time he thought of this beast as his god, and how it seemed so deranged now as he stood in preparation to kill the monster, his mind as clear as it had ever been standing there on the foggy banks of Tippin's Point. "I hope I am right about this, Officer Benitez. I truly do. As for the name, going forward, I think we should call it the Croatoan."

"Why does that sound familiar?"

"Danny!"

It was Samantha's voice, and she sounded close. Danny couldn't yet see her through the dense fog, so he stared in the direction of her call, and then gave a wide, beaming smile when she breached the mist and appeared like a ghost, smiling herself.

In her hands, she held the largest conch shell Danny had ever seen.

Chapter 35

Nadie awoke to the scream of one of the colonists, a voice she was only able to distinguish by the shrieking cries of the name of the woman's savior as she shouted his name again and again in a plea for his mercy.

Jesus Christ.

There was only terror in the woman's appeals for pity though, and Nadie immediately thought of her Numohshomus' stories.

A second voice of distress rang through the wigwam, this one indistinguishable in terms of people or tribe, and it was immediately followed by several more, the cacophony of screams building to a melody of horror which resounded from every direction of the village.

The vocalizations were mixed now, of colonists and Algonquin, men, women and children, all shouting as if a torch had suddenly been set to the world.

It was the Croatoan. Nadie knew it as she knew her own mother's face. Samuel Cook had unleashed the beast of myths onto the village.

Something suddenly banged against the outside of the wigwam and Nadie opened her mouth to scream, but she put a hand there, immediately stifling the cry.

What good will silence do? she thought. Death itself, had arrived, there to collect her spirit for all of eternity. The monster of her childhood, the legend of the sea that her Numohshomus had spoken of for years had been born into existence, arriving now, at this moment, to destroy her people and the invaders from the east.

Another strike against the outer wall.

"Matunaagd!" Nadie screamed, but her husband was already standing beside her, the thick stone head of a tomahawk held away from his body, shoulder height, ready to kill.

Nadie put a finger to her mouth and crept to the lone window of the hut, trying to get a view of what was occurring outside. But the fog of the morning was like a bloom of cotton, making the village look as if it had been lifted from the earth and placed upon a cloud.

"What is happening, Nadie?"

Nadie looked at her husband, bewildered that he hadn't yet come to the obvious truth. "It is the Croatoan, Matunaagd. It has come for us, just as we feared it would."

Matunaagd swallowed and nodded, accepting the conclusion without argument.

Matunaagd took one step toward the opening of the wigwam, then another, until he was close enough to lift the leather covering which protected the house to the outside.

"Matunaagd, no!"

"I have to help them, Nadie. Those are our people. They are dying."

"It will kill you, Matunaagd." She looked away. "It will kill us all."

The screams of pain and panic raged all around Nadie and Matunaagd's dwelling, flying above the wigwam like wayward spirits, and the pair looked at each other with a knowing farewell in both of their eyes.

"I will come back," Matunaagd assured, averting his gaze to the floor as he spoke.

Nadie nodded, accepting the lie.

Matunaagd pulled back the thick hide that formed the door of the wigwam and, as he did, an imperiled scream erupted from the other side.

Matunaagd didn't hesitate, acting on untainted instinct as he lifted the tomahawk quickly and in one sweeping motion brought the weapon down fiercely upon the intruder outside.

He stood motionless for a moment, staring at his kill, his arm stuck in the motion of the lethal blow. Slowly, he pulled his hand away and stepped back, and as he did, Nadie could hear the thud of her husband's victim collapse to the ground outside.

"No." Matunaagd's single word was just a whisper, but it was quickly followed by a low, thunderous bellow of pain. "Nooooooo!"

Nadie felt the first droplet stream down the inside of her cheek as she stepped to the opening of her home, silent as sand as she moved. She looked first to her husband, who had retreated to the far end of the hut and was now crouched in a half-huddle against the wall, staring in disbelief at the slaughter he had just committed. Nadie took a deep breath and turned back to the door, forcing herself to look to the ground outside.

Sokwa lay dead in the dust, her eyes open and tortured, blood streaming through the middle of her face like the melting snows of spring.

Nadie took a step outside and looked to the center of the village where chaos reigned. She watched in stillness as the disorder of the morning spread around her, observing a dozen dead bodies on the ground, lying just below the lift of the fog, as if the vapor itself had been the exterminating poison. And in the broken white of the air she could see people running and screaming, attempting to carry their babies and injured to some fictional place of safety and shelter.

Another scream rang out, and as Nadie turned toward the sound, she saw it for the first time.

The Croatoan.

It had the size and thickness of a small oak, and though its stride was that of a walk, its pace was quick, each tread the length of three made by a man.

Nadie felt no fear standing in her position, exposed to the murderous giant, and as the Croatoan passed by her, it turned and looked in her direction, its eyes catching hers for no more than the breath of a butterfly. Whether it had seen her through the fog, Nadie couldn't know, but *she* had seen *it*, its blackness so complete it was as if the Manitoosh himself were striding past her. She had been spared in that moment, but it felt to her as if the Croatoan had chronicled her, had enumerated her to its registry, promising to return later for the final collection of her heart.

Nadie walked back into the wigwam and toward Matunaagd, grabbing his hand as she brought him to the floor. And there they sat and waited for the carnage to end.

Chapter 36

"What happened here?" Danny asked, rubbing his finger across the open hole at the top of the conch shell.

"I told Jessica, that's my friend who owns the store, why we needed the conch, and she was all over it. She bored out the hole right there in the store. You put your mouth right here and blow." Samantha paused. "And spare me any sex jokes."

"You told her why we needed it?"

"Well, just that we...you wanted it to make calling sounds. Apparently, that's a thing. She knew exactly what I was talking about."

Danny held a suspicious gaze on Samantha for a few beats and then nodded, accepting the answer. "If you say so."

"It's fine. She doesn't care. Just say 'thank you' and let's figure out how we're going to make this work."

"Thank you, Samantha," Danny said, and then turned to Officer Benitez. "Samantha, this is Renata. Renata, Samantha."

The women did their greetings, each giving a joyless smile, a glisten of dread lingering somewhere deep in their eyes, knowing the end of the world could be only minutes away.

"Well, I guess there's no time like this second right here." Danny inhaled and put his mouth to the opening of the shell.

"Wait!" Samantha said. "Did Tracy do her part yet. Is she..?" She looked at Renata and gave a cock of the head.

"I'm all filled in on the plan, Samantha. I know about all of it."

Samantha gave Renata a grin and furrowed her brow. "Really? Wow, the whole plan?" She looked back to Danny. "Yeah, I guess he is kind of cute."

Renata frowned. "I guess. If you're into that sort of thing. Guys, I mean."

Samantha laughed.

"All right, I'm trying to raise an ancient creature from the bottom of the ocean. So, anymore interruptions before I blast this thing?" Danny was irritated that he had to re-load his bow, regain his will, and there was no look of humor on his face.

Both women shook their heads.

"I have to admit," Danny said, creating a bit of tension for the moment. "I'm nervous."

"Don't be," Renata said. "You've already seen it. And this is what you've been waiting for for the last two years. When the time comes, you'll do what you have to."

Danny quivered his head. "I'm not worried about that. I'm worried that it *won't* show. This is the only thing I've got left. If the noise from this shell doesn't bring it out, my fear is that we'll never be able to control it.

"Then blow the goddamn thing, Danny," Samantha said flatly, "and let's find out where we stand."

Danny put the cratered mollusk shell to his mouth, ensuring that his lips were wrapped around the full circumference of the opening, and without another thought or hesitation, he loaded his lungs with air and blew it all out through the shell.

The sound was louder than he'd expected, joyously loud, and the other police officers on the scene now stopped and looked at the group curiously.

"It's an Indian ritual," Renata said, holding the stares of the officers until they shrugged and went back about their business of gathering evidence and searching for clues.

But there was nothing for them to find on the shores of Tippin's Point. The killer was already known; now it just needed to arrive.

Danny held the shell against his thigh and nodded confidently, basking in the resonance of the alarm that still hung on the breeze. If the Croatoan's nature was to respond to such a beacon, if it was indeed drawn to this horn of the sea, then it would come to that call. That was as hearty a blare as Danny could have produced.

"Nice shell, Sam," he said, his stare now locked back on the misty surface of the bay, looking for the first sign of life.

> "It's Samantha. And I'll let Jessie know you approve."
> "So what now?" Benitez asked.

Danny didn't move. "Get the weapons ready," he answered. "And the second you see that thing coming, don't spare a fucking bullet.

Chapter 37

Nadie and Matunaagd exited the wigwam together, and Nadie was almost certain they had arrived in the afterlife. The fog in the air was even heavier than earlier when she saw the Croatoan pass by her, and it now almost blanketed the landscape entirely. She had no sense of how long they had been hiding, how long they had sat waiting for a death that never arrived. Or perhaps it had, and she was becoming conscious to it in this moment.

"What is that sound?" Matunaagd asked.

A scraping noise resounded from somewhere in the center of the village, and it was accompanied by the low murmur of voices drifting in through the clouds.

Nadie shook off the question and walked toward the voices.

"Nadie, wait."

Nadie ignored her husband and continued walking, stepping into a clearing in the haze where Nadie's vision of heaven was immediately toppled. Dozens of bodies—maybe hundreds—were loaded into countless piles in and around the village square, with even more being dragged into other piles. The faces of the dead men and women were a combination of white and brown; all of the haulers Algonquin. The only talking being done was in the form of instruction, mainly about where the next corpse should be placed.

"What is happening?" Nadie said finally, her question subdued, directed to no one in particular. There were perhaps fifteen of her tribe that she could see working, all of whom ignored her.

Except for one girl, whose eye Nadie caught.

It was Jania, Sokwa's sister. She pointed to one of the men beside her, directing him to take the body of Elyoner Cook to a pile near the edge of the road. The left half of Samuel's mother's face was missing, exposing the white jaw and cheekbone of her skull, her blue eyes remaining intact in their sockets. She looked like she was smiling, and Nadie reflexively smiled back as the corpse was dragged quickly to its temporary place of rest.

Jania approached Nadie, and as she stood before her, there was no expression on her face. "There is much to be done, Nadie," she said, her words curt, stoic.

"What happened?" It wasn't the right question, but it was all Nadie could think to say.

Jania looked around her and back toward the men and women pulling the twisted, bloody bodies into heaps of dead flesh. She turned back to Nadie, her eyes overwrought, and then shook her head, unable to find the proper explanation. "There are twenty of us remaining. And you. The Manitooshes stole the rest."

Twenty left. If Jania's number of survivors was correct, Nadie could see nearly all of them in her current view. They were all Algonquin.

"I am looking for Sokwa," Jania said, a glisten of hope in her voice.

Matunaagd was now beside his wife, and as he began to speak, Nadie shook her head and interrupted. "I'm sorry, Jania, your sister is dead. Her body is just there." Nadie pointed toward her wigwam, bowing her head in an act of shame, which Jania inferred as reverence. Matunaagd had killed Sokwa, but now was not the time for that revelation. And perhaps that time would never come. She shot a glance toward her husband and gave a warning shiver of her head.

Jania nodded at the news of her sister's demise, still showing no expression of grief or emotion in her eyes. She then said, "We will need your help. Both of yours."

"What is it you're doing?" Matunaagd asked.

Jania looked around the scene as if searching for the impetus for such a question. "We cannot leave the village this way. The white men are returning. Perhaps not in this cycle, but one day. And this massacre will bring war to our shores."

"So what then?"

Jania shrugged. "We're going to burn them. All of the bodies, foreign and native. And dispose of the ashes."

"But...what will you tell them when they return?" It was Nadie, the nausea building in her belly and throat at the thought of such an endeavor. "Where will you say they've all gone?"

Jania smiled now, narrowing her eyes, searching for the jest in the question. "We won't be here, Nadie. We have to leave this land immediately."

"To go where?"

"I don't know. Another home. To the big lands of the west. And once there, we'll disperse. And pray when the men of England do return, they won't seek vengeance. But they will seek it. And have it eventually. Perhaps not upon us, but upon others. All we can hope to do now is survive for ourselves."

Nadie stared into the square as the first torch was lit, grimacing as the hair and clothing of one of the elder colonists—Stephen Crowell—took to the flame. The orange blaze then caught the trouser leg of Stephen's brother Isaac, and within seconds, the pile of a dozen dead Englishmen, women and children was a conflagration of human flesh and bone.

"Where did it go?" Nadie asked. "What happened to the Croatoan?"

"Croatoan." Jania said the name in a whisper, feeling the full texture of the word in her mouth.

Nadie nodded.

Janie's eyes filled with tears now, finally showing the first effects of the trauma. "It killed them so fast, Nadie. They could not run. They could not fight them. The children...Sokwa."

Nadie pulled Jania toward her and hugged her tightly, allowing the young woman to set free her tears upon Nadie's shoulder.

Before her weeping had ended, Nadie pushed away from Jania. She looked at her curiously—this girl who had organized the preservation of her people by instituting the morbid plan that was now burning all around them—and asked, "Them?"

"What?" Jania wiped a tear and shook her head, confused.

"You said, 'they couldn't fight them.' Who else, Jania?"

"There were two. Two of these monsters you've named."

Two.

Nadie had seen only the one pass, but the carnage that lay all around her was more suggestive of the number Janie had just mentioned. "Where are they, Jania? These two Croatoans? Where have they gone?"

Chapter 38

Danny felt the vibration of his cell phone but didn't bother to look at the number. He didn't want to take his eyes off the bay even for a second. After all, he had made the call to the Croatoan, so if it did arrive on this beach, it was now his responsibility.

The fifth and final silent ring ended and, after a pause of a few seconds, began again.

Danny instantly knew something was wrong and fished the phone from his pocket. He looked at the number and saw it was Tracy.

"Tracy, where are you?" he answered.

"I'm where you told me to be, boss. Down at the beach in front of your house. Holy shit, Danny, you need to get down here now. It's coming. It's coming right. Fucking. Now."

"What...what are you talking about? The god? The Croatoan? But...it was in the bay. The boy was killed here last night." Danny was more ruminating than conversing with Tracy.

"Well, then you can come down and tell it yourself, because it's coming. I can see its head. Oh my god, its head is out."

Danny could picture it in his mind, the large cranium breaching the water.

The black and purple man.

His breathing turned to heavy panting, but not from the feeling of addiction he'd felt in his previous life, but of an empathetic terror for what Tracy was experiencing.

"I'm coming, Tracy. I'll be there in five minutes. Get the hell out of there. Don't watch it. Don't try to study it or look at it or follow it. Just go. Now. Please."

"It's okay, Danny, the sheriff's got his pistol on it. But we could use a little more firepower, so bring that twelve-gauge."

"Tracy, run!" Danny shouted to the phone, but there was no answer on the other end. Tracy was disconnected.

"Jesus, Danny, what's happening?" Samantha asked.

"Stay here, Sam. Keep an eye on the bay." Danny turned to Renata. "We have to get to the ocean. My house. It's coming. It's rising now."

Chapter 39

Samuel finally reached the eastern shore of the island, and by now his energy was all but spent. He could barely exhaust another breath as he brought the boat to a point where he could touch his feet to the bottom and pull the canoe to shore. He had never been a strong swimmer, a weakness about which his father had always reminded him, and with his muscles at near exhaustion, his only choice had been to use the broken oar to bring him in.

He lumbered over the hull and stood in the water, listening for the screams of the tortured victims somewhere up the hill and through the woods. But there was only the drone of the forest, meaning either the slaughter was over or he was too far away to hear.

But he wasn't too far, he knew that, which meant the massacre had ended.

That was all right, Samuel thought. The Croatoan—Croatoans—were still alive, about that he felt sure. And, if for any reason they weren't, if the colonists and natives had slayed them during their defense, then there were more gods in the sea. There must have been. This was an assumption, of course, that more existed, but in his heart, he knew it was true.

And the conch, which he now gripped tightly in his hand, would be his invitation.

Samuel pulled the canoe to the bank and then collapsed to the muddy shore. He lay with his cheek to the ground, continuing to listen for distress calls from the colony, hearing only silence instead.

He wanted nothing more than to sleep, but there was no time for such luxuries, so he willed himself to his feet and walked over to the cluster of oleander bushes where he had stashed the Woman of the Western Shores' book.

It was still there, untouched, and as he picked it up and began his walk back to the colony, he saw the first plume of smoke rising to the sky.

There were survivors.

Samuel smiled at the signal, and he stumbled wildly through the tree line until he was on Kitchi's secret path back to the colony. He wanted to run, but his body simply wouldn't allow it, so he took large, heavy steps, spitting and gasping for air as he went, nearly toppling on several occasions, but gathering his footing each time. He could smell the fire now, and he recognized it as burning flesh. *Whose?* Samuel thought, fighting his mind that it wasn't that of his gods.

Then who?

He began to weep as he struggled with each step, feeling as if the world were pulling him from behind, trying to suck him back toward the sound. He was perhaps only ten minutes from the colony, but he had to stop to rest.

Samuel found a cedar tree beside the path and walked to it, putting his back against the trunk and closing his eyes. He dozed off for only a moment when the crackle of tree branches woke him, and he suddenly felt energized with fear and anticipation. He stood and listened, the smoke from the colony now thick in the sky above, as if the colony itself were on fire. It was bleeding into the forest now, combining with the fog to make the world a sea of white.

Another crackle and then a movement up ahead.

Samuel stood motionless now, squinting his eyes, trying to focus his vision through the smoke and fog that was smothering the trees of the forest.

And then he saw the first Croatoan, its eyes piercing the blanket of mist as it moved into a gap in the fog. Another step and Samuel could now see the ragged points of its colossal teeth, grinding in abnormal directions, stabbing down as if punishing its mouth with its own fangs.

There was another crunching sound in the trees, this time to Samuel's right, just off the path. He turned to it, and there he saw the second of the gods, splitting the branches and coming directly toward him, quickly.

In a second, Samuel's emotions cycled through surprise and joy and fear, as well as a few others he couldn't quite describe. This was the purpose of his life. His religion. And as both monsters drew within a few feet of him, he smiled.

And then he ran.

The burn in his legs and lungs was suddenly gone, replaced with a feeling of vitality as he descended the path back toward the sound, but as he navigated one of the moderate curves of the path, his foot caught a root, sending him tumbling to the dirt and the book to the leaf litter of the forest.

Samuel tried to get to his feet, but his left leg was no longer viable, and the bone that connected it to his foot was now sticking out through his skin. He crawled on his knees now, looking back to the path but unable to see the source of the loud crunching sounds that were following him.

His eyes drifted down over his bloody leg and the splintered bone protruding outward, which had now begun collecting dirt and leaves as Samuel labored toward the sound.

The sound.

He could now see it through the trees and fog, and within moments, he was back on the beach. With a strength he would never have believed existed within him, Samuel dragged himself back to the canoe, and then launched it to the water and climbed inside.

He looked back to the forest, and there he saw the greatest vision of his life. The two Croatoans stood tall at the perimeter of the tree line, like two purplish-black demons cast upward from Hell by the Devil himself.

The beasts from the sea began to approach, first one and then the other, and Samuel brought out the oar and dropped the blade to the water. He looked back to the gods, and then, behind them, and then, as if from some impossible dream, a wheelbarrow breached the fog and emerged from the forest, and behind it Nootau's mother, Nadie stood.

She stepped to the beach and stopped, and Samuel could see in her eyes she had no idea she was behind the monsters during her journey down the path from the village.

Nootau's father emerged next, and Samuel could see Nootau's mother make an 'X' across her mouth, telling him to stay quiet. His expression was similar to his wife's, surprise and incredulity.

This was Samuel's chance, he thought. There *were* survivors, just as he had known, and now he could witness once again the beautiful brutality of the Croatoans.

"There!" he screamed, pointing his finger as he pushed himself up onto his one functioning foot. The move made his head feel light, as if the pain and loss of blood were slowly robbing his brain of nutrients. But he held on to consciousness, determined to convey the signal to the Croatoans that their prey lurked just behind them.

But his call only brought the beasts toward Samuel more quickly, and they were now only steps from the shore and the canoe.

"No!" Samuel cried, "They're behind you. Just there." He pointed again, but this time the motion threw off his balance and he stumbled backward, catching his foot on the stern seat, sending him splashing backfirst into the water.

When he raised his head above the surface, he could see the chest of one of the Croatoans approaching him, as the head of the other dipped below the surface.

The last thing Samuel saw as he felt the claw of the first Croatoan pierce his gut were the faces of Nootau's parents, their eyes unblinking as they watched the second monster sink his teeth into the top of Samuel's head.

Chapter 40

The ocean beach in front of Danny's house was less than a five-minute drive from the spot on the bay where he stood currently, but by the time he and Renata Benitez arrived at the shoreline, Tracy and Sheriff Calazzo were nowhere to be found.

"Was this some kind of a joke?" Benitez asked. "Because if so, it's a pretty goddam bad one."

"Look at that," Danny said, pointing down the beach about twenty yards.

Danny and Renata walked to the spot where Danny had aimed, and he saw the tracks instantly. They were footprints. Croatoan footprints, freshly made, and they were leading up toward the dunes that rose high in front of Danny's house.

"Oh my god," Renata whispered. "It is real."

"So, you're just *now* believing me?" Danny asked rhetorically.

They followed the tracks quickly, and within a few steps, Danny spotted it, just on the other side of the dunes, its blackened body rupturing the camouflage of the sea grass that sprouted in every direction from the sandbanks.

The Croatoan.

"There," Danny said, his voice breathy and excited. He took another two steps to get a clear view beyond the mound, and there he could see Tracy, maybe ten yards beyond where the Croatoan stood, writhing in the sand, wounded.

Almost in unison, Danny and Renata began running toward her, Benitez with the shotgun pointed straight toward the sea beast, cocked and ready.

And then a blast gashed the air.

It was a gunshot, and following the report, Benitez collapsed to the sand in a heap, sending the shotgun sailing to the ground in front of her.

Danny stopped in mid-stride. "What..?" He turned in a full circle, perplexed. "How did..?"

"If I was you, I wouldn't move no more than an inch, boy." A voice called from somewhere above Danny.

Danny didn't move, not even to look up toward the voice. He knew instantly it was Calazzo.

"Not unless you want to join your friend, Tracy, there. Friends for dinner, maybe?" Calazzo let out a bellowing laugh at this joke, which, under other circumstances, Danny might have found funny.

The sheriff was standing on the porch of Danny's house, and Danny figured out what was happening in seconds.

The goddamn sheriff.

Calazzo had seen the Croatoan rising from the waves, just as Danny had done that first day at Rove beach, and now he couldn't look away. The sheriff had witnessed the majesty of the sea god for himself, and now he wanted to capture the full magic of its destruction.

Danny could see Tracy clearly now, as well as the substantial wound in her leg. It was from a bullet, unquestionably, in the back of her right thigh, and she was bleeding profusely, the darkened sand stained all around her. She had probably tried to run from the Croatoan, Danny thought, like any normal person, but Calazzo had already been charmed, and rather than risk the beast disappearing, he had shot Tracy, hoping to lure the beast to its wounded prey. And afterwards, Calazzo had taken his perch up above, hoping to witness the final execution with a bird's eye view.

Danny studied the Croatoan now, which seemed to have become paralyzed by the sound of the pistol. It hadn't turned toward Danny yet, still focusing on the quarry at its feet.

Danny didn't have a plan, but he was also out of time. Two women were down. He didn't know the status of Benitez yet—it was very likely she was dead—and judging by the lack of fight, Tracy didn't have much time.

"Were you going to kill it afterwards, sheriff?" Danny asked, getting straight to the point, not wasting time on questions to which he already knew the answers.

The sheriff scoffed. "After what?"

"After you watched it kill my friend. Were you just going to shoot it in the head?"

"Hadn't really thought it all out, I guess. But my goodness, will you just look at that thing. Have you ever?"

"I have," Danny said. "A couple of times. It is majestic. I can't argue with that."

"I'd say it's even more than that, Danny. I'd call it divine."

Danny knew exactly how the sheriff felt.

"You can stop here, sheriff. You can. It's not too late. You can still exit this scene without too much trouble. I'll vouch for you. I know what you're experiencing. I've been there. It's not your fault. It's like a drug."

"Drug addicts go to jail too, Mr. Lynch."

"What then? What will you do?"

The sheriff was silent as he looked down at the Croatoan, which had now taken another step toward Tracy, seemingly over its disorientation from the gunshot. The sheriff then swallowed hard, blinking and shaking his head as he looked down on the victims below.

Danny could see Sheriff Calazzo's mouth curl down in a frown, and his confident, fanatical eyes suddenly turned abstemious. It was the face of a man who had suddenly recognized his sin and was now facing the horror of his actions.

"I'm sorry," he said, and then pointed the gun at the creature and shot at it, striking it at the shoulder just beside its huge neck.

Danny didn't know whether to run or watch, but it really didn't matter. He couldn't move. It was as if he'd been tied down and forced to watch a scene in his life play out on a movie screen, and whatever decisions he made in his mind were incapable of being carried out in reality.

And then the sheriff took a step forward to the edge of the rail, and Danny could see the events of the next few seconds play out before they happened. But there was little he could think to do about them.

"Sheriff, no," Danny said, using a tone that he might have taken with his accountant as they reviewed the year's taxes.

The sheriff nodded once and smiled knowingly. "I only have the one left. Tell them I'm sorry."

Sheriff Calazzo then lifted his pistol and placed it against his temple, and then blew a hole through his head.

Chapter 41

Tracy couldn't see the suicide, but at the sound of the gunshot, she screamed, and with that shriek, the Croatoan took another plodding step toward her, outstretching one massive arm, the five-inch claws at the end of it ready to clutch and crush.

Danny ran immediately toward Tracy, knowing in that instant he was going to die. Thoughts of Tammy entered his mind, and, as was always the case when he thought of his wife, he could hear the sounds of her final screams, see the pain in her eyes. But those memories would be ending soon. He would be with her now. If not in spirit or heaven, about which he was still agnostic even in these final moments, then in punishment. In justice. It was his turn to die as Tammy did, feeling the squeeze of the monster's hands on his neck, smelling the death of its mouth as Danny's own life drained.

"Hey, fucko!" He was perhaps two steps from the beast now, this 'sighting' that he had discovered one mundane morning on the shores of a sleepy beachfront town on the east coast of America. But it turned out to be no discovery at all. This was an ancient thing. Alive—somehow—existing in the darkest waters since the time of the earliest settlers. And certainly long before them, if Danny had to guess.

And then it had returned. To the shores of the Atlantic. Whether Lynn Shields was the first to see it or if there were more before her, Danny couldn't know, just as he could never know the reason it had chosen to re-emerge in this century at all. Or perhaps it had always been here? There was certainly more evidence waiting to be found. If one looked hard enough, Danny surmised, evidence of the Croatoan would probably turn up in every culture in the Western hemisphere. Maybe beyond.

But time was needed for that type of research, and Danny knew his days were short.

The Croatoan reacted instantly to Danny's heckle and turned toward him, taking only a moment to shift its focus away from Tracy. It immediately reached for Danny's neck, opening its mouth as it came, releasing from its gums a row of fangs that looked as if they'd been transplanted from some mutant piranha.

Danny turned to run, hoping to lure the creature toward him and away from Tracy, but he misjudged the creature's dexterity and speed, and before he could take a second step, the monster had him by the back of the shirt and was now pulling Danny toward its body.

Danny closed his eyes as he felt the massive fingers grip his left shoulder, and then a quiet peace closed over him as he waited for the crush of his skull, wondering what thoughts, if any, would appear as his brain collapsed.

Boom!

The blast from behind him sounded like dynamite, and for a moment Danny thought it was the sound of life itself expiring.

And he was right.

The grip on Danny's shoulder released, and his momentum from the struggle caused him to fall forward into the sand. He was facing to his right, and a half-second later, he watched as the Croatoan fell into view, collapsing beside

Danny, a large piece of its head completely missing, strands of red and orange brain matter popping like fireworks from the dark head of the beast.

The Black and Purple man was dead.

Danny turned to see Renata standing above him, the shotgun pointed down at the Croatoan, pumped and ready.

Danny blinked severely, making sure he was seeing the correct person in front of him. "He missed you?" Danny asked. "But...I saw you go down."

"No, he hit me. Right in the center of my chest." Renata pulled her shirt apart at the buttons, exposing the bullet-proof vest beneath.

"He must have known you were wearing it, right? Calazzo? He knew?"

Renata nodded, the sadness clear in her eyes. "He knew."

Danny could see there was a lot Renata Benitez would have to explore in the months and years to come, about trust and honor and being a police officer. But today, Danny thought, and forever more, she was a hero.

"Shit," Danny shouted, standing up in terror. "Tracy!"

"I've already called the ambulance," Renata said, putting up her hands to steady Danny. And, as if on cue, the sirens of the emergency vehicles began their broadcast in the distance.

Chapter 42

Renata rode with Tracy to the hospital, while Danny drove back to Tippin's Point to check on Samantha. The yellow tape was still blocking off access to the bay, but of the half-dozen police cars that had been dispatched to investigate the murder of the teenager, only one remained. The rest, no doubt, had been sent to Danny's house to explore that spectacle. At this point, Danny figured, he was going to have to change his name; no one in their right mind would ever let him live in their town again.

With only the single car at the scene, Danny figured Samantha had also heard the news and was now on her way to the beach house, and as he turned the car back toward the road to head home, he could see from the lot someone standing on the beach.

The air was still too thick to identify the person, but as he exited his car and approached the shoreline, he could see it was Samantha. She was alone, standing still, staring into the waters of the bay. It was a look Danny knew well.

"Samantha?"

No reply.

"Samantha, we...we did it. Renata, she killed it."

Samantha turned to Danny and then back to the water. She pointed a finger to a spot maybe thirty yards out. Danny followed the point and, through a gap in the fog, he could see it. The black head that had changed his life forever. The picture he had taken with his phone at the ocean of Rove

Beach, which had created such chaos in his life, was being re-enacted now upon the bay at Tippin's Point.

Danny thought of the police car in the parking lot, and without averting his eyes from the bay he asked, "Where is the officer that was here, Samantha?"

Samantha was silent as she watched the Croatoan submerge completely, exhaling fully once it was out of sight. She closed her eyes for a beat and then looked at Danny, her eyes now narrow with pleasure. "He's gone," she said smiling. "He's gone."

Chapter 43

Nadie dumped the last wheelbarrow full of human ashes into the bay and walked the path back up to the village. The fog had lifted and there was little evidence that anything out of the ordinary had ever happened there.

But there had been a great deal of death on this land, and even if the remaining members of her people had nothing to fear from the next wave of Englishmen that would be arriving one day, she knew they could never stay. This land had been claimed by devils. Manitoosh. It belonged to them now and perhaps always had. And there were vast lands to the west. Lands, legend told, that stretched further than a man could walk in thirty moons. Too much land to stay where they were now, living in the gloom of monsters.

Nadie gathered with Matunaagd and Janie and the remaining members of her tribe in the village center. All of them had a bladder slung across their shoulders and a small sack filled with food and a few sacred items. The rest of the village they left as it was, looking commonplace, cleaned of the dead and destruction that had littered the ground only a day earlier.

The smell of burning flesh was still heavy in the air, and Nadie looked once more at the cursed ground of her home and then spat on the soil.

She nodded once to Matunaagd who turned and led the small group toward the outskirts of the now vacant village. Nadie followed in the back of the pack, and as she passed the last of the tall medicine trees that sat just inside the perimeter of the village, she noticed a single word carved near the bottom of the trunk. The word was written in the letters of the English, and Nadie knew it was only Jania who could have carved it.

Croatoan.

Whether it was as a warning for the settlers who would be arriving, or a clue for the writers of history, Nadie didn't know.

But Jania did. And perhaps one day she would ask her.

Dear Reader,

Thank you for reading! I've always loved the idea of historical mysteries, especially ones that, even with all of today's information sharing and technology, still can't quite be solved, and the Lost Colony is a perfect example of that.

The Origin was a lot of fun to write for that reason, since it allowed me to posit my own 'theories' about what may have happened to those early American settlers.

I hope you enjoyed it!

If you liked The Origin, please leave a review for it on Amazon.[1]

The story will continue with book three scheduled for release in the summer of 2019.

To stay in touch with me and learn about my other books, giveaways and special sneak peeks, subscribe to my newsletter[2].

1.   https://www.amazon.com/Origin-Sighting-gripping-monster-thriller-ebook/dp/B07HNNG6JC/

2.   http://www.christophercolemanauthor.com/newsletter/

OTHER BOOKS BY CHRISTOPHER COLEMAN
THE GRETEL SERIES
Gretel (Gretel Book One)[3]
Marlene's Revenge (Gretel Book Two)[4]
Hansel (Gretel Book Three)[5]
Anika Rising (Gretel Book Four)[6]
THE THEY CAME WITH THE SNOW SERIES
They Came with the Snow (They Came with the Snow Book One)[7]
The Melting (They Came with the Snow Book Two)[8]

---

3. https://www.amazon.com/Gretel-Book-One-Christopher-Coleman-ebook/dp/B01605OOL4/

4. https://www.amazon.com/Marlenes-Revenge-Gretel-Book-psychological-ebook/dp/B01LX8R3LD/

5. https://www.amazon.com/Hansel-Gretel-Book-Three-Mystery-ebook/dp/B072L8C5SN/

6. https://www.amazon.com/gp/product/B0784MXFHD/

7. https://www.amazon.com/They-Came-Snow-Post-Apocalyptic-Survival-ebook/dp/B06XPL2Q4L/

8. https://www.amazon.com/gp/product/B07FCW6C2H/r

SUBSCRIBE TO CHRISTOPHER COLE-MAN'S NEWSLETTER[9]

---

9. http://www.christophercolemanauthor.com/newsletter/

Made in the USA
Monee, IL
12 June 2021

71072899R00171